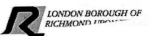

ANNALIESE AVERY

THE
DOOMFIRE
SECRET

■SCHOLASTIC

Published in the UK by Scholastic, 2022
Euston House, 24 Eversholt Street, London, NW1 1DB
Scholastic Ireland, 89E Lagan Road, Dublin Industrial Estate, Glasnevin,
Dublin, D11 HP5F

ISBN 978 0702 30606 8

A CIP catalogue record for this book
is available from the British Library.

Printed by CPI Group (UK) Ltd, Croydon, CR0 4YY
Paper made from wood grown in sustainable
forests and other controlled sources.

1 3 5 7 9 10 8 6 4 2

www.scholastic.co.uk

For Jason,
who has shared with me the passing of time,
and the discovery of eternity in a moment.

"Quam bene vivas refert non quam diu."
Seneca the Younger

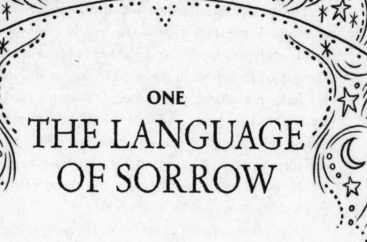

ONE

THE LANGUAGE OF SORROW

Sorrow was speaking to Paisley Fitzwilliam. It called to her from deep inside as she led Odelia and the others through the crisp cold streets of Lower London. Keeping to the shadows, they moved swiftly.

"Paisley, are you all right?" Corbett asked.

Odelia tutted loudly at him. "Of course she's not all right. Would you be, if your mother had just died and your brother had been carried off by Krigare to the icy Northern Realms on dragon-back?"

"No, I guess not," Corbett said in a low voice. "But it's what people ask, isn't it – *'are you all right?'* not *'would you like to talk about your loss and grief?'*"

Paisley said nothing, then looked away from him, glancing over at Hal. Odelia was by his side, one hand firmly wrapped around the top of his arm as she guided him through the streets. He was still in his Krigare uniform: dark-coloured, dragon-scaled leather trousers and a military tunic. It got cold riding high through the air on the back of a dragon, and the leathers were warm, offering protection from the elements as well as from enemies; there wasn't much that could pierce a dragon's hide.

Hal smiled sadly at Paisley, his single eye glinting in the early morning light, the angry red scar that ran from the top of his head under his eyepatch and all the way to his jaw puckering. "In the Northern Realms, when we lose a loved one, we celebrate their life, we remember the way that they lived, and we tell the stories of their deeds – the same deeds that are recorded in their Krigare marks, if they are lucky." He gestured to the icy blue tattoos that ran up his neck and up into the shaved sides of his hair; the band of dirty-blond hair that ran down the centre of his head was long and plaited in a way that reminded Paisley of the older Dragon Walkers she had seen in the vaults of Kensington Above.

Paisley took a step towards him. "You don't get to tell me how to grieve. You don't get to tell me about loss. My brother isn't here because your people took him! I will not allow him to become another blue mark on anyone's body. You, Hal Northman, are going to help me get my brother back – I'm sure I'll be able to trade you for him. But if you do anything to jeopardize me getting Dax back, if you add to my grief in any way, we won't take you north with us; we will leave you here for the King's Men to deal with."

Hal had stopped smiling. He set his jaw and looked solemnly at Paisley.

"That seems like a sound plan. Similar to something I might do myself, if I were in your position."

Paisley turned away from him and the others and closed her eyes tight. Her head filled with images from the night before: the fight in the observatory at Greenwich, mother's machine, the experiment. The Dark Dragon stabbing Paisley in the heart.

She remembered what it had felt like as she had slipped into the Veil – distant and vast. How she had seen her father, and he had sent her back, back to face the Dark Dragon, back to watch her mother die and Dax be taken, back to the realization that Uncle Hector had betrayed them all.

When she thought about her mother lying in the rubble, her eyes closed to the world for ever, it was as if she could see it but couldn't feel it just yet. It felt distant, as if it had all happened to a different Paisley: maybe the one she was before she went in the Veil. She found the distance comforting and was scared of what would happen when she felt her loss.

The freezing-cold streets of Lower London felt as if they were pressing in on her. Mother was dead, Dax was gone, and deep within herself she felt empty; it was as if the black Veil rifts had reached in and taken away a vital part of her, as they had done the Dark Dragon's arm, leaving a sticky patch of nothingness in their wake.

"Paisley?" Corbett touched her shoulder.

She turned on him. "Look, I'm not OK, Corbett. I mean, obviously I'm not OK. My mother. . ." She took a deep, rattling breath in, then breathed out slowly, her breath fogging like dragon smoke in the chill morning. "But Dax needs me, and I need him." She could hear her voice tremble, and coughed as she pushed down the lump at the back of her throat.

"So, right now that is what I'm focusing on: getting to Dax."

Paisley glared over at Hal. Everybody knew that the people of the Northern Realms were barbaric, uneducated, and not to be trusted. History was full of their teachery against the Empire of Albion and the Chief Designer, and now they had Dax.

Paisley felt her anger rise as she looked up at the floating borough of Kensington Above drifting overhead, its large snow-globe-like dome glinting in the clear, bright-blue winter sky. So much had changed since they had left the floating borough. How would her track have bent if she and Dax had never visited the Dragon Vault, never set out to save Mother? Would Mother still be alive? Would Dax have been taken? Paisley sighed. There was no escaping one's track; whatever she would have done, she was sure that eventually the cogs of the Celestial Mechanism would have brought her here.

"Where are we going?" Odelia asked, alert, her body tense, as she held on tight to the Krigare. Paisley looked from Hal to Odelia and realized that the streets of Lower London were just as unsafe for her as they were for him.

5

"Home's not far," Paisley said.

"Are you sure that is wise?" Odelia asked. "The Dark Dragon might try to find you there."

"True. But I don't know what else to suggest. We shouldn't be out in the open like this, just walking around on the streets. If the King's Men find us. . ."

"I agree with Paisley," Corbett said, looking over at Hal and Odelia. "And we can always check out the house to make sure the coast is clear when we get there."

"And once we know we are safe we can come up with a plan to be reunited with Dax," added Odelia.

Paisley gave a small smile to both Corbett and Odelia. She knew that there was a gaping hole inside her that her mother had left, even if, at the moment, she couldn't feel it. She also knew that when she did, Odelia and Corbett would be there to help her from falling into it.

She gave Hal a wide berth as they continued on, but she kept her eyes on him, checking that he wasn't putting any of them in danger.

"What are you looking at?" Paisley asked as she glimpsed Corbett staring up at the sky. He was wearing the coat that Roach had left behind after the fighting at the observatory, and it looked large and bulky on Corbett's smaller frame. The collar was turned up, and so was his face, as his hands dug through the many pockets before pulling out a small pair of binoculars and peering through them.

"What is it?" Paisley asked.

Corbett lifted an arm and pointed into the early morning sky. "You see that star?" Paisley nodded. "Well, it's not a star!"

"Is it Comet Wolstenholme?" Paisley asked. Something tightened in her chest as she thought of the comet that her mother's machine had just pulled towards the Earth.

"No, it's not a comet either. It's a planet, and it's not supposed to be there."

"What? How is that possible? Where is it supposed to be?"

But Corbett never answered. As he had been looking through the binoculars, he didn't see that Odelia had suddenly paused at the kerb ahead of him. As he bundled into her, she swiftly twisted to one side, but his inertia carried him into the road. Corbett fell, arms out, ready for impact, but he never reached the ground. Hal grabbed the back of his coat and held him suspended above the road, his feet still on the kerb. Paisley turned her head in unison with Corbett's to see the fast-approaching omnibus heading straight for him. He let out a scream as she lunged forward to help just as Hal promptly pulled Corbett to safety. The omnibus passed in a blur.

"That was close!" Paisley said, as she placed a hand on Corbett's arm. Paisley's heart was racing as she looked at the receding omnibus. "Are you both all right?" she asked. If anything had happened to Corbett or Odelia, Paisley was sure that she would be in even more trouble than she already was. She needed them, and not just to help her get Dax back, she realized.

"You saved me!" Corbett said to Hal as he stood staring at him in disbelief.

"Yes, thank you, Krigare," Odelia said to Hal with a nod of approval, before she snapped her head to look across the street.

Paisley saw what had made Odelia halt: two Men of the Yard in their black-and-red uniforms were making their way across the road towards them. They were staring at Hal; his ice-blue Krigare marks and dragonhide uniform made him an easy target to spot on the quiet early morning streets.

Odelia stepped in front of the Krigare, shrugging back her cape and resting her hands on the hilts of her curving swords.

"Stay where you are in the name of the George!" the Men of the Yard called.

"Run!" Odelia yelled. The four of them turned and ran back the way they had come, pounding through the streets of Lower London with the Men of the Yard behind them, blowing on their whistles for assistance.

Odelia swiftly outran them all, taking the lead, steering them away from danger. Paisley was not surprised to find Corbett close behind the Dragon Walker, the fear of the situation making him run fast. Paisley ran along behind Hal, making sure he was following the others. She wasn't about to let him use this as an opportunity to escape.

Paisley glanced over her shoulder: the Men of the Yard were in hot pursuit as Odelia led them towards a covered market full of stallholders setting up for the day.

Paisley grabbed her satchel as it swung out wildly, knocking a passer-by who yelled at her. She noticed how her body felt strong and agile, better than new.

She was sure that if she wanted to she could have easily outrun Odelia, the pain of her wounds from the previous night a distant memory.

She glanced behind her and saw that the man she had hit with her satchel had stumbled into the Men of the Yard, holding them up.

"Stop those kids! They're Krigare!" one of the Yardmen shouted.

The stallholders rallied then, and Paisley realized that she and Hal had been cut off from Odelia and Corbett, who were both running for the exit on the far side of the market building, being chased by a man holding a baguette and another in a butcher's apron.

Hal came to a stop, looking about. Paisley pulled him along with her as she skidded left between the stalls, avoiding the group of people in her way, as she headed for a smaller side exit, Hal following close behind now. She leaped up on to a flower cart and turned to help Hal. He jumped up after her, and the two of them ran along the adjacent stall before jumping down on the other side.

Paisley could feel a strange electrica surge in the air, as if her fear and anxiety were stretching their way out as she and Hal ran for an open side door. When they were just metres away, the door slid into place, trapping them. Paisley looked at Hal, his breathing coming fast, his blond braid whipping about him, his single blue eye narrow and searching as he crouched a little, arms wide and ready for trouble. Then he straightened up and his face became smooth, and his eye widened.

Paisley turned to see that between her and Hal and the people chasing them was a black Veil rift, large and looming and incredibly dark as it sucked in all of the light around it.

Paisley stepped away from it, feeling the door at her back and Hal beside her.

"It looks like the things from the observatory. Do you think they followed us?" Hal asked.

Paisley stared in disbelief. "I don't know. I mean, maybe. I've never seen anything like them before last night. I think they might be the Veil – not the whole thing, just pockets of it, like little drops spilling into our world . . . or something."

Paisley remembered that she had heard her father's voice inside one of the black clouds as it had moved close to Uncle Hector in the observatory. Her father who had died four years earlier, her father whom she had seen when she was in the Veil.

Paisley unconsciously reached her hand towards her chest, feeling the space where the Dark Dragon's blade had sliced into her body.

She watched the fear in the faces of the people on the other side of the black rift as it grew and split in two. She felt something tug her towards it.

She realized that she was tethered to it in some way, connected on a level that she could not understand or make reason of, but that she knew to be true just as she knew that water was wet and that love sometimes hurt. Paisley's eyes grew wide as one of the clouds shot towards the crowd; they ran and jumped behind stalls for cover as the other rift headed straight for Paisley. She stood stock-still as the cloud of seemingly unending blackness glided towards her, smooth and undaunted in its approach.

Hal threw her down to the ground and out of the way as the Veil rift glided over her head, buzzing like the low hum of an electrica light. As it made contact with the door behind them, Paisley watched with fascinated horror as the rift absorbed the parts of the door that it touched, pulling the matter from the door into the blackness with the crackle of an electrica spark. Then the hum was gone and so was the rift, leaving behind a large hole in the door. The edge of the hole in the wood was smooth and precise, as if it had always been there, this gap in the world.

Hal was straight back on his feet, pulling Paisley through the gap. She froze, watching in terror as the other rift grew and made its way silently forwards. The stallholders and early morning shoppers were screaming and running as the rift sucked in everything it came in contact with, before vanishing as quickly as it had arrived.

Outside was chaos, people running away from the market, calling and screaming.

"Come on, we have to get away! More of your Yardmen will be here soon." Hal dragged Paisley down a nearby street. Then another and another. They ducked into an alley to catch their breath. Paisley doubled over, her flame-red curls falling in front of her face.

"Those things, you think they are, what?

Gateways into the Veil?" Hal asked, a single eyebrow raised over the top of his eyepatch.

"Yes— No, not gateways... I don't think you would want to travel through them; you saw what happened to the door. I don't think that anything good lies within them," Paisley said. "If Mother were here she would be conducting some kind of experiment, trying to find out how they ticked, and what they were made of." Paisley's hands were over her heart again as she remembered the pull of the rift and the string of connection that she had felt.

At that moment, Odelia dropped from the heavens, carrying Corbett in her arms. Paisley was relieved to see them both, safe and unharmed.

Odelia let go of Corbett, and he moved away awkwardly as she folded her magnificent dragon wings smooth to her back and threw her cloak over them.

"Here." She thrust a large, moss-green shawl at Hal. He took it, wrapping it to form a hood, his Krigare marks hidden in the shadows, his dragonhide uniform covered as the shawl reached down to his knees. "What happened? Why was everyone running away from the market?" Odelia asked.

Paisley looked at Hal and shook her head. "The Veil rifts, the ones from the observatory ... they were here."

Odelia gave Paisley a serious look. "Curious," she said. "The Men of the Yard are distracted; we should make the most of the confusion."

Paisley led them once more, but this time she stuck to the back streets and twisting passages, and they headed to her home in bursts of motion between the shadows.

Despite the empty cobbled walkways, Paisley kept looking all around her, not for the Men of the Yard but for any sign of the black Veil rifts. She thought of the connection she had felt to them, and shuddered at the way they had obliterated everything they touched, as if what had been there never was, leaving behind that same gaping hole in the world that Mother had.

TWO

THERE'S NO PLACE LIKE HOME

The door was already open when Paisley made her way up the steps to her home.

"Hello ... Mrs Keene?" she yelled as she pushed the door wider. "Dax?" The hope in her voice was met with silence and she felt foolish.

Odelia put out a hand to stop her from going into the hallway, then pulled one of the curved swords from her hip and gave it to Corbett.

"Watch the Krigare," she told him as she pulled the other sword and began to make her way into the house.

"Wait, why do I need a sword?" Corbett asked.

"How else will you stop him if he tries to escape? With your overwhelming fighting skills?"

Corbett held the sword at an awkward angle and pointed it in Hal's direction.

Hal gave a small lopsided smile and held up his hands. "This really isn't necessary. I have nowhere to go and, surprisingly, I think I'm safer with all of you than I am out there with the Men of the Yard," Hal said, giving Paisley a serious look.

Paisley ignored it and followed Odelia into the house, Hal close behind her, as Corbett kept the sword pointing at the Krigare's back.

Odelia swept through the downstairs rooms, declaring each one clear with a nod towards Paisley, then she made her way upstairs.

Paisley entered the library. The last time she had been in the room was with Dax; he'd had the maps of the Empire of Albion spread out on the table, surrounded by those of the Northern Realms and the Empires to the East. Now the table was bare.

The door to Mother's study stood ajar and Paisley felt a jolt in the pit of her stomach as she saw a shadow move in the room. She quickly crossed the library and pulled open the study door. No one was there, but a window was open and a cold winter breeze sent the curtains flapping about.

Paisley rushed to the window and stuck her head out, looking into the back garden. The snow had been disturbed, and Paisley fought the impulse to jump out the window and track down whoever it was. Instead, she shut the window with a bang and turned, looking around the room.

"What's wrong?" Corbett asked from the doorway, Hal was just over the threshold, looking about the study.

"Someone was here," she said as her eyes darted over the shelves, looking for anything out of place.

Mother's study was as neat and tidy as she had left it, before being taken by the Dark Dragon. Paisley took a step towards a bookcase, running her long pale fingers over the spines of her mother's books, closing her eyes for a moment as a wave of loss ran over her.

Corbett was observing the room too, looking for anything out of place; as her mother's apprentice, he was familiar with the study and its contents. Hal started walking around the room, taking it all in, and as he reached Violetta's desk, he lifted a small dragonhide book.

"My mother's journal," Paisley said as she held out a hand to Hal. He extended the book out towards her, and then pulled it back as she reached out further for it.

Paisley held out her hand and fixed Hal with a no-nonsense look. "Give it to me," she told him.

"Sorry, I was kidding, I shouldn't have done that, here," Hal said, placing the book into her hand.

Paisley turned the journal over, running her fingers over the velvety, soft interlocking scales of the dragonhide.

"But didn't your mother have her journal when she was taken by the Dark Dragon? How did it get here?" Corbett asked, then Paisley darted back to the window and pulled it open.

"Roach!" Paisley yelled as she leaned out of the window. The world was silent. He was no doubt long gone by now. She slammed the window closed, and felt tears prick at her eyes. *How dare he come here. How dare he.* She held the book close to her chest. The house didn't feel like home any more: all the warmth had been sucked from it like dead nightsilver.

Odelia came in and stood next to Corbett. "All clear," she said.

"Well, someone's been here." Paisley gestured with the journal. She flipped it open, and it fell on a page full of Mother's elegant handwriting and a drawing of the Heart Stone that had been inside the watch.

Tucked in between the two pages was a crisp white envelope with the seal of the Mechanists on it. Paisley flipped it over and was surprised to find her name typed on the front in Old Celtic.

Her mouth ran dry.

"What is it?" Odelia asked.

Paisley lifted the letter from the book, and as she did, she felt something shift within the envelope. Her heart sank. She broke the seal and pulled out the letter within. She read aloud:

Paisley Fitzwilliam,

It has come to our attention that the Chief Designer has seen fit to bestow you with a second set of stars. Your rebirth has created a new track in the world, and a new set of stars have been called to govern it. This act is highly unusual and has, to our knowledge, never occurred in the Mechanism before. However, the Chief Designer's intentions are always clear and true, as is your track; may it keep you as your stars guide you.

It is the life's work of us Mechanists to ensure that the stars of fortune guide all along their track; we do not judge, nor pass judgement, but we are here to offer illumination to any who call upon us.

Please proceed to your nearest Mechanist chapel at your earliest convenience to receive your second stars, and rest assured that as the scriptures of the blueprints dictate, "all tracks lead the way, and all stars are guiding."

Smooth turnings,
Astrom Fe Stars

Paisley's head spun like the tighter circles of the Celestial Mechanism. She had lived for almost fourteen turnings without any stars to guide her, with no destiny to head towards, no track firmly beneath her to follow, a trackless, starless wanderer in the world. How she had wanted her stars, wanted to be just like everyone else. A few days ago, there had been a fleeting moment when she had been excited that the Chief Designer had bestowed her stars – she had felt as if she was finally like everyone else in the Empire.

But then her stars had taken so much from her and given her nothing but trouble. She wasn't sure that she could bear it if her second stars held more of the same.

"A second set of stars! I've never heard of such a thing," Corbett said.

"You've never known anyone to outlive their stars either; slipping into the Veil and returning," Odelia said with a raise of her eyebrow.

Paisley felt as if there was a trembling in her track. From the moment when she had placed her hand into the schematica and the stars of her destiny had been tattooed on her wrist – as was done for all citizens of the George – so the world had spun away from her.

"Your stars say that you will fail. Your stars say, Paisley Fitzwilliam, that, before the end of your

fourteenth turning, your cog will cease, your track will end, and you will die." Her stars had declared that, and they had been right:

The Dark Dragon had stabbed her, and she had died, but she had returned too.

Paisley felt a hot worry pass over her as she tried not to think about the presence of the Veil within her or how her first stars had lit her track towards the Veil. As she folded the summons letter, crisping the edge of the thick parchment, she wondered if she would have died and returned if she had never received her stars. She stuffed the summons into the envelope, the small copper coin winking at her. She felt a hot surge of defiance towards her new stars; they were taunting her with a destiny that she had no control over, that she had no choice in, that like the last set of stars might lead her to misfortune. She thought of the last time she had seen her mother as she scrunched the letter in her fist, feeling the metal coin solid in her hand, before stuffing it into her satchel.

"You are going to get your second stars, aren't you?" Corbett's eyes were wide.

Paisley hesitated for a moment. "No, no I'm not.

What good did my last set do me?" Paisley said, feeling angry at her stars and angry at the Chief Designer for giving them to her. "My last stars told me I was going to die, and, well . . . we all know how that worked out. I think my life was just fine before I got any stars, and I'm sure I'll do perfectly well without them now."

Hal gave a little *ha* as he leaned up against the bookcase, and Paisley fixed him with a look.

"This is how we live in the Northern Realms," he explained. "No stars to guide us, no Mechanists to tell us what our tracks are. We forge our own lives through the deeds that we do, just as our ancestors did in the days before the Mechanism."

Paisley shifted uncomfortably on the spot. She hadn't thought about the parallels between her starless wonderings and the way the barbarians of the North lived. She'd spent most of her life feeling as if she had no direction, and the idea of not having a track to follow made her feel adrift, even now, after everything. But she couldn't go through with it all again.

"Don't you want to know what's waiting for you along your track?" Corbett asked.

Paisley shook her head as Odelia said, "Your stars might say something important; they might give us some insight on what's to come, on how to be reunited with Dax, or how to destroy the Dark Dragon."

Paisley squeezed the summons again, feeling the coin hard in her hand. Maybe Odelia was right, but what if her stars were dark again? What if they said she would never see Dax? She couldn't bear knowing.

"Aye, or even some information about the comet and what's happening to the Celestial Mechanism." Corbett suddenly turned and walked out of the study and back into the library, passing the sword back to Odelia as she moved out of his way. He headed for a shelf and pulled out a volume from the collection of astrojournals. He placed it on the table and began turning the pages, flattening down a double spread of mathematical calculations and numbers. "I need something to write on," he said as he reached into the pocket of Roach's coat and began searching for something, pulling out a small metal tin, a piece of string, a photogram of a small girl with curly hair and a big smile. He stuffed them all back in his pockets before asking Paisley, "Do you have a piece of paper and a pen?"

She located them for him, and the moment he had the pen in his hand he started to scribble down a series of numbers from the astrojournal and then work out some complicated equations.

"Is this about the planet you saw before, when we were by the market? The one you said wasn't supposed to be there?" Paisley looked over his shoulder at the open page full of columns of coordinates, each number the location of a celestial object within the Mechanism at a given time and date. Corbett looked up from the book, and Paisley could tell by the look on his face that something was wrong. "I need to talk to someone about this. I need to get some data about what's going on out there in the Mechanism."

"What do *you* think is going on?" Odelia asked, her arms crossed over her chest.

Corbett took a deep breath. "To be completely honest with you, I don't know." He nodded towards Paisley with a sad smile. "Your mother, she would have understood it, but I've only just started my apprenticeship, only just begun to understand the workings of the Celestial Mechanism."

"But you think that something is wrong in the Mechanism?" Odelia pressed.

"Aye, well, this morning I saw one of the wandering planets, only it was wandering in the wrong place – this calculation confirms it. I think, and I really hope that I'm wrong, that when the Dark Dragon made us pull the comet towards her, we moved more than just Comet Wolstenholme. You see, I used the coordinates from the previous night. Professor Fitzwilliam had designed the machine to influence the comet, to move it from its track and pull it on to a new one. I thought that by using the old coordinates, by pointing the machine at the space that the comet had been in – rather than where it was – that whatever the machine did to influence the comet would miss and not have any effect on it. But I forgot one thing: the machine was being powered by two pieces of the Heart Stone joined together. The energy of the two combined is ... huge, and the effect that that had is bigger than we could have expected. I think that somehow we moved more than just the comet. Somehow we altered the Celestial Mechanism."

Hal let out a long whistle. "Your Mechanists are going to love that!" he said with a sly smile.

"What does that mean?" Paisley asked. "Did . . . did we break the Mechanism?" Her eyes were wide and face pale.

"By all the cogs, I hope not," Corbett said, fear edging his words. "But we definitely did something. The blueprints say that the Chief Designer created the Celestial Mechanism to keep all within it safe. By bringing order to the chaos that existed before."

Hal gave a snort and folded his arms as he rested against the large table in the library. "It wasn't chaos. Our people, the people of the Northern Realms, we keep the stories of the past alive; we know of the freedom that there used to be in the world, in the whole universe, in all the universes. Before the Chief Designer set the tracks of the Celestial Mechanism into motion and tried to confine us all to our stars, there was a different type of movement in the heavens, one that flowed and ebbed like a tide, or a dance, and we were all part of that."

Corbett shook his head. "How can you say that! From all the historical accounts we have, we know that the chaos never served anyone. Celestial

Physicists have proven that the chaos of the cosmos from before was destructive, and Antemechovian Historians have detailed records showing this. The Celestial Mechanism brought order, and once the George had banished the Great Dragons, every track was able to thrive along its predestined path. If we *have* broken the Mechanism, then the tracks could be disrupted, and chaos could return."

"Good," Hal and Odelia said at the same time, then looked at one another.

Paisley narrowed her eyes at Hal, then looked at Odelia with surprise, before turning to Corbett. "What do we need to do? How do we fix it?" she asked.

Corbett rubbed his hand over his forehead. "First we need to know what we're up against. The Celestial Physicists on Greenwich Overhead will have all the relevant data. They also need to know that the Dark Dragon used your mother's machine and forced us to reproduce the experiment with a much greater power source. Even if they can figure out what is happening, they may not be able to figure out the why, without us telling them, and if they don't know how this happened, they might not be able to fix it." Corbett pushed his glasses up his nose and looked at Paisley. "Even if they do know, they still might not be able to fix it."

Paisley swallowed down the lump in her throat: the idea of being responsible for changing the universe was *terrifying*.

"We don't have time to go to Greenwich Overhead," Odelia said. "We need to get moving. The Men of the Yard are looking for the Krigare." She gestured at Hal with her head. "The Dark Dragon will be looking for all of us, and we need to get to the Dragon Lord – to protect him. I am as eager to see the fold of the mechanism as the Krigare is, but it is written that all events must play out among the track of the Unknown Unfolding, forged into the Unseen Tracks of the mechanism by the Mighty Mother Dragon Anu. And Dax will play his part; reuniting with him is our priority, not fixing the Celestial Mechanism!"

"Dax is the Dragon Lord!" Hal said, raising the eyebrow above his eyepatch.

Paisley ignored him. "Odelia's right. Getting Dax back is the most important thing here; we can't waste any time."

Corbett slammed the book shut. "Look, we're going to need to gather supplies and come up with a plan to go north and get Dax back, right?" Paisley nodded. "Well, I can get to Greenwich Overhead and find the information that I need in the time it takes you to do that. There's a maglectrica train that leaves King Star Station every hour. I use it when I travel home to see my family. We can be on the five o'clock train up to Inverness and be at my parents' forge in time for a late supper. That will put us closer to Dax. In the meantime, I'll get the information I need, and tell the Celestial Physicists on Greenwich Overhead what has happened, and you lot can find supplies and rest." He looked over at Odelia and then pointedly at Paisley; she could tell that the two of them were worried about her.

Paisley looked over at the clock; it was still early morning and a long time before the train would leave, a long time for her not to be moving towards Dax. Below the clock was a photogram of her father taken shortly before he died. In the photogram he was wearing his knightly regalia and on his left lapel was a single nightsilver star marking him out as one of the Knights of the Round: the First Knight of his order and one of the thirteen advisors to the George. In the photogram, Edmund Fitzwilliam looked just as he had done when Paisley had seen her father in the Veil. She remembered what he would always say before going on an expedition with his knights: "Preparation is the key to a successful journey. If you don't prepare, you might as well not bother setting out at all."

"OK, Corbett. You go and get what you need from Greenwich Overhead. We'll get all the things we need for the journey north, and we'll meet you at King Star Station by five p.m."

THREE

STARS AND DARK STRIPES

Roach had jumped out of Violetta's study window as he had heard Paisley enter the library. He'd caught a quick glimpse of her through the half-open study door, followed by Corbett Grubbins and Hal Northman.

As Roach made his way around to the front of the house, he remembered having first seen the Krigare when stealing Soul Fire in the Northern Realms. The giant fire diamond had been used to power the region through the harnessing of the stone's intrinsic electrica energy.

Although Soul Fire was not exactly a fire

diamond: it was in fact one quarter of the Heart Stone which legend said was once the heart of the Great Dragon Anu! Anu, the Mother Dragon from whom all other dragons came, the dragon whose breath had forged the unseen tracks of the Celestial Mechanism at the command of the Chief Designer.

Roach wasn't sure about the validity of the myths, but the Dark Dragon was. She was thousands of years old and was once one of the four Soul Sisters, protectors of the Heart Stone, the essence of the soul of the Great Mother Dragon Anu. After the Dark Dragon tried to deceive her sisters and claim the Heart Stone for herself, it was broken into four pieces and scattered across the world. She had been searching for the four pieces ever since. It was the Dark Dragon who had bid Roach to steal Soul Fire from the Northern Realms, which was where he had first become acquainted with the Krigare Hal Northman.

Roach was sure that there was a score that would need to be settled between the two of them. The Krigare had lost his eye by the time Roach had taken Soul Fire, but not his dragon. Hal had then been head of the Krigare, and it was under his watch that Roach had committed his theft. However, it was a turn in the Mechanism that had led the Dark Dragon to a second piece of the Heart Stone, in the care of Violetta Fitzwilliam.

Roach had reached the front of the Fitzwilliams' house when he heard Paisley shout his name. For a moment he paused and imagined Paisley, her flame twist hair flying as she called his name.

Roach shook his head and started walking away from the house. He was sure that Paisley had found the journal, and within it was the destiny token the Master of Stars had made at the Dark Dragon's request.

The Master of Stars had been resistant, the old Mechanist arguing that it was irregular for anyone to receive a second set of stars. But, as always, the Dark Dragon won in the end.

Roach adjusted the collar of his smart coat, as the thick wool irritated his neck, and from the pocket he pulled a small tin. He opened it to reveal a swarm of sleeping cogroaches and a small electrica display. On the display was a solid dot.

Roach stood at the end of the street and watched the house as he held the tin and sent out his intention. He'd found that the cogroaches responded better when he tried to empty his mind and think only of what he wanted them to achieve. He focused on how he would feel when the cogroaches had done his bidding, and after a few moments a small glowing dot broke from the single dot on the screen and started moving away from it. Roach knew that the stationary dot belonged to the cogroaches that were deep in the pockets of his other coat, the coat that Corbett Grubbins was now wearing. The single moving dot had split in two; they belonged to the cogroaches he had just stirred into action.

He heard them before he saw them: the quiet whirling of their electrica-fed clockwork wings, two of them carrying between them a photogram of his sister, Clara.

Roach waited for them to land in the tin before he took the photogram, stroked it, then placed it safely into his inside pocket. He glanced down and saw that there were four dots on the display now, each one representing a cogroach that he had given an intention to; they would now do everything they could to stay with Paisley, Odelia, Hal and Corbett.

Roach watched the dots for a moment, then snapped the tin shut and went on his way.

He had an appointment, and the George was not a man that you kept waiting.

*

Inside the house, Paisley pointed Hal and Corbett in the direction of her father's closet. Odelia handed Corbett back her curved sword.

"Hurt the Krigare if he tries to leave," she told him.

Corbett fumbled with the sword, before aiming it in Hal's general direction. Paisley saw Hal glance at the sword and shake his head with an amused smile, but he put up his hands and allowed Corbett to guide him into the room, the sword pointing the way. Paisley showed Odelia to her bedroom.

"You're a little taller than me," she mused. "You might be better off with something from Mother's wardrobe instead?"

Odelia had already crossed the room, thrown open the doors to Paisley's closet and was rifling through, holding dresses and skirts up against herself.

"I think this will do," she said, holding up a grey

skirt that on Paisley brushed the top of her high boots but on Odelia just cleared her knees.

Paisley found her a soft, pink silk blouse, then stopped as Odelia took off her cloak and extended her wings.

"Hold it out by the shoulders," Odelia instructed as she took her sword from her hip. She made two slashes in the air and the back of the blouse gently flexed as two vertical slits appeared.

Paisley helped Odelia negotiate the blouse around her wings, then turned to find something to wear herself.

"Odelia," Paisley said as she stood awkwardly undoing the buttons of her shirt, dried blood flaking off and falling to the floor, the bloodstain now a soft brown rather than a bright red. She held her hands out and looked at the russet-coloured flakes covering her shaking hands.

Odelia took a step closer. "Are you worried about what you might see?"

Through the material, Paisley could feel the wound left by the Dark Dragon's dagger. She held her hands over her heart – it wasn't an open wound, but it wasn't healed either; the same as the large gash from where the Dragon Walker she'd fought at the Natural History Museum had sliced her back with her claw. She could feel something when she flexed her shoulder blades together, something that filled the gap and sunk deep into her, just like with the wound to her heart.

"I ... I think that when I ... when I slipped into the Veil, something happened to me." Paisley remembered seeing her father and how he had reached out towards the light, cupping some of it in his hand, and then pushed it into Paisley through the wound in her chest.

"And I think that I bought some of the Veil with me when I came back. I can feel it, inside me. And ... at the market when the rifts formed, they were just like those at the observatory, but I was more aware, even though I was scared, and I could feel it; I could feel it connected to me in some way." Paisley looked expectantly at Odelia through a blur of tears.

Odelia took a step towards Paisley and hugged her, wrapping her wings around her and holding her tight.

"I remember when my Dragon Touch first started

to bloom. I was six and I was so scared, and alone. I couldn't tell anyone; my family were zealous in their belief in the George and the Chief Designer's vision. But you are not alone, Paisley; you have me and Corbett, and soon we will be reunited with Dax. Whatever this is, we will face it with you." Odelia kissed Paisley on the top of the head and stood back.

Paisley wiped her tears. Odelia was right, she wasn't alone. She gave Odelia a small smile and felt a warm rush of friendship and love flood into her. Odelia made her feel braver than she thought she was capable of.

Paisley took off her blouse, turning to see her back in the mirror. She saw a black seam running across her skin, as if the Veil rift had filled up the void, forming a scar. It looked like liquid, impossibly black with a soft shimmer to it – as if it were moving inside her. Paisley felt a little nauseated as she looked at it.

Odelia extended a finger and reached out towards the scar.

Paisley flinched. "Wait." She picked up her hairbrush from her vanity unit. "Use this first, to test that it's not like the Veil."

Odelia took the brush, gently running the handle of it down the hard and ridged scar. Then she reached out a long finger and touched it. Odelia's touch sent a soft shimmer running over it, like wind on the surface of a deep, dark lake. Paisley could feel it rippling inside her; it wasn't an unpleasant feeling, but it was an unfamiliar sensation that made her feel self-conscious and awkward.

She reached for a clean dress and quickly pulled it on.

"I've never seen or heard of anything like this before," Odelia said, her voice full of awe.

Paisley didn't have the same feelings; she was scared of the Veil inside her, and worried about what it might do.

"I'm sure it's nothing. Besides, we have other things to worry about," Paisley said, her voice sounding sharp as she fastened the belt of her dress. "We need to prepare for our journey north. We need to focus on getting Dax back. All of this –" she gestured to herself – "all of this can wait."

Odelia nodded but didn't look convinced.

"How do they feel about the Dragon Touched in the North?" Paisley asked. "All I know is that they are a barbaric, trackless people who deny their stars and the Chief Designer."

Odelia looked at Paisley in contemplation for a moment. "Are you worried that they will find out about Dax's Dragon Touched leg?" she asked flatly. "There has always been an uneasy truce between us Dragon Walkers and the people of the Northern Realms – we do not enter into hostilities, but we are not allies. The Dragon Touched of the Northern Realms are not persecuted as they are in the Empire of the George, but I think that they are not fully trusted either. After all, if it were not for the Mother Dragon Anu, then the Chief Designer would not have been able to create the Celestial Mechanism – and for this reason, they see Anu as the root of all their problems, and by extension blame us Dragon Walkers, for we are the Daughters of the Dragon and patiently walk the tracks of the Celestial Mechanism that she created waiting for the unfolding to begin."

Paisley wasn't sure why the people of the Northern Realms resisted the Celestial Mechanism, but she was sure that if they were to discover that Dax was a Dragon Touched boy that he would be in grave danger, for even the people of the North would know of the prophecy of the Dragon Touched Boy, that the Dragon Walkers believed he would restore the Great Dragons to the world, who have the potential to create and destroy destiny and the tracks of the Celestial Mechanism. So if they were to find out about Dax, about his Touch, unlike the people of the Empire, the Northmen would not want to kill Dax; quite the opposite, they would want to use him to bring about the end of everything the Chief Designer had created. Paisley found this revelation strangely reassuring.

FOUR

SCRAMBLED DRAGON EGGS

Paisley followed her nose and the grumble of her stomach down to the kitchen.

"Mrs Keen," she called out as she entered.

Instead of seeing the jolly housekeeper, she found Hal, alone next to the stove.

"Where's Corbett?" Paisley asked.

Hal turned towards her with a smile; he was wearing an apron and dropping sausages into a pan while scrambling a big bowl of eggs.

"He just left. I made him some food. He said he needed to get going and to give you this." Hal reached inside the pocket of the apron and pulled out a note. "Oh, and this is for the Dragon Walker." He handed Paisley Odelia's curved sword, with a deliberate wink of his eye.

"He left you alone," she said, eyeing Hal with distrust.

"Yeah, I guess he figures that I have nowhere else to go and that I know this is the safest place for me to be. And he's right, in a way."

Paisley stared at Hal as he began opening all the small pots in Mrs Keen's spice rack and smelling them.

She broke the seal on Corbett's note and read:

Paisley,

I know how you feel about your stars, and you more than anyone have good reason to distrust the track that the Chief Designer has forged for you, but I can't help thinking that Odelia is right. She usually is – but don't tell her I said that!

There may be something in your stars that will help us along the way, and if I'm right, if we have done something to alter the Celestial

Mechanism, we are going to need all the help that we can get.

> *See you at King Star Station,*
> *Corbett*

Paisley folded the note and stuffed it into her pocket as she pulled her satchel off her shoulder and placed it down on the table with a *clunk*.

It wasn't far to the Mechanist chapel. And maybe Corbett and Odelia were right: her second stars might give them some insight on the future, who knows they could even be brighter than her first . . . but they might not. They might be just as dark and bring more worry. Her second stars might be of no more use to her than the first ones had been. She ran a finger over her first star track, tattooed on her wrist in their strange semicircle, the stars of her fate dictating her death.

She glanced over at Hal, his icy blue tattoos marking the deeds he had done, rather than a track of stars signalling what he was destined to do. She wondered if this was not a better way to live, with all you have done shining brightly – not the promise of what you were going to do in time.

She pushed the idea of claiming her second stars from her mind and down into her dress pocket, where her summons and star token sat heavy.

Odelia entered the room, her arms ladened with weapons. "I found these," she said, handing Paisley a sword and a small dagger.

"Do I get one?" Hal asked.

"Only if you are going to use it to cut sausages," Paisley answered.

Odelia pulled some things from her pockets: a pair of scissors, a hairbrush and a pot of make-up foundation that Paisley recognized from her mother's dressing table. Paisley resisted the urge to snatch them from her and put them right back where they should be, where Mother should be.

"I found some things to help us disguise Hal too," Odelia said as she turned and placed the things on the other end of the table.

"I'm wearing this strange outfit that Corbett gave me, what more do I need?" Hal removed Mrs Keen's apron and Paisley took in his clothes as he pulled on the collar of the white shirt, his green tie shifting below the navy-blue waistcoat. He had on a pair of grey trousers and navy shoes, and a matching grey blazer. A navy coat hung on the back of a nearby chair.

"For starters, we need to cover your Krigare marks." Odelia pulled out a chair and gestured to Hal to sit in it.

"I never really believed the rumours that Dragon Walkers torture their prisoners, but now I can see it is true," he declared as he sat down, then swivelled to face Odelia. "If you cover my marks, no one will know what kind of person I am."

"I thought the people of the Northern Realms were known by their deeds. You'll just have to show us all who you are," Odelia said, raising her eyebrows. "Right now you are showing me that you are stubborn and whingy."

Paisley gave a small *ha* as Hal crossed his arms over his chest. "It is more than just that." He nodded up at Odelia. "You Dragon Walkers shave your heads when you are in training, you are only allowed to grow and braid your hair like a warrior when you have earned the privilege, and to have your braids removed or to grow your hair before you have proven yourselves would be unthinkable."

"That is different," Odelia said as she fixed Hal with a steely stare.

"How is it different!"

"Because when we are in situations of danger we adapt that part of us." She gestured towards the wig on the table. "My sisters will lose their braids and wear the fashions of the empire if needed. They will cut their hair too if it is necessary." Paisley watched as Odelia flinched at the idea. "We do these things when we need to, not because we do not value our way of life, but because we want to preserve it. Covering your Krigare marks will preserve your life. It will change who you are on the outside for a time, but not who you are on the inside," Odelia told Hal.

"Fine, cover my marks," he said. "But you are not to cut my hair!"

Odelia began to use the make-up to cover the ice-blue tattoos on Hal's neck and up into his hair.

"I don't think you need to worry about not being able to show people *what kind of person* you are; everyone knows that the people of the Northern Realms are trackless rebels, out to destroy the Chief Designer and the Mechanism. That they would sooner stop a track they crossed than try to understand it. And I'm sure that soon enough we will see that in your track with or without your Krigare marks," Paisley said, not hiding the contempt in her voice.

"Yes, this is true, we are eager for the demise of the Chief Designer and the Celestial Mechanism. We don't deny it," Hal said.

Odelia stopped applying the make-up and looked over at Paisley. "And everyone believes that Dragon Walkers are starless, greedy, selfish, and a threat to all in the Empire. Is that what you think I am?"

"No, not at all!" Paisley said.

"Then why do you believe this view of Hal, if you do not believe the Empire's view of me?" Odelia asked as she returned to covering Hal's Krigare marks with a little more tenderness than she had used before.

"But ... you've been guarding him, you've been passing your sword to Corbett and getting us all to keep watch on him. Why have you done that if *you* think his intentions are good? His people took Dax!"

"I did that because we need him. He can help us get Dax *back*; that is of paramount importance.

But keeping him under watch doesn't mean that I think he's wrong or bad. I respect him as a warrior; I just don't agree with his motivations. The Empire has taught you that the Northern Realms and all in it are bad, including Hal, and you believe them. But if I have learned anything during my almost sixteen turnings it is that every track has more than one edge."

"Are you saying that we should trust him?"

"I am saying that maybe you shouldn't be so quick to *not* trust him. He hasn't tried to attack us, or escape; he was useful at the market, and he's being very useful now by cooking."

Paisley shook her head. "But his sister took my brother! And if he had protected Soul Fire, then none of this would have happened. And I don't trust him because . . . because I'm scared about Dax and I need. . ."

"Someone to be angry at?" Hal offered.

Paisley looked down at her satchel. She could feel her tears welling and was determined not to let them fall.

She got up and started to turn the sausages in the pan; they were browning nicely now.

"Your brother will be treated well."

Paisley put the spoon down with a slam and turned to face Hal.

"You don't get it! I was supposed to look after him! He's little, and he'll be scared, and he's all on his own. I'm responsible for him. I'm all he has in the whole world, and he is all I have too. Father has been gone so long, Uncle Hector betrayed us all and our mother. . ." Paisley started crying. "Our mother just . . . died!" Odelia left Hal and went over to Paisley, and gently guided her to a chair.

"There is nothing that Hal or I can say or do to fix this. But we can move forward with you, and we can pledge you our swords. I have a personal interest in bringing down the Dark Dragon and her minion Lorena."

"Me too," Hal said. "The Dark Dragon sent Roach to steal Soul Fire on my watch, and I will be avenged. We 'barbarians' are not as uncivilized as you may believe. We have much honour, and your brother will be well cared for, and when we get to my father's lands, I will see that he is freed."

"And after we get Dax, we will track down the Dark Dragon and deal with her," Odelia said.

Paisley shook her head. "I promised my mother

that I would keep the Heart Stone safe, that I would keep it from the Dark Dragon, that I would find the other parts to keep them safe too."

"Then we will do that first, and then have our revenge," Hal said with a smile.

Paisley felt instantly better. Maybe there was something about this jolly Krigare that she had been too quick to judge. She remembered how he had pulled Corbett from the road when the omnibus was coming, how he had followed her through the market when he could have got away, and how he had pulled her to safety when she had been frozen by the fear of the Veil rift.

Paisley looked from Odelia to Hal and felt ashamed as well as sad.

"First things," Odelia said. "Let me finish disguising Hal, then he can finish cooking while you and I plan what to pack for our journey. I saw some excellent knuckle dusters in your father's armoury; they are definitely coming with us, and you should take these throwing stars."

Paisley took them from Odelia and turned the metal stars in her hand. She felt better when she had a plan.

"There are four large canvas rucksacks in the attic, from when Father used to make us go camping," Paisley said. "We can use them to carry the supplies we need."

Paisley pulled her satchel towards her and started unloading it as Odelia tried to persuade Hal to cut his hair.

"Your braids are too much of a giveaway," Odelia reasoned. "Do you want to keep them, or your life?"

"Both," Hal said.

"You can put them in your pocket and keep them with you," Odelia suggested.

Hal shook his head. "No."

Odelia sighed. "You are stubborn and foolish."

"And you are blunt and brutal," he said.

Paisley gave a small smile and looked at Odelia as she wondered if the Dragon Walker took that as a compliment.

"How about we upbraid them and brush them straight? We can style them in a way that makes your hair look shorter. Some of the Knights have long hair, but not quite as long as yours, and they never braid it," Paisley said.

Hal was silent for a moment. "As soon as I am

in the Northern Realms, I will rebraid my hair and wash off the make-up covering my marks."

"Yes," Odelia said, "and I will stretch my wings and remove my wig."

"Well, you might want to be a little cautious. Not everyone in the Northern Realms is a fan of the Dragon Walkers!"

Odelia looked at him, her eyebrow raised and a hint of a smile dancing on her lips.

"OK, I get it," Hal said as he pulled at one of his braids and began to unplait it. Odelia helped him unpick the many-plaited braid, then began to brush his hair flat and style it more in keeping with the Empire's fashions.

Paisley left the objects from her satchel strewn across the table as she went to turn the sausages again; they were almost cooked, so she removed them from the heat. Hal's eyes fixed on the dragon egg that she had pulled from her satchel and placed on the table.

"Where did you get *that*?" he asked in the same breathy tone that Doc Langley had used when he had seen the egg.

"It was in my family's trove on the floating

borough of Kensington Above. My brother found it; we think it belonged to our mother, although I guess my father may have discovered it – he studied Dragonology when he was a younger man. It used to be covered in nightsilver." Paisley paused. "It used to be a lot shinier too," she said, lifting the egg to look at it more closely.

"Whoa!" She almost dropped it. "I think that something moved inside it!" Paisley exclaimed, her eyes wide.

Odelia had stopped brushing Hal's hair. He stood up, moving around the table to Paisley's side, his eyes not leaving the egg. "May I?" he asked, hands outstretched.

Paisley hesitated, then handed over the egg, and Hal let out a sharp, excited breath.

"We showed it to an expert, Doc Langley; he's a Dragonologist. He thought that it might be a Great Dragon egg!"

Hal nodded. "I think he's right! I have never seen an egg like this before! How did you manage to get enough dragon fire to heat it?"

"Sorry?" Paisley asked, bewildered. She looked to Odelia, who gave a slight shrug.

"This egg has been fired, heated in the breath of a dragon," Hal said.

Paisley thought back to the observatory. "Maybe it was your dragons – the ones from the North, when they were fighting the Dark Dragon?"

Hal shook his head. "I don't think so. It needs to be a sustained flame to start the transition phase."

"Lorena!" Odelia said, her lip curling as she said the name of the former Dragon Walker. "She used her breath to heat your mother's watch so that the Dark Dragon could destroy it! When she did that, everything around it was caught in her breath. I remember your dragonhide satchel was close, and. . ." Odelia looked at Paisley.

"The egg!" they said in unison.

"Yes, of course, it must have slipped out of the nightsilver case while it was in the bag." Paisley looked at the mottled grey egg. Hal was holding it outstretched as Paisley and Odelia leaned in to look at it, the electrica light above the table bathing it in a soft amber. The egg suddenly shook in Hal's hand, and both he and Paisley gave a little start. Odelia raised an eyebrow.

"What do we do with it?" Paisley asked.

"Nothing, there's nothing you can do. It's started to gestate, and in a few weeks it will hatch and there will be a dragon."

"A few weeks!" Paisley said.

"Well, as long as the Great Dragons follow the same gestation times as the dragons of the North, although I suppose it might be quicker or slower."

"Doc said that not much was known about Great Dragons; after all, no one has seen one since the first George vanquished them to the Veil," Odelia said.

"We should make a sling for it," Hal suggested. "We can take it in turns of carrying it."

"That might draw too much attention," Paisley said. "We can just keep it in my satchel for now." She held it open, and Hal reluctantly placed it in.

As she sat back down, Paisley felt the weight of the egg and the responsibility that it came with. A Great Dragon would only add to the danger that they were in, and she worried about what was in the track ahead of her.

Hal moved the sausages back on to the heat and added the waiting saucepan. He melted the butter in it, then poured in the scrambled eggs.

Paisley wondered if it was a little wrong of her to

eat them, as she sat with her satchel on her lap and the dragon egg resting in it ... but she was far too hungry not to.

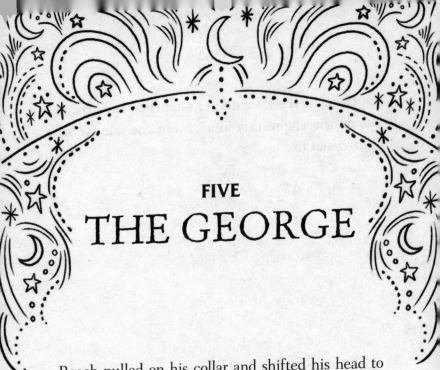

FIVE

THE GEORGE

Roach pulled on his collar and shifted his head to one side as he walked up to Lord Hector. But it was more than just the tightness of his best shirt and the sound of his shoes clipping on the marble of the palace floor that made him feel uneasy.

He had made a few visits to the palace with Lord Hector, always at the Dark Dragon's request. On their first visit, Roach had been amazed to find that Hector needed no invitation: he was immediately admitted and eagerly entertained.

However, today there was something stirring in the palace. The knights seemed tense and alert, their hands resting on the hilts of their nightsilver swords, their fighting armour fixed and ready, helms lacking the usual plumage and flare. They looked utilitarian – ready for trouble.

Hector glanced at Roach. "Did you bring it?" he asked.

Roach reached inside his coat pocket and pulled out a small wooden box. He handed it to Hector.

"He's refusing to meet with us without it," Hector said. "Did you see her, Paisley?"

"Yeah, Briefly," Roach said as he turned his attention to the painting in front of them. It was of one of the early Georges: lance in hand, nightsilver armour glistening.

Hector turned to look at Roach. "How was she?" he asked.

Determined, angry, scared. Upset that you, a person she trusted, the only person she thought she had left to guide her through the Mechanism, betrayed her, Roach wanted to say, but instead he shrugged his shoulders. "As well as can be expected," he replied.

Hector turned to face the painting too.

At that moment a tall, thin man walked in through the double doors to the lobby. He wore the green-and-black livery of the George's household and gave a short, sharp bow.

"The George is in the Throne Room, Lord Hector." The steward stood to one side and held the door open, ushering them through.

Roach hesitated for a moment as the hairs on the back of his neck began to tingle; he could feel that something was coming along his track, and he wasn't altogether sure about it.

Beyond the doors, the palace took on a different feel. The opulence was still there, but the light and warmth had been replaced with a deeper, darker richness.

The soft ivory colour palette had been usurped by dark blues and greens. The walls still boasted gold-edged paintings of the Georges throughout the ages, gallant men on horseback in full nightsilver, but the paintings looked more serious, their subject matter making Roach feel uncomfortable. One showed an image of a past George with his lance in his hand and his quarry underfoot, but instead of a dragon it was a woman, a Dragon Walker with wings like Odelia's. She wasn't strong and fearless like the Dragon Walkers Roach had seen; she looked scared and frail, her wings shredded as well as her clothes.

Roach looked away.

At the end of the corridor there was another set of huge doors, covered in stars and the golden looping tracks of the Mechanism. The steward opened them both, then stood to one side.

It was even darker beyond the doors. The muted winter sun pushed feebly through the windows, wearing the colours of the stained glass as it danced weakly on the polished floor of the throne room.

Roach looked into the shadows cast by the pillars that held up the painted ceiling. Looking up, he could see the story above him; it was the same story that echoed through every picture frame, tapestry, statue and mural in the palace. The first George being chosen by the Chief Designer, the stars of his destiny marking him for greatness, signalling him as the ruler of the empire, as the destroyer of the Great Dragons and the upholder of all that the Celestial Mechanism stood for.

Roach tugged his coat straight, then clenched his fists as they moved towards the throne.

It was nothing like the Dark Dragon's throne;

hers was forged of nightsilver and constructed from the teeth of a Great Dragon, dark and powerful – like the gaping jaws of the dragons themselves. The throne of the George was all the golden swirls and arching tracks of the Celestial Mechanism. Wandering stars made their way around the top of the throne on unseen clockwork cogs, and in the centre, above the twists and turns of destiny, floated the King Star.

Roach raised a quizzical eyebrow, unsure of how the nightsilver star was suspended; electrica-magnetism, he supposed.

The King Star, dark and mysterious. Every citizen of the Empire knew about the star, and when a child was given their stars, their parents would hold their breath in anticipation or dread. To be marked with the King Star was to be singled out as the next George of the Empire.

The future George would then be taken from their family and brought up in the splendour of the palace. Educated in high politics and warfare, society and economics, the future George would learn how to be the King of Albion and all its Empires. The New George was known as the George Ascending, and from the moment of his appointing by the Chief Designer, the current George would be responsible for preparing the George Ascending for his future position.

Roach knew that the current George had received his stars when he was only a few days old. He'd been born in Ohio, Amerika, and the Mechanists had whisked him across the sea to Albion before his parents had time to register what their son was destined for. Most had praised the Chief Designer for anointing a ruler from the Amerikas. The new young George had helped to quell the rumours of rebellion and the thoughts of independence from the Empire. But like all ideas, the dream of autonomy for the Amerikas was not destroyed, and now, as the George sat on the throne he'd occupied for almost one hundred and twenty years, Roach wondered if he was mulling over the whispers that had reached across the wide Atlantic, far fiercer than the tentacles of the krakens that mighty ocean homed.

The George was a frail old man lost in his track. Slumped in his throne. His skin ashen and thin as gossamer, hanging off the angles of his bones, his purple veins bulging in his hands, his once-black hair now white and not as tightly curled, his chestnut eyes muddy puddles searching the Veil for things he would no doubt soon see.

Roach had never been this close to the George before; usually he waited in an antechamber while Hector conducted the Dark Dragon's dealings.

Hector gave a small cough that echoed its way to the ear of the George.

"Ah, it's you, is it? So she's sent it at last, Lord Hector."

Roach followed a step behind as they approached the throne, the wandering stars continuing along their tracks like flies above the head of the George.

Hector bowed low; Roach followed suit. "My mistress sends her greetings."

The George unsteadily made his way to his feet and shuffled along the thin, blood-red carpet that led to the throne. "And is she pleased with me? I have done as she requested and have my men assembled. They await her instruction even now." He glanced off to a door on the left, lifting his shaking arm in its direction. Roach wrinkled his nose at the miasma of old age that wafted from the George.

"She is most pleased and sends a token of her

thanks, along with new commands." Hector reached inside his coat and pulled out the small wooden box.

The George lurched towards it, and Hector moved the box just out of his reach. "Will you give your word that you will do as she asks?"

The George was focused on the box, his hands still stretched out. "Yes, yes, I will do anything she wants, just give it to me." Clots of white spittle flew from the George's lips.

Hector gave a cruel smile as he offered the box to the George. Not hesitating, the old man lurched forward, snatching and almost dropping it.

Roach watched with slight horror as the George fumbled with the catch, then discarded the box and the note inside, pulling out a small phial. He held it up to the light and swirled it so that the red liquid coated the glass.

Roach had seen the same dangerous look now on the George's face many times before outside the poppy houses, and even on his own mother's face once or twice after Clara had been taken, when he had been too slow to stop her from visiting them.

The George scrabbled with the silver stopper, sending it bouncing on the marble floor as he drank down the deep red liquid. A moment of bliss filled his face as he licked his lips and closed his eyes, sighing deeply.

Roach knew what the phial contained. It was identical to the one that sat in his pocket: the Dark Dragon's blood. The power that the blood of the Dragon Touched held was spoken of in hushed rumours, as were the experiments being done on the Dragon Touched that the Men of the Yard captured.

Roach felt his jaw clench as he thought of Clara.

The George suddenly pitched forward, letting out a groan of despair as he fell to the floor.

Hector took a jump back as Roach moved forward.

"What's happening to him? Did you poison him?" Roach accused, crouching and reaching out a hand towards the George as he began to convulse, his kingly robes thrashing around and covering him from head to toe.

"Far from it! The George has received the Dark Dragon's gift many times and each time he does, his reaction is more violent. Step back, let him be, he'll be calm soon enough," Hector said.

Roach pulled back his outstretched hand but

remained crouching. "This reaction has happened before, then?"

"Yes," Hector said, rolling his eyes as if he was bored. "More and more lately."

The George stopped thrashing and lay as still as death.

Roach looked about the throne room for help, but Hector placed a hand on his shoulder to stop him.

"Give the George a moment," he said.

After an anxious breath or two, the King of Albion began to stir. He sighed, his voice lower than it had been. He twisted, his movements more smooth and graceful. He pushed himself to his hands and knees, his face down. His head was now uncovered and Roach could see that his hair was now full of tight curls, each one soot-stroked black. The George crouched, then stood and turned to reveal a man who looked under half his previous age: his face was strong and plump once more, his eyes darker and sharper, his glistening black skin full of vitality and a warm lustre.

The George in front of Roach now looked like the one he recognized from stamps and coins and photograms. Roach marvelled at the sharp vicissitude of youth and suddenly realized something: that the long track of the George's life had nothing to do with his stars and everything to do with the Dark Dragon and her blood! Roach cast his mind back and remembered from his lessons on Georgian antiquity that the early Georges did not live as long as the recent ones did. It was generally accepted that the early Georges, especially those who were battling dragons, rebellions and lands outside of the Empire, had shorter tracks because the Chief Designer had filled their destinies with much heroic peril. But now he thought about it, Roach realized that the Dark Dragon, although she appeared to be a young girl, was older than all of the Georges combined; had she been sustaining the later Georges with her blood? Manipulating them in exchange for long tracks? Keeping their cogs turning till the next George Ascending was given the King Star? Roach shook his head, trying to remember exactly when the long tracks of the George had started. Then he wondered if the Dark Dragon's involvement in the tracks were planned by the Chief Designer, or if her interference was of her own doing?

"Tell her not to wait that long again; my years are

quick to catch up with me of late," the George said to Hector, his newfound youth making him bolder than he had been a few minutes before, his voice deeper in more than just tone.

"With all respect, my Georgeness, you have no power to dictate to the Dark Dragon."

For a moment, the face of the frail king passed over this younger version, and he knew it was true: the George was as much a pawn of the Dark Dragon as Roach or Hector were.

The George smoothly leaned down and scooped up the box, retrieving the note within. He read it, his face becoming harder as his eyes tracked down the page.

Whatever it was that she was asking of the George, the George didn't like it one bit.

SIX

THE ROUND ROOM

The newly young George led the way out of the room, the stars on the throne still bussing along their track as if nothing had changed. The servants greeting him with civility and calm. His steward bowed low; only the shift of his eye in Hector's direction let Roach know that the change in the George had been acknowledged.

"All of your knights have been assembled for some time now, as you instructed. They are eager to see Your Georgeness," the steward said as he led the way.

"As they should be. We have been detained with

matters of the Mechanism that only those with the mark of the King Star can understand," the George said, his voice deep and commanding.

Roach got the impression that the George had used the "*matters of the Mechanism*" as a frequent excuse for keeping people waiting, but as ruler of the Empire of Albion, he was sure that everyone had to wait – everyone except the Dark Dragon, that was.

Roach and Hector halted behind the George as the steward opened a set of great double doors.

Roach looked in and saw a perfectly round room. He had heard of this room; it was the stuff of legends. In the round room of the George, many great dragon-slaying expeditions had been planned. In this room, the empire was commanded. In this room, the will of the Chief Designer was executed.

The round room had been built on top of the entrance to the lair of the Great Dragon Brōga, whom the third George had vanquished, then set about building the palace over her home. In those early days, the Old Celtic term *Wyrm* was often used instead of *dragon*, and the room was dubbed the Wyrm Room.

Beneath the palace were the twisting tunnels of

the dragon's lair, and Roach knew that if he were to follow them he would eventually end up in the Dark Dragon's throne room, the former central chamber of Brõga.

But the entrance to the tunnels had long been closed with a large circular seal that covered the floor of the Wyrm Room. It showed an image in coloured mosaic glass and metal of the third George and Brõga locked in battle.

On top of the seal, in the middle of the room, stood an equally perfect round table. The dark polished wood shone as the electrica lights that flooded the room bounced down on it.

The table sat fourteen, each seating separated by a groove that radiated out from the centre like the arms on a cog. In each of the grooves lay a sword that belonged to the knight occupying the large, wooden high-backed chair in front of it. Save one, the occupants of the chairs came and went, but the chairs themselves remained, each one carrying the symbol of the order that the knight headed; some carved in wood, some cast in brass, gold, nightsilver or copper.

The King's Men stood as the George entered.

Roach couldn't help noticing a few quizzical eyebrows rise as they appraised the George.

Every child in the Empire knew the names of the King's Men, their offices and titles. They were the most powerful men in the Empire, besides the George. Roach had lost count of how many times he and his childhood friends had played at being knights.

When he had been younger, Roach had always chosen to be the First Knight of the Order of Valour. Back then, the Knight of Valour had been Sir Richard Dench, but Roach wasn't sure who the young man in the seat with the copper heart was now. He had stopped playing knights when Clara had been born, and the stars of knights often burned bright and short.

Next to the new Knight of Valour sat another young man, maybe a year or two older than Roach himself. Above his seat was a compass made of brass and steel. Paisley's father had once sat in that seat, when he had been the First Knight of the Order of Exploration.

There were thirteen Orders of Knights, each represented at the table, each with a voice on matters of vital importance to the Empire.

There were two empty seats at the table. One had the nightsilver King Star above it, and it was where the George now took his place, pulling his ornamental sword from his belt and setting it in the groove in the table. The other empty seat was directly opposite the George.

In the groove lay the fragments of a shattered nightsilver sword, and in the dust- and cobweb-covered chair sat the ancient skeletal remains of Sir Jacob Pew, the first and only Knight of the Veil.

From his history lessons, Roach knew that Sir Jacob Pew had died at the hands of the first George upon his appointment as head of the Order, his remains placed on the chair. Sir Jacob Pew was destined to serve the George in the Veil for all eternity, and his Order composed of all the knights that had ever fallen in battle – all knights that died in the name of the George were destined to continue to uphold their tracks in the Veil. It was believed that they helped to keep order there and stopped any of the Great Dragons who might try to return to the Celestial Mechanism.

The other chairs were occupied by men of various ages: some, like the Knight of Valour a little older than Roach, most around Hector's age, some old enough to be Lord Hector's father, a few his grandfather.

Roach continued to trace the faces of the knights as he followed Hector, heading towards a set of empty chairs in a row that lined the wall of the round room enclosing the table and that only broke for the double door. In these seats sat the paladins and squires of the knights, some with pen and paper ready to scribe.

The George waved a hand, and everyone sat with a small muttering.

As they did, the knight in the chair in front of Roach turned and gave a stern look to the person sitting next to Roach, a small boy of about twelve, juggling his pen and rustling his paper as if his stars were shaking his track.

Roach recognized the knight: Arch Architect Harman, the Knight of the Celestial Mechanism, with the golden tracks of the universe sitting above his chair.

Roach disliked all Mechanists almost as much as he did the Men of the Yard, and as he sat staring at the back of Arch Architect Harman's chair, he couldn't help but think of how satisfying it would be to use the golden tracks that hung above the Mechanist as a noose.

Arch Architect Harman was the first to speak. "We hope you are well, Your Georgeness. We had heard rumours that you were in ill health."

There was a hint of provocation in his voice, and Roach was sure that the George heard it too, as the George smiled dangerously at Arch Architect Harman and said, "There are always rumours about my stars and my track, but, as you can see, both shine brightly and I am in fine health. No need for you and your Mechanists to go looking for a new King Star; I am sure that the Empire is safe with me for a few more turnings yet." His voice was deep and rich as it rolled around the room, and the knights before him nodded and laughed in good humour.

Roach saw the look the George gave Harman as the First Knight of the Mechanism replied, "Of course, I am sure that the Chief Designer cast your King Star with strength and longevity when he bestowed it upon you. Not all the past Georges have had such lucky tracks."

"It has come to our attention," the George said,

breaking his gaze from Arch Architect Harman and casting his eyes around the table, "that last night my empire was attacked." The George paused. "The Northern Realm sent its Krigare here, to Albion, to London, to my doorstep. Last night our skies and shores were polluted by those barbarians and defiled by their dragons."

The old man in the chair with the sun above it began to speak: "My Georgeness, we of the Order of Illumination have received no such intelligence. If this were true—"

"Do you doubt me?" the George asked.

"No, my George, it is just. . ." The old man stopped and looked behind him, beckoning to one of his squires. A strong-looking, bearded middle-aged man left his seat and crouched low to the old man, and they whispered to each other before the bearded man bowed to the George and left the room in a hurry.

The George continued: "As you all know, the Northern Realms have become increasingly bold since the disappearance of Soul Fire. They quite wrongly believe that we have taken it."

Roach shifted uncomfortably in his seat.

"The mere thought of our knights in arms has so far kept the North at bay, but I have reason to believe that the Northern Realms are responsible for more than violating our territorial integrity. I have received intelligence that they are responsible for the death of one of my citizens, the wife of a fallen knight, no less: Professor Violetta Fitzwilliam. And before they killed the professor and fled, taking her young son and her colleague Dr Langley with them as prisoners, they forced her to conduct an experiment with the Great Comet Wolstenholme that will place us all in danger. Sir Hugh, what do you and your scientist make of that?"

Roach watched in steady disbelief as the George ran through the intelligence that Hector had brought to him, truths that the Dark Dragon had twisted. Not for the first time, it crossed Roach's mind, as he sat in the round room with the tunnels of the Great Dragon below it, how ironic it was that this George, the latest in a long line whose track marked them out to defend the Empire against dragons, was taking orders from one.

Sir Hugh cleared his throat. "My George, Professor Fitzwilliam was killed in an accident on the borough of Greenwich Above a few days ago, she could not have—"

"Was the comet's track altered last night?" the George demanded, as he stared at Sir Hugh.

"Why, yes, in quite a dramatic fashion – actually I need to speak to you about—"

"And didn't Professor Fitzwilliam alter the course of this comet once before?"

"She did, my George, but—"

"And is anyone else capable of doing such a thing?"

"No, not to my knowledge, Your Georgeness."

The George gave a small smile as Sir Hugh looked flustered.

"Then let us assume that my intelligence is correct, that the Krigare infiltrated our defences, that they harmed our people, and they moved the comet. To what end?"

Sir Hugh coughed again.

"Sir Hugh?" the George said with a wave of his hand.

"As I said, we did detect a significant movement in the comet last night, and we have had our best mathematicians process the numbers many times, and it would seem that the comet is heading straight for us, towards the Earth, towards Albion. There is a possibility that its track may miss us, and we all hope that the Chief Designer has made that so, but there is also the greater possibility that it will not. We have also made some other observations, other changes to the Celestial Mechanism that appear to have happened at the same time, changes that I am deeply concerned about." Sir Hugh shook a little as he spoke, and Roach could feel his anxiety flooding the room, with everyone except the George looking anxious.

"I see," the George said, his jaw set, his eyes hard as he looked at the scientist. "It would seem that the Chief Designer is testing us. It would not be the first time that our ability to follow our tracks has been challenged. We will not fail. We will not fall from our tracks!"

At that moment the bearded squire of the Order of Illumination re-entered the room and hurried over to the Order's old knight, and he began to whisper in his ear.

"Tell us all, man!" the George bellowed.

The bearded man stood up, swallowed, then gave

a small bow. "Your Georgeness, the Krigare were sighted in London last night, in Greenwich, at the old observatory to be exact, and again this morning at a nearby market. Our squires have evidence that some sort of experiment was performed at the observatory. The Krigare appear to have destroyed the machine afterwards and ... and there was some indication that the Dragon Walkers were also involved."

The George stood up quickly and brought a fist down on the table. "The Krigare in league with the Dragon Walkers? Ahh, those women have flouted the rules of the Empire for too long, it makes sense that they would align themselves with our enemies. No more. We will not tolerate these actions of the Northern Realms and its allies, the Dragon Walkers.

"Faithful Knights, my anointed King's Men, it was written in the stars of your destiny that you were to serve me and protect our great Empire. The time has come for you to see your stars fulfilled! Ready yourself for war."

SEVEN

THE PROMISE
OF THE
GEORGE

The destiny token weighed heavy in Paisley's coat pocket as she led the way to King Star Station. The track in front of her was dark and foreboding: somewhere ahead of her was Dax, but the way to him looked impossible.

The scriptures said that a track is travelled one step at a time. Put one foot in front of the other and trust in where the Chief Designer may lead you. But Paisley wasn't sure that she trusted the Chief Designer. Her track had been full of disappointment and sorrow from the moment she had received her first stars; she worried that her second stars would trick her too.

"Which way?" Hal asked as he shifted his backpack from one shoulder to the other. Paisley looked about, collecting her bearings and escaping her thoughts.

"This way." She pointed and continued on.

The streets were becoming busier and busier. Paisley pulled her dragonhide satchel closer to her, protecting the egg inside by clutching the bag with her arm. But the backpack kept catching on people as she made her way forward, and she glanced behind every few moments to check that Odelia and Hal were still with her as the throng of people increased.

"What are all these people doing here?" Odelia asked. "Is it normal for you all to collect like this in groups? Lower London is very strange."

Paisley shrugged. "I have no idea what's going on," she said as she tried to see what was drawing everyone together up ahead.

The crowd ebbed and flowed, and before she knew it Paisley was being caught up in the gathering of people. Instead of heading for the train station, she found herself being diverted. She pushed against the flow of the crowd, but for every step she took in the right direction, she took three or four in the wrong.

Looking around, she could no longer see Odelia or Hal. Paisley felt her breath catch as she turned her head from side to side, looking for them. She pushed her way towards a nearby building and climbed the stairs to get a better view. As she scoured the crowd, she wondered if Hal had used this opportunity to slip away. She frantically looked for him amongst the people, worried about how she might get Dax back without him, but Hal was the first to find her.

"Where's Odelia?" Paisley asked.

Hal started searching the throng of people too. "There she is!" He pointed deeper into the crowd, further ahead, and there she was, pushing her way not towards Paisley and Hal but away from them in the direction that the crowd was heading. Paisley looked over the top of the gathering and her heart sank.

"The gallows!" she said, nudging Hal in the side, then pointed at the raised platform ahead. There, surrounded by jeering people, was a hanging gallows.

"What's happening?" Hal asked.

Paisley could feel a tremble coming over her.

Her palms were slick and her breathing was choppy. "Dragon Touched, the King's Men are about to hang..." But Paisley couldn't finish her sentence; she looked at the empty noose and all she could imagine was Dax, with his dragon leg, dangling from the rope.

"We've got to get to Odelia! If they find her, they'll just add an extra rope!" Paisley descended the steps, then pushed and nudged and shoved through the crowd, Hal following close behind her, until she eventually reached Odelia.

"Odelia!" Paisley grabbed the Dragon Walker's arm and tugged on it. Odelia smoothly pulled her arm away and glared at Paisley, her brows low and eyes dangerous. Paisley felt a lump in her throat as she worried over what the Dragon Walker might do as she pushed on through, making her way to the front of the crowd facing the gallows.

"Odelia, please!" Paisley followed her and suddenly the crowd erupted into a loud cheer. A door had opened in the wall that ran along the back of the raised platform, isolating the streets of London from the prison beyond. Paisley's gut twisted as she saw two women being led up on to the platform.

"Marea!" Odelia said as she stared at the younger of the two women. Both were wearing thin white dresses that made Paisley's flesh goose with cold.

The older of the two women slipped as she walked up the stairs, ankles and wrists shackled. Marea stooped down and helped her to her feet as the Men of the Yard nudged each of them onwards and the crowd jeered.

Paisley felt the lump in her throat grow larger. She found it hard to breathe, her ears filling with the angry shouts.

"Kill the dragons!"

"Hang them!"

"End their tainted tracks and put out their blasphemous stars!"

"Please, Odelia, I don't want to see this!" Paisley said as she sought out and pulled on Odelia's arm again.

"I can't leave," Odelia whispered as she leaned in and moved her lips close to Paisley's ear.

"You can't save them!" Paisley hissed. "There's too many people."

"I know that!" snapped Odelia. "But those are my sisters: I have to bear witness to the dimming of their stars."

Paisley looked back at the gallows, to see the younger woman, Marea, standing defiantly in front of the crowd. There was no sign of her Dragon Touch, but Paisley could clearly see deep-green scales the same colour as the evergreens of winter covering one side of the older woman's face and neck, spreading under the thin white cotton dress she wore. The touch continued down her left arm to her shackled hands and claw-like fingers.

The green scales reminded her of Dax's. She pushed away her tears.

"Odelia, if they find you, they will hang you too," Paisley told her in a scared whisper as the crowd around her pushed and jeered.

"Paisley is right," Hal said. "You'll do your sisters no service by joining them. You place me, Paisley and your Dragon Lord in danger by being here."

Paisley could see the conflict passing over Odelia's face as she stared straight at Marea, and in that moment the Dragon Walker found Odelia in the crowd. Their eyes met and the smallest of nods passed between them, and Odelia softened; she began to cry, and in a small voice she said, "May Anu keep your stars forever burning, sister."

Then she began to turn away from the gallows and Hal grasped both Odelia's and Paisley's hands and led them both back through the crowd, the people around them eagerly occupying the place they left behind.

Paisley could hear the dull shouts of the crowd as she kept her eyes forward and followed Hal, his hand tightly on hers, Odelia on the other side, her face streaming with tears.

As they exited the crowd and turned the corner on to King Star Station Street, the three of them stopped still as a mighty cheer from the crowd filled the world.

Paisley's chest felt tight, her free hand clenched in a fist that she used to dash away her tears. That could have been Dax up there, or Odelia, and what would their crime have been – being different? To be nothing more than who they were? How could she or anyone allow such a thing to happen? She instantly regretted not trying to save the two Dragon Walkers, not fighting until they were free. But where would that have got them? Where would that have got Odelia and Hal?

As the crowd continued to cheer, and Hal led

them both towards the train station, Paisley swore on all the stars that if she had broken the mechanism, then when she fixed it, she would do all she could to make sure that nothing like this would ever happen again.

EIGHT
KING'S STAR STATION

Paisley stood next to Hal on the platform, still shaking. She looked at the train in front of them and blinked several times as she tried to take in the scene of normality around her. People going about their days moving along their tracks when a few streets away... She took a deep breath and rounded her fingers into fists.

Above the platform was a large clock and a placard announcing the six o'clock train to Inverness. They were an hour late meeting Corbett, and Paisley continued to scour the train station for him, even though she knew he wasn't there.

"I've never seen a train like this before," Hal said. Paisley realized she had looked at the train several times but hadn't actually seen it: she took in its olive-green paint, its sleek lines and soft curves, solid and imposing. It had no wheels like conventional trains; this train used electrica-magnetism to levitate above the rails.

"This type of Maglectrica is called a Laithwaite. There's not much waiting about when you're on one, by all accounts," Paisley said, focusing her mind on something bland and trivial. "They have lots of them in Amerika, but this is the first one in Albion. Mother told me they were planning to build a track over the sea to Frankia." The thought of Mother made Paisley catch her breath.

"I wonder what it will feel like when we are travelling?" Hal said, walking towards the carriages. The Laithwaite gave a gentle hum as it sat, waiting to fly down its track.

"Well, we're about to find out. Come on, Odelia should be in there by now," Paisley said as she checked the number on the carriage alongside that on her ticket and opened the door for Hal to enter.

The carriage interior was very grand and

reminded Paisley of the elegant hotels and restaurants on the floating borough of Kensington Above. Odelia was already sitting in their carriage; Paisley had decided it was best for them to enter separately and that Odelia might need a moment to herself. When she reached her, the Dragon Walker was as quiet and composed as Paisley had ever seen her, but the tension around her felt tighter.

Hal collapsed into the plush green velvet seating opposite Odelia with a weary sigh of relief. Paisley cast her eye around: the walls of the compartment were panelled in dark wood and the soft electrica lighting reminded Paisley of the library at Uncle Hector's club.

"All is safe," Odelia said, not taking her eyes from the platform beyond the window. "I did a sweep of the train and found no sign of the Men of the Yard."

Paisley pulled off her backpack and stowed it in the luggage rack before sitting next to Odelia. She took her satchel off and quickly checked on the dragon egg before nestling her bag beside her.

"And no sign of Corbett?" she asked. "Are you sure that he would have got the earlier train?"

Odelia gave a small sigh. "Yes, we told him we

would be on it, and he may not have had time to check the whole train for us before it departed. Otherwise, he would have been waiting on the platform for us; you know he would." Paisley nodded: it was true, Corbett would never have left without them if he'd known they had been delayed.

"I'm sure he'll be waiting for us at Inverness when we get there," Odelia said. Paisley could imagine him now, sitting on a bench on the platform, hugging Roach's coat around him and constantly checking his watch.

A whistle on the platform blew and the bang of carriage doors shook the train. The light hum increased a notch, and Paisley felt a little thrill of anticipation rise inside her as the train rose slightly. Then it began to glide forward slowly.

She looked at Hal and saw a broad smile crinkling his scar. "Wow, what a peculiar sensation," he said as the world started to hurtle past the windows faster and faster and the train soundlessly and smoothly gained speed. It felt as if they were stationary and it was the world that was moving past them.

For a second Paisley remembered experiencing a similar sensation when she was in the Veil. Then that thrill of excitement morphed into one of fear as Paisley sensed a little fizzle of electrica . . . and there in the middle of the carriage hovered a small, dark Veil rift. Odelia's hand was in hers.

"It's all right, Paisley," Odelia said, soft and calm. "You don't need to be scared or worried. We're on our way north, we'll meet Corbett, and then we'll get Dax."

"Dax," Paisley said, staring at the rift.

"That's right, Dax. I want you to close your eyes and think of a happy memory, one of just you and Dax."

Paisley screwed her eyes up tight, blocking out the rift, thinking of when she and Dax had recently built the Orrery for the day of small turnings.

Paisley felt Odelia's grip relax, and after a few moments she opened her eyes to see that the Veil rift had gone.

"How . . . how did you know that would work?" Paisley asked Odelia.

"I didn't, I just remember you saying that you'd felt scared when the rifts appeared at the market. I wondered if changing the way you felt, focusing on a different emotion, would make any difference."

"Looks like it did," Hal said. He was a little paler than he had been and sitting a little further back in his seat. "So, you can make these rifts?" he asked Paisley.

"I have no idea how or why, but yes, I guess so."

They sat in silence for a long moment and then Hal stood up. "Who's hungry?" he asked.

"I'll go," Paisley said. "If someone sees you, they might realize who you are." Paisley made to stand but Hal held out a hand and said to her in a perfect new Celtic accent, "Do not worry so, dear Paisley. I am a Krigare, and we have many talents."

Odelia handed him some coins from her purse. "Besides, it would be a good test of Odelia's skills in camouflage," he added in his own accent before exiting the compartment to hunt for food.

Paisley looked at Odelia. "Do you trust him?" she asked.

Odelia nodded. "We're on a train travelling very fast; I don't think he will try to escape. Besides, I gave him very little money, he has no allies, and no friends to help him – except us. He will return."

"Is he our friend now, then?" Paisley asked.

Paisley thought about Hal and the way he

97

had stayed by her side in the market, how he had helped them to prepare for the journey, given them information about the dragon egg, and how, in the middle of the crowd, when both she and Odelia had frozen, he had pulled them both away from the gallows.

"I haven't decided if he is my friend yet, but I know he is not my enemy," Odelia replied.

When he returned, Hal was carrying three fresh-cooked pasties and three cups of hot chocolate. He handed them out, then pulled a copy of the evening edition of the *King's Herald* from under his arm and placed it on Paisley's lap.

ENEMIES OF THE EMPIRE, the headline read, followed by drawings of suspects who looked very much like Paisley, Odelia, Corbett and Hal – before his makeover.

Paisley almost dropped her hot chocolate as she snatched up the paper and began reading aloud:

"The *King's Herald* has learned that last night the heart of our Empire was attacked by a small group consisting of Krigare and Dragon Walkers. The attack took place near to the capital and ended the track of at least two people. The intelligence we have gathered here at the *Herald* suggests that the attackers may have had bigger plans, with some suggesting that the George may have been the intended target of the attack. However, the tracks of the assailants did not bend that way, and, with no new King Star having been bestowed to a track, it is unlikely that the Chief Designer would have ever allowed such action.

Arch Architect Harman commented, "As we all know too well, both the Krigare and the Dragon Walkers defy the ways of the Mechanism and do not live by their stars. An attack against the Empire, against the George, and the Chief Designer, would not be something that they would hesitate over."

The Men of the Yard have issued images of four individuals believed to be two Dragon Walkers and two Krigare, who are known to still be at large in the Empire. If you see these individuals, contact the authorities immediately. They are thought to be armed and trackless."

Paisley lowered the paper so that they could all see the pictures.

"They totally got my Krigare markings wrong!" Hal said as he jabbed a finger at the paper. Paisley couldn't see them under all the make-up that Odelia had applied, but was sure Hal was right. "How will anyone know who I am?" he complained.

Paisley gave a light chuckle. "We don't want anyone to know who you are, or any of us for that matter."

"I think the pictures all bear a passing resemblance to us; we should be wary," Odelia said, standing up and pulling the blinds of the compartment down so that no one could see in from the corridor.

"What about Corbett?" asked Paisley, suddenly worried.

Odelia checked her watch. "His train will be reaching Inverness in a few hours. He'll be with his family and safe, and we'll be there soon enough. Besides, this is the evening edition of the *Herald*, so no one on the earlier train would have seen it."

Paisley hoped that Odelia was right.

Hal had taken the paper from Paisley, and with

a pencil he started correcting the tattoos on the drawing.

"You said that a Krigare is known by their actions, that they let them shine in the world," Paisley said to him.

Hall looked up from his mark-making and nodded. "This is true."

"Then why are you so worried about the picture?"

Hal gave a shrug. "It is important to me. In the North, our marks are part of our heritage, our traditions, who we are as a people, but they are also who we are as individuals. These marks are not me, and I don't want to be misunderstood by anyone who sees them or for people to judge me because they have the wrong opinions of who I am."

Paisley wriggled in her seat. She had misunderstood Hal; she had misjudged him. "Hal, anyone who spends any time with you will be able to see that you are a good person, that you are trying to do what is right within the circumstances that you find yourself in."

"You think I am a good person?" Hal tipped his head to one side, taking Paisley in with his single eye.

"I do."

A moment of understanding passed between Paisley and the Krigare as they moved away from being foes and somewhere closer to being friends.

"Tell me about your marks," Paisley said as she pointed to one of the tattoos on the drawing. Hal began to tell Paisley which aspects of his life each of the ice-blue lines and symbols meant. She sipped her cocoa and ate her pasty as he spoke, and she in turn told him about herself.

Odelia added little to the conversation; she read through the paper, and after a little while, Paisley felt her nodding beside her.

Of the two of them, Hal had been the first to fall asleep, but Paisley had no doubts that if any trouble arose both he and Odelia would be ready. Paisley drifted off to sleep, safe in the knowledge that Odelia and Hal were close, that they were moving ever closer to Dax, and Corbett, too.

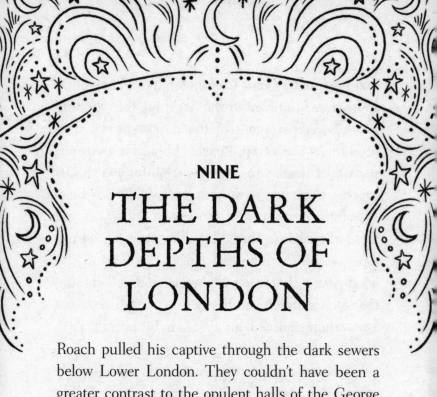

NINE

THE DARK DEPTHS OF LONDON

Roach pulled his captive through the dark sewers below Lower London. They couldn't have been a greater contrast to the opulent halls of the George that he had traversed a few hours before.

Lord Hector was just assisting the George and his First Knights on their war strategy when the tin in Roach's coat pocket gave a low hum. Roach opened it to find that the cogroach that was sitting in the pocket of Corbett Grubbins was on the move, and in a moment so was he.

"This would be about ten times easier if you just cooperated," Roach said as he pulled on a rope that was tied around Corbett's hands. The young apprentice stumbled in the dark, his feet slipping on the wet pavement of the damp sewer as he tried to get away from Roach. "Look, I've told you, she wants to *see* you. She has a job for you. It's in your best interest to do it and not kick up a fuss, all right!"

Corbett began thrashing about, tugging on the rope again. Roach turned quickly, pulling off the hood that had covered Corbett's head and shining the electrica torch into his face.

Corbett squinted, his glasses in his pocket, a gag around his mouth.

"Seriously, you don't want to mess with her. Or me, for that matter."

Corbett began to yell loudly through the gag.

"It's no use, no one can hear you down here." Roach cast the electric light around so that Corbett could take in the tunnel. "No one is coming to rescue you. Your friends are all on a train heading North. She knows that; she knows lots of things, most of which I've told her, like all about your older brother, Norris, and how his stars have marked him out as a Alchesmith and he'll take over your family forge at

Ord. How he'll most probably marry his sweetheart, Effie, if the Mechanists decree that their tracks are compatible. Be a shame if anything upset their stars. . ." Roach's voice echoed in the tunnel.

He could tell by the look in Corbett's eyes that he hadn't been expecting Roach to know about his family. It was easy to be strong when it was just you, when only you might suffer, but when it was those you loved at risk, things were different.

Roach began walking, and Corbett dutifully followed through the twisting tunnels deeper and deeper under the heart of the city towards the Dark Dragon's lair, the once home of the mighty Great Dragon Brõga.

The Dark Dragon sat on her throne of nightsilver, the glistening white teeth of a Great Dragon fused into the black metal, sharp and sinister.

Roach watched as Corbett's eyes darted around the chamber, taking in the octagonal walls, and the ornate patterns carved on each one. Roach wondered if Corbett could read the symbols hidden in the patterns of the walls; he was, after all, a scholar, a celestial physicist in training, and he knew a lot more that Roach ever would.

"Bring him to me!" the Dark Dragon called as she saw Roach enter the throne room.

Roach moved to Corbett's side and grabbed a hold of the top of his arm, manoeuvring him towards the octagonal raised platform in the middle of the room where the throne sat. It was as dark and light as the little girl sitting on it. The crisp white teeth of a great dragon, who had died at the hand of the third George thousands of years ago, cast into the black nightsilver metal of the throne. The Dark Dragon looked tiny as she sat on it, her black dragonhide boots not reaching the ground. Her hair was as dark as the nightsilver of the throne, and her skin as white as the teeth. She smiled sweetly at Roach and Corbett as they moved closer to the throne, all innocence. But Roach knew that even though she looked like a harmless little girl of nine or ten, she was actually older than the teeth that she sat on.

"Listen to me," he whispered. "You never want to anger a dragon, especially this one. Do everything she asks, and she might just spare you."

Corbett turned to look at Roach, his eyes wide. With his bound hands he reached into his pocket, pulling out his glasses. Roach took them from him and smoothly wiped them clean on his coat before putting them on Corbett's face. The glass lens on the right had a crack running down it from when Roach had first apprehended Corbett as Corbett made his way from the Aerodoc towards King Star train station.

Roach stopped in front of the Dark Dragon, on the step below her throne. Corbett stood, defiant, not taking his eyes from the beautiful little girl in front of him as Roach removed the gag.

"Corbett Grubbins," the Dark Dragon said, her voice sweet and light as she smiled at him and slipped from her throne. She wore tall dragonhide boots over a pair of trousers and a jacket that would not have looked out of place on one of the King's Men. Draped over her shoulders was a black cloak with a blood-red lining to match the detail on her uniform.

The Dark Dragon walked to the edge of the platform, standing above Corbett, her head level with his.

"You are quite extraordinary," she told Corbett, her smile radiating awe for the young apprentice. "The nightsilver machine that you made for Violetta

Fitzwilliam was of the highest craftmanship I have ever seen."

Roach watched and Corbett's face altered, the fear and worry softening as the Dark Dragon continued to praise him.

"I have been alive for a very, very long time. I walked this Earth before the First George's King Star was even born. I watched the original Alchesmiths' search for the secrets of the unseen metals, those precious metallic elements thought to have been crafted by the Chief Designer and forged by Anu to create the tracks of the Mechanism. I saw how the Alchesmiths passed their teachings along the track from student to student, and I was there when the secrets of nightsilver were first found. I witnessed the First George forge his lance, and with it, slay Ealdordóm, the first Great Dragon to fall. But never in all my turnings have I seen someone as skilled with nightsilver as you."

Corbett's lips flicked into a brief smile before he clamped them shut again, the flattery flushing his cheeks pink. Roach watched as the Dark Dragon worked her magic.

"And not only are you skilled in Alchesmithery, but you are also training to be a Celestial Mechanist!" The Dark Dragon looked at Corbett with big eyes full of wonder. "I bet there isn't much that you can't do or don't know about."

Corbett smiled then, and Roach knew that she had him.

"I bet you can make anything out of nightsilver."

"Well, maybe not *anything*."

"You made the machine, and that was very complicated," the Dark Dragon said.

Corbett nodded in agreement.

"Do you think you could make something for me?" she asked, sweetly and innocently, her childlike enthusiasm lulling Corbett into a false sense of security and superiority. Roach had seen the Dark Dragon work this trick many times before; he'd even fallen for it himself once or twice.

"What would you like me to make?" Corbett asked.

"An arm," the Dark Dragon said, her bottom lip starting to tremble a little and tears filling her eyes as she pulled back the cloak to show the material of her tunic as it folded tight against the stump of her arm, abruptly ending a hand's width from the top of her shoulder.

"Does it hurt?" Corbett asked.

The Dark Dragon shook her head. "It did, but not now. I've lost limbs before, you know. Fingers, a hand once, and a leg, but they all grew back within a few hours. It's my Dragon Touch, you see; it keeps me young and whole and connected. But when the Veil took my arm, that was something different, and I can't seem to grow it back. You are so skilled and so clever, I know you could do it; you could build me an arm out of nightsilver, and it would be strong and powerful, just like the one I lost. Could you do that for me? Could you build me an arm?"

"Yes, yes, I suppose I could do that for you," Corbett said with a wistful look.

"Will you?" she asked.

"Aye, of course."

Roach wasn't sure if Corbett had agreed so quickly because of his warning or because the Dark Dragon had manipulated him so well.

"Good." The Dark Dragon smiled sweetly. "I'd like to give you a gift," she said, her eyes dry now. "It is a special gift, one reserved for only a few. It has the power to enhance the abilities and nature of whoever I choose to bestow it on."

Roach began to shift about beside Corbett, fearing what was about to happen. He wondered if he should push Corbett aside, or warn him. But to do that would incur the Dark Dragon's displeasure, and he needed her; he needed the Dark Dragon to succeed and be victorious. If she were ever to break down the Veil and bring back the Great Dragons, the dead would come with them – Clara. And Corbett was part of that plan. Roach took a small step away from him.

"You, Corbett Grubbins, are intelligent and skilled. With my gift, your mind will sharpen, your intellect will expand, your skills will deepen. With my gift, we will be for ever linked, you and I. Would you like that?" she asked.

Whatever stupor Corbett was in, Roach was sure that he was not thinking clearly. Corbett nodded to the Dark Dragon and parted his lips to reply to her, but before a word could escape his mouth, she had grabbed Corbett with her strong little fingers, wrapping them around his jaw and pulling open his mouth. She hesitated for a moment.

"This was easier before your friend took my arm. But not to worry, for I too am skilled and clever." With that, she bit her small white teeth into the bottom of her lip and beads of dark red blood sprang forth and dropped, one by one, from her lips into Corbett's open mouth.

Roach held the top of Corbett's arms as he thrashed around and gagged on the drops of blood, trying to spit them out.

The Dark Dragon's lip healed in moments, the blood stopping, the skin on her lip returning to a smooth, plump pink. She forced Corbett's mouth closed so that he ingested all the blood. "You will thank me," she whispered in his ear. "My blood will make your brain sharper and body more agile. For a while, you will be full of energy and totally alive. You will be able to work faster and longer and make me an arm that is worthy of me. This is my gift to you – that, and the connection we now share through my blood."

As soon as she let go of Corbett's chin, he spat in her face. Roach was proud of him.

As the Dark Dragon wiped the spittle with her cape, she locked eyes with Corbett. "Roach, take him to my forge. Give him everything he needs to make my arm and finish the work of my last Alchesmith."

Corbett stumbled a little as Roach led him away.

"Don't worry. The initial rush will soon pass, and when it does ... well, just don't like it too much. Remember where it comes from; remember who she is."

Roach looked back over his shoulder at the tiny girl sitting on the throne.

TEN

COPPERICH AND BETRAYAL

Roach wrinkled his nose as he pushed open the door to the forge and led Corbett in. The air was stale, and Roach made his way around the room, opening the windows that looked out over the rooftops of London. They had exited the twisting sewers, Corbett drifting along beside Roach as the initial effects of the Dark Dragon's blood gift worked their way out. A door in the sewer led to a twisting staircase that gave way to the forge. Roach had half-dragged Corbett up the spiral staircase, as Corbett stumbled around in a daze.

It was always like this in the beginning: a

confusion of the body and mind, but as with the George, Roach realized that the more often the gift is taken, the more violent the initial reaction, but the quicker the receiver recovers as the full effects of the Dark Dragon's blood takes over – for a time.

Corbett began to walk around the room, taking it all in, shaking his head to clear it every now and again as he fumbled around. Roach leaned against the doorway at the opposite end of the forge, which led into the storeroom.

In the centre was the forge fire – dull and cold, the spent coals littering the bottom of the hearth grey and lifeless; everything bright and warm had been burned out of them. Roach knew how that felt; all that was bright and warm in him had long since been used up. He set his jaw, turned, and slipped into the storeroom.

The walls here were lined with shelves of supplies: large chunks of raw metal, bottles of fine powdered substances, and liquids with handwritten red warning labels shouting caution.

Corbett followed him, appraising one of the shelves, looking over the bottles and boxes and tubs of alchemical substances.

"What is all this?" Corbett asked. "I mean, I know what it is, but why am I here?" He placed a hand to his head. "I'm a little confused."

"The confusion will pass, and when it does, you'll be fine – better than fine! You're here because you're an Alchesmith and she wants you to make her an arm to replace the one that Paisley took, and..." Roach rifled in his pocket. "She wants you to make her some of these, too." He pulled out a tightly rolled blueprint.

Crossing to a nearby workbench, Roach unrolled the blueprint to show the plans for a clockwork dragon about the same size as a large eagle. "She has a large colony of them at her control. Your predecessor finished most of them; this was the last flock." Roach nodded towards a shelf where eight mechanical dragons sat in varying degrees of completion. Corbett walked towards them.

"There should be plenty of parts over there, and all the things needed to make and cast the parts you don't have. Of course, you'll have to make the nightsilver and the copperich— Oh, you'll be needing this." Roach put his hand into his coat and pulled out a small glass phial full of a sticky, deep-red liquid.

"Is that hers?" Corbett asked, licking his lips.

Roach nodded and thrust the phial at him. "Don't get any ideas! You'll need it all to make her arm and the rest of the mechanical dragons."

Corbett carefully took it and quickly stowed it on the shelf with all of the other alchemical elements.

"Who made these?" Corbett asked, running a hand over one of the mechanical dragons in appreciation.

"Her last Alchesmith."

"And what's copperich?" Corbett asked as he turned back to Roach.

Roach looked at him blankly for a moment and then gave a little *hmph* of surprise. Raising his eyebrows, he said, "Thought you'd know all about that, being a man of science and all."

He beckoned Corbett to follow him as he walked to the back of the storeroom and ascended a small rung of wooden stairs that led up to a mezzanine in the rafters. On one side was a small cot piled with thin blankets and dirty sheets, and on the other was a long desk, littered with papers and books.

Roach flicked on the switch and electrica lights bathed the desk, while the cot remained in darkness.

Corbett began to lift the papers to the light, examining them one by one. He found the blueprints for the cogroaches; the plans were drawn in exquisite detail and painted in silver, brass, nightsilver black and. . .

"Copperich," he said, running a finger across the paper that showed the outline of the cogroach and a copper-coloured network of twisting metal that ran within it. "I saw this metal in your cogroaches on the roof of Paisley's home, but I didn't know what it was then – still don't, to be honest."

Roach joined Corbett at the desk and pulled open a drawer, and amongst the pencils, paints, brushes and paper was a dragonhide journal similar to Violetta's. In the right-hand corner of the journal were two nightsilver initials, RH, that had been forced into the dragonhide.

Corbett ran his finger over the cold embossing of metal as Roach handed it to him.

"It's all in there," Roach said as he started searching the wall of tacked-up images and writings. "And somewhere up here there should be an article he wrote, published in some journal in Amerika. Explained it all; that's how she found him." Roach glanced over at the cot and the bundle of blankets.

"He who?"

"The Alchesmith, Russell Hertzsprung."

"Russell Hertzsprung!" Corbett said with a slight chortle. "You mean the Mysterious Alchesmith of Main?"

Roach lifted an eyebrow. "He might have been a little odd, but sometimes I think he was the clearest thinker in all of the Mechanism. Ahh, here it is. . ." Roach tugged a page from the wall, leaving behind a clean cream square where it had been.

"*Practical Applications of the Entanglement of Deeper Self with the Particles of Copperich Extracted by Phytoleaching Fungi,*" Roach read aloud before handing it over to Corbett, who blinked several times.

"Yeah, there's a lot of long words there." Roach smiled. "Russell told me how when he was a young man he had emigrated to Amerika and travelled the whole of the Empire's lands there, and beyond, to a small group of volcanic islands. And there he found some igneous rocks – copper sulphate or something – all broken up and scattered in the soil in tiny bits. Now, this weren't no normal copper, and

119

Russell suspected that when the volcano had formed it had been near a seam of firestone, and the rocks had a tiny amount of firestone embedded in them, or mixed, or something; he called it coupled?

"The particles were small, too small for you to see without an electrica microscope, but growing on the soil was a type of fungus, a kind of toadstool that Russell had never seen before." Roach reached down and opened a small cupboard, pulling out a metal box.

Inside were small shrivelled toadstools, grey and puckered. Roach took one from the box, holding it by the top between his finger and thumb.

"When he picked one of the toadstools and turned it over, he found this." Roach turned the toadstool, and as he did a flash of copper shone in the electrica light. The gills on the underside of the toadstool were all made from the copper metal. Corbett took in a breath and extended a finger.

"Careful, the metal gills are fragile and break off easy. Besides, this is the last of his stash. Anyhow, Russell said that the combination of the fire diamond and something in the phytoleaching – the way that the toadstool extracts the metal from the soil – made the copper richer and gave it properties that normal copper just don't have."

Corbett was scanning the article; he looked up and nodded to Roach. Corbett had lost some of his dullness now, and Roach could tell that the Dark Dragon's gift was about to get started.

"Russell said that he then used the same process of forming nightsilver, but instead of using silver and such he used this volcanic toadstool copper, marrying it with the host's blood and everything to make a new metal – copperich. He even thought that it might be one of the unseen metals of the Mechanism, the invisible material that creates the tracks of the universe that everything moves upon, the planets, the stars, us. Of course they laughed at him for that, but he was on to something. Copperich is similar to Nightsilver but different, like night and day. Where nightsilver is strong and full of the power of its host, the copperich is, what did he call it – yielding."

"Aye, it says here that the marrying of the host and copper produced a metal that was weak, easily manipulated and broken, but that the entanglement allowed a far greater interaction from the host, and that they were able to influence the metal in ways that made it a symbiotic element." Corbett looked up from the paper, his eyes wide. "The Theoretical Scientists at Greenwich Overhead have been working on trying to do something similar for decades – but the Mysterious Alchesmith – he's already done it!" Corbett snatched up the drawings of the cogroach again and held them up. "I wondered how the cogroaches worked; it was like they had minds of their own!"

"Not of their own; it was my mind, that's what they're linked to: *intention*." Roach pulled out the tin from the inside of his pocket and opened it. It was empty.

Then Corbett startled as he felt something crawling on him. He looked down to see that the cogroaches that had been in the pockets of Roach's coat were crawling out and flying over to him. Then they all landed in the tin, settled themselves, and lay still and inanimate – completely lifeless.

"How?" Corbett asked.

Roach shrugged. "I just think about what I want them to do, or maybe *think* isn't quite right. *Imagine*, I imagine what they will do and how they will do it and they just do it. Russell tried to explain it to me once, that thoughts have energy or something, a kind of echo through space and time and that we're just not sophisticated enough to know it is happening. . . I'm sure it's all in there." He pointed at the journal, his eyes lingering on the nightsilver lettering.

"Where is he now? Russell Hertzsprung?"

Roach stood up straight, pulling his shoulders back as he sniffed. "Dead. I came to see him about a month ago and found him. He was very old – he hadn't been right for a long while. She'd told him that she'd give him the gift and set him free after he'd made a copy of Violetta's machine, but he never got round to it. That's why we had to snatch Violetta and her machine, you see."

"So now I have to stay here and take his place? Make the Dark Dragon an arm and an army of large mechanical dragon spies?"

"Well, not really spies, not like this one." Roach held out a small dragon spy that didn't belong to him. "And more of a flock than an army. Russell had worked out all of the designs for them; it's just up to you to finish them. The arm, though – well, I'm sure that you can sort that out, a smart lad like yourself."

Corbett's eyes lit up as jubilation filled his face. He snatched up a copperich toadstool. "I can use this!" he said with a smile.

Roach nodded; the gift was working its magic now. He turned and left Corbett. As he reached the door to the forge, he looked up and saw that Corbett was flicking through Russell's journal.

"A word of advice, Corbett. Don't skimp on the arm. Don't give her anything but your best work. She'll know, and it won't be you that she takes it out on, it won't even be Paisley, or Odelia. It will be your mum and dad, and your brother, Norris. It will be your family forge at Ord, and it will be bad."

Corbett met Roach's eye, and Roach knew that he understood.

Roach felt a small vibration in his pocket and opened the tin with the cogroach tracker in it to see that the three dots representing Paisley, Odelia and Hal had stopped moving. He furrowed his brow.

"I'll be back tomorrow," Roach told Corbett. "There's food and supplies down here. I'd get to work if I were you; she won't want to be kept waiting."

He locked the door as he made his way down the

stairs, thinking of Russell, thinking of how the Dark Dragon had promised to set him free so many times, and how he had asked Roach to help him.

Roach slipped a letter from his pocket that he had lifted from the back of the journal before handing it to Corbett. The letter was addressed to Russell's son and granddaughter; Roach had a pile of them under the floorboard beneath his bed. Each time he had taken one, he had promised to post it, and each time he had lied.

Now he thought of Russell in the Veil, and wondered if the old man now knew of his betrayal.

ELEVEN

THE UNEXPECTED STOP

A soft nudging woke Paisley. She sleepily looked out into the night, the black engulfing the train as it smoothly made its way northwards on a cushion of electrica magnetism. Even the thick white winter snow that covered Albion was hidden in the gloom. The electrica light in the cabin was off, making Paisley feel as if the darkness of outside had seeped into the cabin while she had slumbered. Odelia slept next to her, bolt upright and still as the stars that shone in the unfathomable heavens above. Hal sat slumped opposite, his arms folded, his chin resting on his chest, the soft deep breaths of sleep filling the cabin.

The nudging came again as Paisley absentmindedly reached out to the side of her; she had half expected to find Mother's hand, softly rousing her from sleep as Mother used to do on winter mornings when Paisley was too warm in bed to wake up, but all she found was her satchel.

Suddenly she was wide awake, thinking of Mother but also pulling her satchel on to her lap, reaching inside to touch the dragon egg. It felt much larger than it had been at the house. She searched for the nightsilver casing that was in the bag too. Paisley held the egg in one hand and pulled out the casing with the other; the egg was almost double the size of the case now.

Paisley placed the egg against her cheek and felt how warm it was. She closed her eyes. It felt so soothing, just like the gentle caresses Mother had woken her with.

Then, from inside, the egg gave a little *thud*. Paisley jerked away from it, her heart rate shooting up and dropping the nightsilver case to the floor with a *clang*.

Hal and Odelia were on their feet, Odelia with her blades drawn, Hal with his fists up.

"Sorry, it was just me," Paisley said. Odelia flicked on the electrica lighting in the compartment and for a moment they all blinked in the harshness of the light.

"The egg, it's grown again!" Paisley said. "And I can definitely feel something moving about in there now. This morning it was just a motion, but now it's a thud!"

"Not a something, a dragon," Hal said as he reached out his hand and placed it on top of the egg.

"A dragon," Paisley said as the realization caught her that inside the egg was something real and special, something that needed her in much the same way that Dax did.

They all stood still for a moment, and then Hal gave a laugh, his eyes widening as the dragon inside the egg moved.

"Odelia, feel this," Hal said as he took Odelia's hand and placed it against the egg.

Odelia looked as if she was about to protest and remove her hand when the dragon inside shifted. She broke out into one of her rare and fleeting smiles, and Paisley saw how Hal smiled back, and, in their excitement, the two of them locked eyes for a little longer than a moment.

Paisley looked from Odelia to Hal and then back again.

"What?" Odelia said, raising her eyebrows.

"Oh, nothing," Paisley said with a smile, which faded as she felt a shift in the motion of the train. "Wait, is the train slowing down?" she asked, her voice sounding too loud in the small compartment. "Perhaps we're at the next station?" she added in a smaller voice.

Odelia shook her head and turned off the electrica lights in the compartment. "This is supposed to be a non-stop train to the Wall and beyond." She quickly stood and straightened her wig as she pulled on her coat and moved to the window.

Paisley followed Odelia's lead, pulling on her coat and placing the satchel over her head, tucking the egg safely back inside. Hal grabbed their backpacks from the luggage shelf.

The train slowed quickly and came to a halt, the carriage rocking slightly. They were at a small village station; the train was too long to fit into the platform, and their carriage was left stranded on the magnetic tracks. Paisley could see a few malting buildings around them, and beyond them the scattered houses and cottages of the village.

Odelia had pushed up against the glass, her face reflected in the window, her keen eyes scanning all the way to the platform five or six carriages down.

"The King's Men!"

"Knights?" Hal asked, a note of excitement in his voice.

"Yep."

"Knights! Are you sure?" Paisley asked as she pushed her face up against the glass too.

"I'm sure. Two guesses who they're looking for," Odelia said.

"OK, we can still get away," Paisley said as she picked up her long scarf and wrapped it around her neck, tying it in a succession of knots while her mind raced. They couldn't get captured. She looked at Odelia and Hal and could feel the weight of the dragon egg in her satchel. There was more at stake than rescuing Dax.

Paisley adjusted the strap of her satchel to hold the egg closer to her. "Right, as soon as all of the knights get on the train, we will pull open the window, drop to the ground and run for that small building over there." Paisley pointed to a store shed sitting in the shadow of the large maltings next to it. "Odelia, let us know as soon as they are on board."

Paisley could feel her heart beating rapidly, and tried to calm her breathing, but as she did she became aware of the electrica in the air. She surreptitiously looked around the compartment for any sign of a Veil cloud.

"Three are on board, one has stayed on the platform watching the train."

"Right. OK, that changes things, no window. Follow me." Paisley turned, pulled open the compartment door, and looked down the corridor that ran the length of the carriage past the other closed compartments. Paisley rushed towards the back of the train, away from the station. Through the windows that flanked the corridor she could see that the land on the opposite side of the train was open farmland, but a few carriages down it gave way to some trees that were not too far from the train tracks and looked as if they formed the edge of a woodland.

Paisley continued to travel down the carriages, Hal and Odelia following along behind her, soft-footed and stealthy till they reached the luggage cart. Paisley paused as she opened the door, hoping that there wasn't a porter inside. The carriage was empty save for suitcases and boxes.

"Here." Paisley pulled open the large sliding door on the side of the carriage that was used for loading the luggage. The cold night air was full of an earthy, sweet smell from the maltings. She sat on the floor of the train, her legs hanging over the short drop below, and for a moment she wondered how she was going to get north to Dax now. She'd walk all the way to the Wall and beyond if she had to.

She dropped down from the luggage carriage and into the snow. The snow came up past her knees, and Paisley hesitated, looking around at the white expanse in front of her. It would be hard going, and the Knights would easily be able to follow their trail; they might even see them from the windows of the passenger carriages as they crossed some of the farmland.

"Wait!" Odelia whispered down to her, as she took off her cloak and handed it and her pack to Hal. "I'll come back for you," she told him as she reached down and pulled Paisley up and into the air.

Paisley barely had time to register the sensation of flying before she was on the ground again, Odelia depositing her on the edge of the forest. Then she returned for Hal, flying high and fast to avoid anyone on the train seeing her.

Paisley stood inside the treeline where she could see the full length of the train, two carriages down from where she had escaped. The King's Men were searching every compartment, swords out, armour on. Odelia and Hal were still on the train; she could see them talking animatedly as the King's Men entered the carriage next to the luggage compartment.

The electrica feeling around her increased, and she looked behind her to see a small Veil rift forming. Paisley tried to ignore it, turning back to the train. She bounced on the balls of her feet, her fists clenched. She couldn't lose Odelia too.

Paisley cupped her hands around her mouth and gave a soft *hoot*, and Odelia swung her head back to look at her. Paisley motioned towards the carriage. Odelia looked in that direction, then grabbed Hal and pulled him off the train.

The sliding door slammed shut, sending a deafening sound into the night. Paisley dropped to the ground, shifting her satchel out from underneath her as she lay in a bank of snowy fallen leaves, a wall of drifted snow covering her from view. She hoped that the Veil cloud was not too big or obvious as it floated somewhere above her.

She sneaked a look at the train and saw Odelia and Hal standing on the top of it. The King's Men were in the carriage directly below them. They had the door open and were looking out at the marks that Paisley had made in the snow, then out across the white expanse, baffled.

Paisley ducked back down and held her breath.

"They must still be on the train. Continue the search," she heard one of the men instruct, his voice carrying in the still night followed by the slamming of the door once more.

Moments later she heard Odelia's soft wing beats above the trees. Paisley looked up and followed Odelia's dark outline in the sky through the bare branches. She was glad to see that the Veil rift had fizzled out, although the tingle of electrica was still present and she could feel it coursing through her body. She stopped mid stride as she realized that every time she formed a Veil rift, the connections were becoming stronger. She was becoming more aware of the rifts and the effect they were having on her. Paisley gulped, swallowing down her thoughts and fears, and carried on walking in the direction that Odelia had flown.

A little way into the wood was a thinning in the trees, and Paisley found Odelia there, taking her cloak back from Hal.

"You are very strong," he told her. Paisley smiled at the admiration in his voice.

Odelia fastened her cloak and took her pack from the Krigare, but said nothing.

"That was close," Paisley said as she reached them.

"Yes, well, Hal wanted to stay and sacrifice himself so that we got away," Odelia said, her disapproving eyebrow raised.

"I was being gallant," he said.

"Foolish," she said. "Warriors do not divide their forces when their numbers are low and chances of success in their mission even lower."

"Oh." Paisley hadn't really thought through their chances of succeeding; for her there was no option for failure. She had to be reunited with Dax.

"Don't you see, I could have thrown them

135

off, told them you were going somewhere else – Amerika, maybe!"

"Yes, of course, we were going to Amerika on a train travelling north! All you would have done is get yourself hanged."

Paisley shuddered as she thought of the gallows. "Let's just walk. We're heading north now." Paisley pointed at the heavens. "So, let's keep following the North Star through the trees, and then we'll find out where we are and figure out what to do next."

They set off at a fast pace, as the snow was not so deep here, just a light splattering in amongst the more densely packed trees.

Hal was quiet, and Paisley couldn't tell if he was in a huff or not. Every time she looked in his direction, he looked alert and on guard. If Odelia had spoken to Corbett like that he would have been sulking about, snapping the twigs and rustling all the leaves he could find, making Odelia scowl at him even more.

Paisley missed Corbett, in the silence of the wood. She hoped that he was safely on his way to his family's forge and that she'd be reunited with him, and then Dax, soon.

TWELVE
SAFE AS WAREHOUSES

Paisley shifted her dragonhide satchel as she followed Odelia through the edges of the walled city of York. They had been walking for the best part of a day, pausing every now and again to rest or eat from their supplies. They had kept to the back roads and trails, as the outlying villages had slowly become thicker, the houses closer together, the roads shorter and more numerous as they set their course towards the Dragon Walker Safehouse that Odelia said was in York. Electrica lights burst into being ahead of them as the crisp night fell, cold and still.

"The darkness will offer us some protection,"

Odelia said as they slunk into the city. Paisley turned her head towards the east and saw her mother's comet small and clear, its tail streaking out behind.

Paisley held her satchel in her arms as the weight of the dragon egg pulled down on the strap, leaving her neck and shoulders sore. Her arms were starting to go the same way. As she held the bag she could feel the shape of the egg inside. It was bigger than it had been on the train, and every now and again Paisley felt a light *thud* from inside as the baby dragon turned and twisted within the egg. Each little jolt from within made Paisley's stomach clench and heart race. She was carrying a Great Dragon; the last time one of these had been seen was thousands of years ago.

"I think it's grown again!" Paisley said to Odelia as they stopped at a junction, the Dragon Walker looking in each possible direction.

"She," Hal said. "She has grown, or they, but not it; the dragon in your egg is sentient and not a thing."

"What makes you think she's grown?" Odelia asked as she squinted at the street sign to the left and made up her mind to go that way.

Paisley gestured to her bag. "Because she feels so heavy and you can tell the egg's bigger."

"I can carry her for a bit, if you would like," Hal said.

She shifted her bag in her arms. "It's OK, I'll look after her."

Hal nodded, and Paisley felt a little bad. He was only trying to help, but then, he was a Krigare; what's to say he wouldn't take the dragon egg and run off to the Northern Realms with it? Paisley felt guilty for thinking that way – Hal had proved himself an ally – but it was also true that the dragon was her responsibility.

"What do dragons eat?" Paisley asked him.

Hal fell into step beside her. "Grass in the summer months. They like to graze. Fruit and seeds, and they like nuts and hay. My Steek-Natt was partial to a turnip or two, though no one thanked her for it." He smiled and gave a light laugh as Paisley worked out what he was saying.

"Oh, I see. I'll be sure not to give my dragon any turnips, then."

They walked on, following Odelia like twin shadows. York unfolded before them, and Paisley saw the tops of the Mechanist Cathedral in the distance and felt the weight of the coin in her pocket, almost as heavy as the dragon egg.

"How will I keep her safe? How will I train her?" Paisley blurted as she thought of her stars, then the egg.

"I can help you with the training – if you want me to, that is," said Hal. "As for keeping her safe, we will do the best we can and just hope that she won't hatch until we are safely in the Northern Realms."

Paisley felt her stomach churn as she thought of what might happen if the dragon hatched in the Empire of Albion, what the George and his knights might do to her. She hugged her satchel a little closer.

"Is it much further?" she asked Odelia.

"I hope not," Odelia said as she walked on in sure strides towards a bridge that crossed the frozen river Ouse. Paisley watched as her shadow changed in the light of the many electrica lamps on the bridge, then disappeared as Odelia led them down on to a dark towpath. The lights from above bounced on the ice, and Paisley could see lines and swirls criss-crossing the surface. She smiled as she thought about how she and Dax had skated across the frozen Thames just a few days ago. When they returned home, she had found her star summons waiting for her. Uncle Hector had taken them out that day. Anger burst in her like flames leaping on a log, and she could feel her body tensing and becoming warm as she thought of all that had happened since she received her stars. She kept seeing Uncle Hector's smile as they played on the ice, Dax's giggles filling her ears. She'd been so happy, and she hated herself for not cherishing the moment more and for trusting Uncle Hector to always be there, just as she had fallen on the ice and he'd picked her up, and she'd felt safe and loved.

The tears had frozen on her cheek before she could wipe them away.

Ahead of them was a large and imposing building that took over the towpath, nestled right up to the water's edge. On the side was a large metal sign which read *The Brothers' Warehouse*.

Odelia walked up to the side door of the warehouse and knocked twice before pausing and knocking three times. She then repeated the pattern twice before stepping back and waiting.

Paisley shifted from foot to foot, adjusting the satchel in her arms as she looked back down the towpath, the electrica lights of the bridge glowing beyond the thick darkness that seemed to engulf the huge warehouse. Five stories high, with a crenellated top and a tower on the end nearest the bridge, it looked more like a small castle than a warehouse. Paisley scoured the large windows, each one cut into the solid stone of the imposing building, but all was dark and quiet inside.

Paisley stretched out her back and shifted the egg in her arms again, thinking about taking up Hal's offer to carry it for a bit, when she heard a lock opening from within and the side door opened. The shadow of a large man filled the doorway, silhouetted in the soft golden glow of lights beyond him.

"Greetings, brother," Odelia said as she reached out an arm, crossing it in front of herself as if in defence, and pulling up her sleeve to reveal her golden bangle.

"Greetings, sister." His voice was gravelly and deep as he copied the gesture, showing an identical bangle which he struck against Odelia's. As the metal rings connected, they let out a harmonious chime that resonated through Paisley, low, with a strange tingle that filled the air and made the atoms in her feel like they were vibrating.

The man stood aside and Odelia entered the warehouse, Paisley following her, and Hal last to enter the small hallway. A little further ahead was another door which led them into the main warehouse space. The light here was more subdued, but Paisley could make out crates and barrels piled high and close together.

"Welcome. I am Rufus, keeper of this house. We are quite full tonight, but I'm sure we can find some room for you and . . . your friends, sister. I don't believe we have ever met before."

"No, this is my first time in York," Odelia said, then introduced herself and Paisley and Hal to Rufus as he led them all through a large storeroom, which gave way to a loading bay, then up a wooden staircase, past more crates, and then through stacks of warehouse stock to a concealed door in the wall.

Paisley felt a little nervous jolt as Brother Rufus clicked a hidden hinge and the wall pushed in, revealing a narrow staircase in the gloom behind the false wall; it reminded her of the hidden passages at home. She glanced at Odelia, who gave her a small nod and then made her way up the stairs with all of her usual surety.

"What is this place?" Paisley asked in a hushed whisper as Rufus followed Hal behind her up the stairs.

"It is a warehouse," said Odelia, "just like many others along the riverbank, but it is also a Dragon Walker safehouse. We Dragon Walkers have many such businesses dotted throughout the Empire of Albion, usually in big towns and cities, some in more rural places, out at the coast where we might have access to the sea. Most deal with trade or commodities. We dragons like to hoard, and we like to barter and bargain – the Dragon Brothers included."

"What's a Dragon Brother?" Paisley asked.

"The Dragon Brothers are the male children of Dragon Walkers. They carry the Touch just as we Dragon Walkers do, even if it isn't manifested; they are still our brothers, they are still part of Anu's legacy, just as are our Unseen Sisters who hold the Touch but do not show it."

Paisley nodded. She'd never really given any serious thought to the way that Dragon Touch manifested. She'd always thought that Dax had just had a big bump of bad luck in his track. But now that she thought about it, about the story of the Soul Sisters, about how one of them was probably her ancestor, she realized that, like Dax, she too carried the Touch. She felt a little prouder all of a sudden, that she was connected to the Dragon Walkers, that she was a Dragon Sister too.

"How many Dragon Brothers are there?" Hal asked from behind Paisley.

"In here, about eight or ten, I suspect. In the world? Many more than you would think. They live in the Empire of Albion, and in the Empires to the East, and a few even live in the Northern Realms. Some keep the way of the dragon and are an active part of our family. Others keep their own way. They are still our family; we will still be here for them, all our brothers and our Untouched Sisters too."

Paisley reached the top of the stairs and stood to one side of the landing, waiting for Rufus to join them. When he did, he gestured for them to enter a door to the right.

The room beyond was large and light and airy. Electrica light filled it from two large chandeliers that hung from the beams, their light bouncing from the gilded picture frames that hung on the wooden panelling of the room. There was a large wooden table over to one side, surrounded by solid chairs richly upholstered. On the centre of the table was a bowl full of fruit. To the side of the table was a large fireplace and around it were three large couches; each one looked soft and inviting, and Paisley longed to fall into one of them.

"Sorry that this room is so small," Rufus said. "You will find two bedrooms through the door at the back, and I or one of the other brothers will bring you some supper, but there may be a slight delay. As I mentioned, we have a full house tonight."

"Tell me, Brother, are many of our sisters here?" Odelia asked.

"The Dragadore are seeking refuge after a mission," he told her, and Odelia nodded, a grave flicker of worry passing over her face.

"Was this party from the Dragadore in the company of Adore Marea?"

Paisley remembered the young woman who had stood defiantly on the gallows; her name had been Marea.

"I will ask the Adore Alyse to come and speak

with you, Odelia. She is leading the party now," Rufus said, flitting his dark eyes in Paisley and Hal's direction. Paisley realized that this man was little older than Uncle Hector. His beard and hair were woven with white, and he held himself with the same surety and strength that she had witnessed in Odelia and the other Dragon Walkers on Kensington Above.

"I will find you some nourishment. Please, make yourselves comfortable," Rufus said as he left the room.

Hal immediately collapsed into the nearest sofa and Paisley took off the satchel and placed it gently on the table.

"Who are the Dragadore?" she asked. There was so much that she didn't know about the mysterious Dragon Walkers.

"The Dragadore are the fiercest and most skilled of us Dragon Walkers. They are trained in warfare to a much higher standard than the rest of us. Those Dragon Walkers who complete the training are given the title Adore to show how much we all respect their skill and sacrifice. To be counted amongst them is to be singled out for greatness by Anu. They perform many dangerous and secret missions to protect and keep us all safe."

Paisley thought of the Order of Mercy. Her father had told her that within the order was a secret faction of knights whose strong tracks and bright stars led them into the Empire of the East and Northern Realms, and that there they undertook tasks that lesser knights could never have managed. Paisley felt that the Dragadore were like these knights.

"Have you ever wanted to join the Dragadore?" Paisley asked Odelia.

Odelia smiled. "I think Anu has something different planned for me. I think that she has something great planned for us both, Paisley Fitzwilliam. But if she wished me to become an Adore, I would not balk at the responsibility."

THIRTEEN
THE DRAGADORE

A different Dragon Brother had returned with some food for them, and when all had eaten, Paisley began to feel a little more like herself, as well as a whole lot more tired. She checked on the egg in her satchel and moved it closer to the fire to keep it warm, then she sat in one of the deep, cosy sofas and felt sleep creep over her.

Paisley wasn't sure how long she had slumbered before the door banged open and a high-pitched squeal filled the room. Paisley shot to her feet, grabbing the poker from beside the fire. Without even thinking about it, she, Odelia and Hal had jumped into the middle of the room, back-to-back, Odelia with her hands on the hilts of her swords, Hal with his fists up.

A dark shape swooped over their heads. Odelia was the first to relax, stepping away just as Paisley realized that the shape belonged to a little girl, a Dragon Walker about the same age as Dax, with the most beautiful blue wings, the colour of dawn to dusk and all that was in between.

"Odelia!" she called as she stopped circling the room and headed straight for Odelia, who caught her and hugged her tight. "Sister, it has been many moons since I've seen you!"

"Three moons."

"That is three moons too many. I have missed you so much!"

"And I you," Odelia said with a smile so bold that it took Paisley by surprise. Odelia kissed the top of the little Dragon Walker's bald head, between her tiny blue horns. "And now you are here! Anu has found a way of forging our paths together again."

"She always does," the little Dragon Walker said. Then she looked at Paisley and Hal. "Who are your friends?" she asked. "Brother Rufus said you had interesting travelling companions." Her gaze lingered on Hal, and her eyes narrowed as she took in the ice-blue Krigare marks on his neck where the make-up had worn off.

"This is Paisley Fitzwilliam. She is a fierce warrior on a mission to be reunited with her brother, who has been kidnapped by the Krigare of the Northern Realms. She is a sister in all but touch, and I would die for her," Odelia said, and Paisley felt a lump in her throat. "And this is Hal Northman. He too is a fine fighter. He has lost his dragon, his Krigare companions, his family, and his country, and we both know what that is like. I am not sure if his life is equal to mine, but he will have my sword if he asks of it. Paisley and Hal, this is—"

"CeCe!" another Dragon Walker called from the door, and the young Dragon Walker slipped from Odelia's arms to the floor. "Adore Alyse told you not to bother Odelia!"

"Is this true?" Odelia asked.

"Yes, but as you said, Anu always finds a way for us to be together. This time she called Adore Alyse away to see to one of the Taken who are sick, just as I was able to creep out and find you."

Paisley looked at the new Dragon Walker and was surprised to see that she knew the girl who was now striding into the room, halting at the fruit bowl and taking a small bunch of grapes.

"You," Paisley said, pointing at the girl with the poker and then lowering it quickly before putting it away in its holder by the fire.

The girl had stopped with a grape en route to her mouth and looked at Paisley with wide eyes.

"You know Never?" Odelia asked.

"Not exactly," Paisley said as she turned back to the Dragon Walker and took a step forward, extending a hand. "Paisley Fitzwilliam," she said as they shook hands.

"Never, Never Jordan."

"I saw you at the shop. The Men of the Yard were there, and they tried to take you, but you. . . I'm glad you got away," Paisley finished as she remembered how Never had stood in her chains and roared, extending her jaw wider than Paisley thought was possible, the roar seeping into everyone around her and making them collapse to the floor. And when Paisley and the Men of the Yard had come to, Never had gone.

Paisley watched as Never put the grapes in her pocket, the colour having drained from her face.

"I'm sorry, I didn't mean to upset you," Paisley stammered.

"It's fine," the girl said. "I'm glad I got away too. Especially after what we've been doing."

"And what exactly have you been doing?" Odelia asked, looking from Never to CeCe.

"We have been freeing the Taken," CeCe said, her voice suddenly small and a little shaken as she snaked her hand up and into Odelia's.

"I see," Odelia said softly as she guided the young Dragon Walker towards the sofa and sat down with her nestled close beside her. "That was very brave of you, CeCe."

"What are the Taken?" Hal asked as he too sat on the sofa opposite.

The room became silent, and Paisley sat on the floor in front of the fire and pulled her satchel with the egg towards her, nesting it in her crossed legs. Never sat on the opposite end of the sofa to Hal and eyed him with distrust.

"The Taken," Odelia said, "are the Dragon Walkers who are found by the Men of the Yard and are taken to be hanged. But before that happens, they. . ." Odelia paused and shifted on the couch as CeCe snuggled closer to her. Paisley had never seen Odelia so uncomfortable before. "More often than not, before they kill us, they experiment on us," she finished.

Paisley didn't know what she was expecting to hear, but it wasn't that. "They do what?" she exclaimed, a cold fire burning through her veins.

Odelia was looking straight ahead. "They take our blood. They test our Dragon Touch. They try to reverse it, or harness it, or take it completely – as if they ever could. They try to rip and beat it from us. If we have stars, they put them out," Odelia said, pulling back the sleeve of her left arm to reveal a round scar. "They burn them from us, they take our track, then . . . then they take our lives."

Paisley felt her hands ball into rage-filled fists.

"Once you have no track, they try to find out what makes your Dragon Touch tick," Hal said, his brow low, his blue eye stormy as he looked at Odelia.

"How dare they!" Paisley could feel the hum of electrica behind her, and the fire guttered and disappeared as the Veil cloud that formed pulled all the flames into it. But it vanished as quick as it came.

Hal looked at Paisley as he got up and restocked the fire, slowly placing each branch in a considered way before lighting it. The room was still and silent whilst he did.

"The George did this to you, Odelia?" Paisley eventually asked.

Odelia shrugged. "His knights, and to CeCe too. That's how we met each other. And when the Dragadore freed us along with the others who were being held at the facility we were in, we were separated, CeCe and I. But our tracks keep crossing."

"Anu has a plan for us, Sister." The young Dragon Walker smiled up at Odelia through her tears.

"How old were you?" Paisley asked.

"I was six and a half turnings when I was taken, and almost twelve when I was freed. CeCe hadn't been there long, a few moons," Odelia said in her matter-of-fact way.

"I was little, so I can't remember much, except the needles and the pain," said CeCe. "And Odelia, holding me when I was scared and sore."

"I remember it all," Odelia said, her voice sounding hollow.

Paisley wiped her tears away. She didn't know what to say. She felt so angry. Angry that this had happened to Odelia and CeCe and other Dragon Touched, angry that it was still happening, that it had almost happened to Never.

They all sat in silence for a long while, and the fire that Hal had made slowly ate through the wood to become a roar which mirrored the rage that Paisley felt, and every time the dragon in the egg shifted and moved she hoped that it truly was a Great Dragon, that it would grow to be big and fearless and unstoppable, and as soon as she and the dragon had taken down the Dark Dragon, they would take down the George.

FOURTEEN

SHADOW THOUGHTS

The warehouse was dark and comforting. Odelia's wings flopped over Paisley as she slept, adding an extra layer of warmth.

Paisley turned her head and traced the outline of her friend's face in the soft glow from the embers in the fireplace. Odelia was strong and striking, and as Paisley watched her sleep, she wondered how anyone could have ever hurt her or any of the Dragon Touched. She had always held a fear that Dax would be found by the King's Men and that when he was, he would be killed. But the reality was that, like Odelia, he would have been experimented on first.

Despite Odelia's warm wing, Paisley shivered. Odelia shifted, her left arm sneaking out from the cover, and Paisley saw the edge of the circular scar where her stars had been burned away. The skin was a solid river of darker and lighter patches puckering in rivets and waves within the circle.

Paisley slid her hand out and looked at the strange semicircle of stars on her own wrist. She thought of the Mechanist coin that sat in her coat pocket. Her first stars had said that she would die, and she had, but she'd also come back from the Veil. She'd not wanted to think too much about that, but now she wondered if she had defied her fate because she had refused to believe what her stars had said, or if it was always in her track to die and return.

Paisley slipped from the bed and silently got dressed. She picked up her coat and boots, and snuck from the room as Odelia slumbered.

What if Corbett was right? What if the coin that sat in her pocket held a clue to the future? What if the stars it would give her would set her on a path to defeating the Dark Dragon? To saving Dax! She started putting on her boots, then paused. What if they didn't? What if the stars said that she would fail again? What if nothing had changed?

Mother's voice filled her ears: *"Knowledge is power."* The echo of a memory reached out to Paisley, as if her mother was guiding her on, sending her towards her stars and the knowledge they held. As if her mother was still looking out for her from beyond the Veil.

Paisley brushed her tears aside as she tied her bootlaces and pulled on her coat, feeling a warm glow inside as she thought of her mother, a glow that was cold with loss at the edges but burned bright and hot in the centre, because Mother had loved her fiercely and Paisley had loved her in return.

Paisley stood up, remembering how her mother had always told her that although she was growing up trackless, everything Paisley did would lead her somewhere, and eventually it would lead her to her stars. She couldn't see her track now, but she was sure that she had one.

Hal said that it was best to live your life the way you wanted. But if the Mechanism was true, then there was nothing you could do to avoid your track. Even if you lived your life your way, you would still be following the plans that the Chief Designer had for you. If the Celestial Mechanism existed, then there was no escaping your track.

She crept to the fire, her satchel sitting in front of it and the egg inside. Paisley pulled back the fire guard and added a few more logs, waiting to watch them catch.

She took out the egg and held it close. "I'm not at all sure if I'm doing the right thing, but I know that if I don't collect my second stars and there was something in my track that would stop me from getting to Dax – or worse, put him in danger – and I could have known about it and tried to stop it, then I would never forgive myself." She stroked the egg, feeling the texture of the shell. She was sure that the little dragon inside was sleeping. "Who knows, my stars might even tell me about you." She smiled at the egg, then her smile faded. "It's best to know what I'm up against, right? It feels like there is so much against me, and not a lot in my favour. I hope my stars shine brightly on my track; I hope they show me the right way to go. I know this sounds silly, but my first stars led me to my father. I can't help but hope that my second stars might lead me to my mother, for just a moment. I just want to see her again, to tell her that I love her." She wiped her tears from the surface of the dragon egg, feeling a little foolish. She knew that mother was gone, but for a moment she wondered what she might trade to get her back. Paisley put the egg back in the satchel and moved it closer to the fire to keep warm, then left.

Paisley's hand trembled as she slid open the concealed door at the bottom of the stairs and moved soundlessly through the warehouse, retracing the route that Rufus had led them along a few hours earlier.

The cold winter hit her as she stepped back out on to the towpath, hugging her arms around her, the token heavy in her pocket as she walked away from the bridge and made her way towards the York Mechster. The tall spire of the Mechanist building stuck up above the city, guiding her towards it. Like the smaller Mechanist chapels, Paisley knew that inside there would be a schematica waiting for her token, ready to deliver the stars to her wrists that would guide her along the track of the Chief Designer's choosing.

*

Paisley wasn't the only one being guided through the city of York that night. Roach had left the Central York Aerodoc Station a few hours earlier and had tracked his way through the city, glancing down at the small green display in his hand every now and again till he found her. The little green dot that was tracking Paisley's movements was dead ahead, across the water, in a large building that backed on to the river.

Roach flicked a switch on the side of his goggles that made the screen in the tin go dark but the rest of the world leap into life, green and eerie in the nocturnal vision. On the side of the building were large metal letters that read *The Brothers' Warehouse*. All the windows were dark, but just then Roach caught a flash of light as a door in the side of the warehouse opened.

He clarified the image in the goggles and zoomed in on the person walking towards the bridge. As the person turned and looked around, he smiled.

It was Paisley.

FIFTEEN

THE SECOND STARS OF PAISLEY FITZWILLIAM

It was dark inside the Mechster. A soft, scattered light glowed from above, and when Paisley looked up, she caught her breath. The high, vaulted ceiling was not like that of the small chapel she visited at home. It didn't have the false artificial glow of electrica lights marking out where the stars should have been in the sky; this ceiling looked like a window on to the Celestial Mechanism. Inky black surrounded myriad stars, each one blazing with its own unique colour and intensity in a scattered band of milky twilight. It reminded her of the times that she had seen the night sky from

Greenwich Overhead and how she had felt small and insignificant as she'd gazed up at the vastness of the Mechanism. She was just a small cog in a much bigger endeavour, turning along her short, paltry track.

Her fingers clasped around the token and her cheeks darkened. For a few moments she had allowed herself to think that she was important. After all, who gets to have a second destiny? As she had made her way to the Mechster, she had wondered if she might find a track waiting for her that was significant in some way, but now, standing under the weight of all those stars, she wondered if anyone's track was truly that.

She felt the same fear creep into her that she'd had when she'd received her first stars – what if they were not to her liking? What if they said she would die again? What if they said she would never find Dax? She couldn't bear that – not knowing would be better. She slipped the coin into her pocket and turned to leave, but as she did, she caught sight of someone darting behind a nearby pillar. She placed her hand on to the hilt of her sword and turned her head upwards, pretending to admire the stars. She edged closer to the pilar, then suddenly rounded on it . . . to find nothing.

She heard a shifting behind and turned the sword up, twisting to thrust the watcher against the pillar, her blade at his throat.

"Roach!" She looked up into his dark brown eyes. He smelled of the damp night from some foreign lands to the East of the Empire, rich with spices and tinged with the salt of strange seas.

Where the Veil-filled scar in her chest was, she felt the tip of Roach's dagger. She looked down at the carved wood handle and waited for the trickle of fear and the electrica static in the air . . . but it never came.

"I've already been killed there once before, Mr Roach. I don't think it will work again."

He smiled and a small *ha* slithered from his lips.

"How did you find me?" Paisley asked.

Roach pouted. "You can't expect me to tell you that now, can you?"

"Well, then, what do you want?" she asked.

"The same things as you," he answered, his bright eyes twinkling in the light from the stars above.

"Oh, I very much doubt that," Paisley said, her

grip on the hilt of her sword unwavering.

"You want to save your brother. You want to travel to the land where he is and claim him back. Well, I had a sister, and I want to do the same. I need to claim her back too." His voice was sure and steady, but his eyes clouded and faltered as he spoke. Paisley felt her grip on the sword relax a little.

"Your sister. . ."

"Clara, her name was Clara. If the Men of the Yard hadn't discovered her. . ."

Paisley felt her heart drop. "She was Dragon Touched."

Roach gave the smallest of nods under the guidance of Paisley's sword's edge.

"She was so small and bright, and I loved her so much. I couldn't stop them. I couldn't keep them from taking her or from tightening the noose about her neck, but I can make amends now. I can get her back, *she* can get her back, from the Veil."

"The Dark Dragon? Oh, I see. You help her, and Clara is your reward."

"I think you'll agree that saving a brother or sister is worth the toil."

So that was why he was in league with the Dark

Dragon: just as she had promised Uncle Hector that he would be reunited with his brother, so she had promised Roach his sister. For a second, a thrill rushed over Paisley: maybe if Roach could get his sister back, she could have her mother back, and her father too! But then she realized what the price of that would be, and how disappointed her parents would be in her for following that track. She felt a pain in her heart, her loss pumping through her veins. She took a steadying breath and looked down, realizing that the blade that had been pointing at her heart was gone, and she pulled back her sword – keeping it in her hand while she took a step back from Roach.

"So, why are you here? Why are you following me? I thought the Dark Dragon would be heading north, after the stone, after Dax."

"She is – she has the George raising an army. He's under her control, and she plans to use him and his forces to take the North with your brother and the stone in it. Then she's journeying to Amerika. She thinks another part of the Heart Stone is there, and she needs it for her grand plan to open the Veil and return the Great Dragons, along with Clara and all the others that she has promised to restore to their tracks.

"But right now, she wants something else. She wants to know what your destiny is. It's why she had the Master of Stars cast you a new coin. You entered the Veil and came back, and she's worried that your stars might stop her."

Paisley shoved her hand into her pocket and tightened her fingers around the token. "My stars?"

Roach nodded.

Paisley hesitated, then she reached out her hand, the copper coin sitting in her open palm.

"I think this is kind of poetic," Roach mused. "After all, I saw you receive your first stars back in Lower London. I watched you place your arm in the schematica, and then I took the scroll of stars from you as you stumbled through the streets."

"You!" Paisley tightened her fist around the coin. "I thought I'd lost them!"

"You did – you'd lost them to me."

"Did you read them?" Paisley's stare was hot and fierce.

"I did." She watched as he squirmed under her

gaze. "She needed them."

"Well, I hope they did her no good."

Roach gave a lopsided smile, his dark hair falling across his face in a mischievous way. "I think that you do her no good at all, Paisley Fitzwilliam. Not your stars, but you. That's also why I'm here, to see how you'll vex her next."

"Really?"

Paisley was not sure at all about Roach's motivations. She squeezed the coin in her hand and hoped that her stars said she would be reunited with Dax, but she also hoped they said that she would thwart the Dark Dragon and all who served her.

She looked over at Roach and felt uncomfortable.

"I hardly think it's right that you or she should know my stars. They're mine to give."

Roach sighed. "My stars say that one I love will fall into the Veil. That I will spend my life trying to prove myself worthy of her, and that one day we will travel our tracks united. See? I've shared my stars with you, even though you have no right to them."

"It's not the same. You took my stars; I didn't give them freely."

They both stood in silence for a while, weighing

each other up.

"Well, I'm not going to just give them to you, and I won't let you take them," Paisley said.

"I could trade you something for them," Roach offered.

"What do you have that I would want?" Paisley asked, then she thought of something. "I want you to do all that you can to keep Dax and my friends safe. So Corbett, Odelia, and Hal too."

Roach turned to face her. "Hal?"

"Hal Northman, he's a Krigare, Prince of the Northern Realms."

"I know who he is, I just didn't know he was your friend."

"Well, he is. But that's not important. What is important is that I'll gladly give you my stars if you promise to help me keep them safe from the Dark Dragon. All of them. Safe."

Roach ran a hand over his chin. Paisley could see that he was thinking through his options. "I will swear on my track that if you surrender your star scroll to me then I will do everything in my power to help your friends and Dax."

"And make sure no harm comes to any of them."

Roach gave a big sigh. "There might be a little harm, but yes, overall, I will make sure no big, scary Veil-stirring harm comes to any of them, if I can."

Paisley held his gaze for a long while. She was sure that he was going to try and take her stars anyway, and if she could have his word then he might just keep her friends safe.

"On your sister's stars?" she said as she extended a hand.

Roach didn't hesitate in clasping Paisley's hand. "On Clara's stars."

Something in Roach's eyes made Paisley believe that he was being sincere.

"It's a deal then."

Paisley took long, sure strides towards the schematica. The middle of the Mechster was adorned with life-size sculptures of the Georges' past, each one watching Paisley as she made her way up on to the dais and to the schematica. It looked very similar to the one that she had used to receive her first stars, only bigger and grander. On the top of the machine were looping circles of gold to show the tracks of the Celestial Mechanism.

The opening where Paisley now placed her left

hand was also ringed in a golden circle. With her sword resting against the machine, Paisley took the token and placed it on the edge of the slot at the top. Roach was standing next to her, and the light from the millions of tiny stars in the ceiling above illuminated the two of them, so she could see him clearly.

"You know what they say," he said with another smile, "a starlit track is easily travelled."

"Let's hope so," Paisley whispered as she let the token slip between her fingers and down into the machine.

The soft blades of the schematica closed, holding Paisley's arm firmly in place as a small, glittering pattern of stars were tattooed on to her wrist. It stung, but Paisley had been expecting the pain this time and kept her face still as Roach watched her.

The clunking whirl of the schematica stopped, and Paisley waited for the blades around her arm to open ... but they stayed in place. She tugged her arm, but it didn't budge.

Then a bell sounded from within the machine, its pitch high and clear as it filled the cold darkness of the cathedral, ringing again and again, calling for attention.

Another bell at the far end of the nave began to ring, and then another and another, uniting in a harmonious discord.

"What's going on?" Paisley asked as she looked about the Mechster, her arm still stuck in place, as she tried to work out where all the bells were.

Then she glanced up, as a deep booming filled the Mechster; the bells in the towers had started to ring too. Then the stars in the ceiling caught her attention. They were all moving, but not as they usually would, not marking out their tracks in the Celestial Mechanism. All the stars were moving towards the centre of the roof to form a single star.

"Oh, no!" she said, and shot her head back around to where the scroll that contained her destiny had just fed out of the machine. She tugged it free with her right hand and read:

"You, Paisley Fitzwilliam, have been chosen to guide and rule us all. Your track is the path of empires, your destiny the fate of all men, your word the command of the Chief Designer. All hail the George!"

Paisley's eyes leaped to the King Star that had formed on the ceiling. Her breath caught in her throat and she felt a cold clamminess come over her. The stars of fate had turned, and she felt dizzy with what they held. She looked back down at the parchment, at the printout of the stars of her track, and there in the middle sat the King Star, as black as the night sky, surrounded by smaller golden stars.

Roach let out a long whistle.

Paisley glared at him.

He gave a mock bow. "Apologies, Your Georgeness."

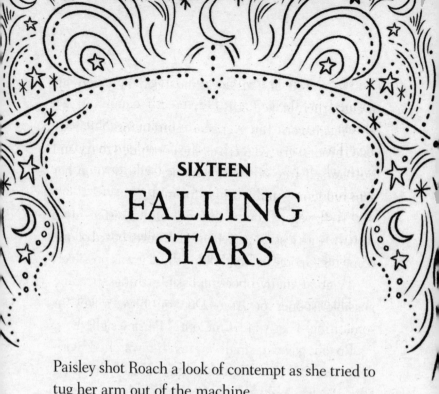

SIXTEEN

FALLING STARS

Paisley shot Roach a look of contempt as she tried to tug her arm out of the machine.

The bells of the cathedral rang louder and louder, and under the noise Paisley heard another sound: running feet. She pulled harder.

A young Mechanist, straightening his robes, his eyes wide, his hair ragged from sleep, ran down the nave, shouting, "All hail the George, ruler of the Empire, chosen emissary of the Chief Designer whose will we be shown in the track of the George— Oh! . . .You're a girl!"

He stared at Paisley as he tried to catch his breath, then looked at Roach.

"Yes, haven't you ever seen a girl before?" Paisley said through gritted teeth as she continued to try and pull herself free of the schematica, the skin on her arm reddening and a bruise forming.

"Well, yes, of course I have. I have a sister – two actually – it's just . . . well, I just ain't never heard of one being the George before. I didn't think it was possible!"

"A great many once-impossible things become possible sooner or later. Do you have a key or something? Can you let me out?" Paisley sighed.

Roach gave a small *ha* as he watched with bemusement. In the glimmering light of the King Star, Paisley could see the young lad glance over at Roach, and redden with embarrassment as he shook his head. "Sorry, no can do. Only the Abbotecht has the means to undo it. You see, there was an incident about five or six Georges ago when the chosen lad scarpered and they had to hunt him down, so now there's a safety feature."

"I would hardly call detaining someone by force a safety feature," Paisley said as she went back to tugging her arm.

"Can you at least turn the bells off? Everyone will hear!"

"Yes, that's the point of them." The young Mechanist beamed, then he saw Paisley's face. "Sorry, miss – I mean, Your Georgeness. I can't stop the bells. The people will want to hear the proclamation! In fact, all the Mechanist chapels, churches, mechsters and buildings in the whole of the Empire will soon be ringing out the good news."

"I've got to get out of here! NOW!" Paisley said as she leaned towards the young Mechanist, who took a big jump back, then she turned towards Roach, her eyes wide and imploring.

"As soon as the Abbotecht arrives, he'll let you out. Then there will a procession all the way to the palace of the George in London, where you will be presented to the Current George, and after that you'll get to say a quick goodbye to your friends and family." The boy glanced Roach up and down. "Then your track will deviate away from all you know and your training to rule the Empire will begin. It's all in the King Scroll." The boy slapped his hand to his head. "I forgot the King Scroll!"

"The what?" Paisley asked.

"The King Scroll. It comes with the star." He pointed at the celling.

"I've never heard of it!" Roach said.

"Well, no, we don't tell everyone everything that goes on when a George is chosen. Where would the mystery be in that?" the Mechanist said, giving Roach a look of disbelief. "Anyway, Your Georgeness, I'm supposed to present it to you! It's full of all the stuff that you need to know about being the George and your track and . . . *everything*, all the secrets of the Mechanism that only the George gets to know! Cool, right? Wait here! I'll be back in a jiffy!" he yelled as he ran back down the aisle.

Roach gave a small smile. "I like him."

Paisley fixed Roach with a stare. "Well, I don't. Did you hear what he said? They're going to take me away and force me to be the George. I need to get out of here; I need to get to Dax."

Her arm had started bleeding now. She dropped her destiny scroll on the floor and reached over for the sword. Roach got there first.

"Give me my sword," she said.

"You're going to chop your arm off?!"

"Don't be so dramatic. I'm going to pry the blades open." She held her hand out expectantly.

Roach took a step towards her. He was so close she could feel how warm he was as he held the point of her sword towards the blades of the machine.

He took a deep breath and looked her straight in the eyes, serious and calm. "Do you trust me?" he asked.

She paused for a fraction of a second before answering, "Definitely not!"

Roach sighed. "Well, then, I'll just have to prove you wrong."

He moved the keen tip of Paisley's sword into the small gap between the overlapping blades and pulled back, turning one out like the petal on a rose. He swiftly moved to the next one, and on the fourth Paisley was able to pull her bleeding arm free.

Roach propped her sword up against the machine, then reached inside his pocket and pulled out a handkerchief. He tied it around her bleeding arm. She held still as his fingers swiftly pulled the knot tight. "There." He moved his hands down her arm towards her hand, and slid a finger over her stars. "Well, I never."

Paisley looked down to see that the half circle

splattering of stars that she had received in her first destiny were joined by a plot of stars that filled the other half of the circle, and in the absolute middle of them all was a black star bigger than all the others — the King Star.

Paisley caught her breath. Then looked up at Roach, holding his gaze.

"You *are* the George," he said, and kneeled in front of her, all jest gone.

The door to the Mechster banged open and a small group of people entered, most in their bedclothes with coats and trousers thrown over the top, some holding electrica torches. They had come to see the new George.

Roach swiftly grabbed Paisley's sword and stood up, pulling her behind the machine.

"What do we do?" Paisley looked over her shoulder at the people walking towards them.

"You do nothing. Stay here. They'll be expecting a boy; I'll lure them off, then you get away."

Paisley didn't have time to say thank you, or ask why he was helping her. Roach was on his feet and running towards the far end of the pews, then off towards the open door.

Voices from the crowd shouted, "There he is!"

"All hail the George!"

"Wait, come back!"

"Your Georgeness!"

Paisley watched as they turned and followed after Roach. He was as quick as a dragon's shadow, slipping out into the chill night. As he left, she realized he had taken her sword . . . and her destiny scroll.

She waited until everyone had gone, then made her way up the aisle. As she neared the door, she heard running. The young Mechanist was back, and this time he had a long golden scroll case in his hand.

"Wait, you can't leave!" he shouted. Then he ran up to her and stopped, trying to catch his breath once again.

Paisley acted without thinking. She pulled the scroll case from him and hit him over the head with it, bringing him to the floor with a *thud*.

"Sorry," Paisley said as she checked he was out cold and pulled him into one of the pews. Taking the scroll case with her, Paisley ran out into the night. Another knot of people were making their way towards the Mechster, and she could see the group who had entered earlier running off in the opposite direction. "The George, he ran away!" she called as she pointed towards the crowd chasing Roach.

The gaggle of people set off in the direction that Paisley had pointed. She started following them and then broke off, darting in what she hoped was the direction of the Dragon Walker Safehouse.

She kept to the shadows, her heart racing. She couldn't be the George, she just couldn't be! But the bells of the Mechster rung out across the city, calling her a liar.

SEVENTEEN

FLIGHT OF THE GEORGE

Paisley sucked in the cold night air. The chill north wind carried a thin drizzle of freezing sleet. The good people of York were exiting their houses with coats and blankets thrown over their nightclothes and milling about, looking into the night at the light that was shining from the top of the cathedral – signalling that the King Star had been bestowed.

Paisley ducked out of a passageway and on to a long, cobbled road that she was sure would lead eventually to the river, and from there she'd be able to find the Brothers' Warehouse, and Odelia and Hal.

There was a knot of men standing around a

tavern called Ye Olde Starre Inne. The door was wide open, electrica light spilling out into the night, illuminating the raindrops like shooting stars. The proprietor, still in his nightclothes and slippers, with his apron over the top, was serving customers.

"Got to toast to the new George," a big, burly man with a pint of ale in hand said to a small cluster of men around him.

He saw Paisley passing by.

"Hey, miss, you'se is going the wrong way. Mechster's that a way, s'where all the commotion is."

Paisley looked away swiftly and increased her pace, which she realized was a mistake as the man watched her with interest, and not more than a second later she heard a little boy shouting, "Pa, Pa, you'll never guess what!" Paisley looked back over her shoulder and saw a boy of eight or nine run up to the burly man. "The George, he ain't a boy, he's a girl, and he's run away!"

The men began to laugh, and although she was further down the road she looked back again and could clearly see the burly man looking at her as another chortled, "Shirking her duty before it's even begun? Sounds about right for a girl – their tracks are naturally more flimsy and frail, after all!"

"Hey, you, wait, show us your stars!" the burly man shouted at Paisley. She turned and quickened her pace again, feeling a cold terror pass over her. The sharing of stars was a private thing; no one ever demanded to see another person's stars. Paisley was sure that these men would force her to show her wrist if they caught up with her, and was terrified that when they did, they would take her straight back to the Mechster.

A few buildings down there was a side alley that led to a narrow passage that ran behind the buildings. Paisley darted through the drizzling rain, the sound of running boots behind her. The passage opened up into another road, this one the same mixture of houses and businesses, with a smattering of people standing about and talking. She ran down the road, then, at a shop called The Imaginarium, she darted into another side alley. She quickly realized the passage was a dead end and came to a halt.

She looked for somewhere to hide, but the alley was empty. She hesitated as she thought of darting back into the street and making a dash for it, and in that instant she felt hands around her waist and a sensation of weightlessness as she was hoisted up into the air.

"Odelia!"

Odelia's midnight wings beat once, twice, and then they were on the top of the flat roof of The Imaginarium, looking down on the alley as the little boy ran in and looked about. His father was soon behind him.

"I was sure I saw her come in here, Pa," he said as they both looked about and then upwards, Paisley and Odelia crouching out of sight.

"Maybe it was the next turn over?" his father wondered as they were joined by another man.

They left as quickly as they had arrived.

Odelia stood up, while Paisley remained crouched, catching her breath and nursing a stitch.

The sleety rain was still falling, and as the light from the electrica lamps of the city shone, they cast huge rainbows. One was shining over Odelia, lighting her dark skin and wings as she shook them out then folded them back, slick against her body. She pulled her cloak over them and pulled her hood up from the raindrops that were running down her bald head.

Paisley thought that she had never known anyone to be in full possession of themselves as Odelia was.

"I guess this has something to do with you?" Odelia nodded towards the Mechster, and Paisley pulled herself up. She could see it clearly from the rooftop – the bell towers ringing out into the night, the light from the gathered stars of the ceiling somehow shining straight up through the roof like an electrica torch, piercing the sky all the way up into the rain clouds and beyond to the Celestial Mechanism.

She swept her eyes across the city and saw many smaller lights shining up to the heavens, too, and she realized that the bells weren't just ringing in the Mechster but all around the city, in every Mechanist building.

What had the young Mechanist said? That every bell in the empire would be ringing, proclaiming that the next George had been appointed by the Chief Designer.

Paisley felt a wave of nausea sweep over her.

She turned to Odelia and lifted her sleeve. "I took the token, I collected my stars, I. . ."

Odelia leaned close to Paisley's wrist, peering

at the mark, and then looked up at her with a wide smile.

Paisley wasn't sure that she had ever seen Odelia smile before, not really smile, not like this. Her face was alight with a broad grin, her eyes sparkling, and, despite all the fear running through Paisley's body, despite every atom in her telling her that she was in more trouble than she could ever wish to be in, Paisley felt herself smile too. She fed off Odelia's excitement and allowed herself for a moment to feel the joy of being singled out and marked as special, without letting in any of the responsibility or the enormity of the power that came with the King Star.

She giggled and felt a little hysterical; Odelia laughed too, her merriment deep and warm.

"Well, I will say this for you, Paisley Fitzwilliam: you were never destined to be born under boring stars."

"No, I guess not."

"I have dreamed of a day when a girl would be marked as the George," Odelia said, her smile turning coy.

Paisley remembered when she was only a little younger than Dax, one of the scholars told them during a history lesson about the choosing of the George: he said the King Star was a sign that the Chief Designer had chosen this person to lead everyone in their tracks. The pupils had set about reciting the names of the Georges, from the first to the present, all ninety-six of them, as well as their places of birth and their titles. She remembered that the forty-second George was called the Bringer of Harmony, after he negotiated peace treaties with the Empires to the North, and the sixty-eighth George was called the Cold George because he was said to have been aloof and distant, keeping to his castle and not endearing himself with the people.

Paisley had asked the scholar if there had ever been any women Georges, and the scholar had laughed.

Almost all the Georges had married, and some had married women, but they were consuls to the George, their stars enabling his to shine brighter.

So, she looked around her at all the other girls, who had their stars and knew their tracks in life, and then she looked at her own wrist, empty, and for a while, despite what the scholar had said, she had a small hope that she would prove the scholar wrong, that when she eventually received her stars that she would have the King Star, that she would be the next George.

She looked down on her stars now. To think that she had gone from a wrist so clear and empty to one chock full of stars and possibilities and action.

"Paisley. Do you understand how important this is, how important you are now? You will have the power of the George, and you can use it to do so much good."

Paisley nodded; Odelia was right, of course. She was sure there were a great many things that she could use it for, not least allowing the Dragon Walkers the same rights as everyone else in the Empire.

"I could, but not right away. I'm only the George Ascending – I wouldn't be the George till the track of the current George has ended. In the meantime, I'd be taken away – trained in high politics and warfare. I'd have little power till my star ascends, less than I have now, and I need to use what I have to get my brother back and make sure the Dark Dragon doesn't get the Heart Stone. Besides, Roach said that the Dark Dragon is controlling the George. And if that's true, I don't want to be anywhere near the George or his men."

"Roach?" Odelia questioned. Paisley told Odelia all about Roach being at the Mechster and what he had told her of the Dark Dragon's plans.

"Odelia, do you wish you still had your track?" Paisley asked shyly. Some people were very comfortable sharing their stars, but most kept them guarded.

Odelia smiled. "I sometimes miss my track. I was destined to dance among my stars. Before my Touch manifested, I was at a school for dancers, and I leaped and twisted. But now . . . now I soar." Odelia looked up into the sky. "We all have a track, Paisley. We all walk, dance or fly along it, even if we cannot see it, even if we do not believe that it is there."

Paisley nodded. "But . . . but what if you don't want your track? What if you would rather walk, dance or fly along a different path, have a different set of stars?"

"Paisley, you are the only person in the whole Mechanism who has ever had the opportunity to follow a different track, to receive a second set of stars. Now, I don't know if that means that your track has changed, or if it has just continued, but we Dragon Walkers know that when the Great Mother Anu fired the tracks, she created them with her breath and bent them to the paths set out by the Chief Designer. The tracks cannot be denied; we see them in the turning of the stars and the twisting of the planets. But we Dragon Walkers also know that within the tracks she hid a plan, a Great Unfolding, she saw what was to come for the Dragons, for the Dragon Touched, for us all, and she sought to change it. That was why the Chief Designer cast her aside. That was why the First George vanquished all the Great Dragons, and why every George since hunts the Dragon Touched. They are scared that one day we will all break free of the unseen tracks that bind us. But, Paisley, to do that we must follow the path Anu has set for us."

Paisley nodded, but she couldn't help thinking of her mother. Mother had moved the comet, she had set it on the motion of a new track, hadn't she? Or were her actions already cast? Already decided by the Chief Designer eons ago, when Anu was instructed to put a kink in the comet's track.

Is that what Paisley's first stars were, a turn in

the track? And what about the King Star? When it came to her stars, nothing made sense to her.

Paisley shook her wrist towards Odelia. "This is not going to stop me from doing the things I need to do, the things I want to do. Dax comes first, then fulfilling my promise to my mother and stopping the Dark Dragon. The Chief Designer's plans will have to wait; I've got my own to deal with first."

EIGHTEEN

MASTERING THE VEIL

The sky in the east was starting to turn from black to inky blue as Odelia landed on the roof of the Brothers' Warehouse and Paisley slipped out of her arms. The bells were still ringing, and the lights from the Mechanist buildings were still shining brightly.

The skylight window squeaked open and CeCe's head popped up.

"You found her!" she called. "Why are the bells ringing? What are the lights for?"

"Trouble," Odelia said as she stepped through the open window and down the short flight of steps.

Paisley pulled the window closed behind her and followed the two Dragon Walkers.

"What type of trouble? Trouble for us, or for her?" CeCe asked, looking back over her shoulder at Paisley.

Odelia led the way into the sitting room, where Paisley had left the dragon egg. "They are one and the same thing," she told CeCe. "Paisley's track is twisted with ours, with everyone's, everywhere. She is going to be the next George; she is going to be responsible for guiding the tracks of the whole Empire, the world, maybe even the Celestial Mechanism."

Paisley paused in the doorway as she took in the gravity of what Odelia was saying. The idea was too big to absorb; she still felt as if she were scratching at the edges of it in her mind. It felt too much to carry, and she would have to do it alone when she ascended to the throne. And just like the past Georges, her track would be longer than normal: Dax, Odelia, Corbett, everyone she cared for would meet the Veil and her cog would continue for many, many turnings to come, alone and heavy with responsibility.

"What have I done?" She felt as if the Mechanism

had just been removed from under her. Her knees felt weak as she reached out a hand, grasped the doorframe and sank down to the ground.

It didn't matter what she wanted to do with her life; her track would never really be her own again, no matter what she had said to Odelia. Whatever she did, her cog would affect the motion of everyone in the Mechanism. She clutched her chest as fear took over, her breath coming fast. The Veil scar on her chest felt colder and more solid.

"I should have never got my stars," she said, shaking her head as a cold wave of panic swept over her. She felt the electrica buzz coursing through her, and this time she could feel the Veil rift forming in the middle of the room. It was large and looming, and as she spiralled deeper into her fear, she could feel it growing.

CeCe yelled and jumped back behind Odelia. Hal scuttled around from the other side of the rift, Never by his side.

"What's going on?" Rufus asked from behind Paisley, as he stood in the hallway, looking into the room at the black cloud of nothing.

"I'll get Adora Alyse," he said, turning and speeding away.

"What is it?" Never asked, staring at the Veil rift.

Odelia took a step towards the rift, tipping her head to one side as she examined it in more detail than she previously had, gazing at the rift in wonder. Then Paisley gave a yelp of fear and Odelia pulled away.

"It's part of the Veil," Odelia said. "It's a long story, but it's coming from Paisley. It's connected to her in some way, connected through her emotions, I think. It's quite remarkable and has the power to destroy anything it touches."

Paisley felt more panicked as the Veil cloud grew again. "I don't think I can keep hold of it!" she cried.

"You need to calm down, focus on your breathing. Think happy thoughts, just as you did on the train," Odelia instructed in a stern voice.

Paisley shook her head; her mind was so full of fear she didn't have room for anything else.

Never kept her eyes on the rift as she moved to Paisley's side and crouched next to her. Reaching out, she grasped Paisley's hand and cupped her face in her other hand. Her touch was cool like a freshwater stream on a warm day.

"Paisley," Never said, her voice deep and

comforting. "Paisley, look at me. I'm going to use my Dragon Touch to help you, OK?" Her eyes were a soft amber colour, warm and comforting. Paisley gave a small nod of agreement.

"Listen to my voice. You are safe. You are calm. You are in control of your emotions."

Paisley felt her breathing steady as Never's voice seeped its way into her, and the words *safe, calm, in control* washed over Paisley repetitively, like waves on a pebbled beach. She could hear Never speaking to her, but she could also feel the words that she said inside her.

"Keep going, the rift is getting smaller!" Odelia's voice drifted to Paisley like the gentle sound of shifting shingle.

"Paisley, can you feel the connection between you and the Veil rift?" Never asked.

Paisley could feel it. It was as if an invisible thread extended out of her, connecting her to the dark rift, and if she travelled along it in her mind she found that she could experience things about the rift. She intuitively knew things about it, just as she had known things about the Veil when she had entered it. She could feel the edges of the rift, she could feel its mass, and the ripples that radiated across its surface in time with the beating of her heart. She felt deep into the black nothingness, and there, surrounded by all of her feelings of worry and fear, she sensed a part that was distinctly other and its eagerness to be free.

Paisley felt herself nod back to Never. "I can feel it," she said, her voice sounding far away and floaty.

"Good. Paisley, can you stop it? Can you make it go away?"

"I don't know if I can."

"Try," Never said. "You don't know what you're capable of until you try."

In her mind Paisley felt the edges of the rift and began to fold them in on themselves, making the rift smaller, and as she did, she imagined all of her fears rushing back into her. But this time she listened to them, and spoke to them calmly.

Yes, things were bad and getting worse, but she had Odelia and Hal, and Corbett too. Dax: she held him in her heart and mind. She would get to Dax, she had to, nothing was going to stop her, not the Veil, her stars, or the Chief Designer. Mother had shown that the tracks could be moved. Paisley would forge her own track if she had to.

"That's it. You are in control, you are safe, you are calm, you have the power to master the Veil rifts," Never told her, and Paisley believed it.

She focused her eyes and watched as the Veil collapsed in on itself. She felt something else flood back into her along with the fear, an understanding that she couldn't quite put her finger on, as if the bit in the Veil that she had sensed in the centre had sneaked into her too.

Paisley took a large breath and felt the tension in her shoulders settle, as the eerie feeling faded back into the dull awareness of the Veil that she had previously felt, and she realized that it was strangely comforting. She looked from Odelia and CeCe to Hal, then Never.

The four of them were staring just past her. Paisley turned her head to see a woman a little older than Mother had been; she had long, golden hair plaited and twisted in intricate waves. She was staring at Paisley with an intensity that made her feel as if she was one of Doc Langley's specimens under an electricamicroscope.

"Odelia, when you told me about your friends you forgot to mention that one of them was Veil Touched!" the woman said.

"Forgive me, Adore Alyse, I didn't know that what Paisley possesses has a name."

"How did this happen to you, child?" Adore Alyse asked as she led Paisley further into the room, guiding her towards the sofas, nodding at Rufus, who closed the door behind them.

"I . . ." Paisley shot a hurried look at Odelia.

"Tell her the truth – about Dax, your mother, the Veil," Odelia said as she settled into the opposite sofa with Hal on one side and CeCe sitting close to her on the other.

Adore Alyse smiled kindly at Paisley. "I can see the truth in your words; they vibrate in colours around you, colours you cannot perceive, but my Dragon Touch allows me to see them."

Paisley started with her first stars and began to tell Adore Alyse everything, from keeping her fate a secret, to the discovery of the comet and her mother's experiment. How she faced the Dark Dragon and lost her mother. She told of Hector's betrayal and Dax's secret. She finished her story with her return from the Veil, leaving her father behind, losing her mother, and then Dax being taken.

Adore Alyse took it all in and was silent in contemplation.

"You called it Veil Touched, what's happened to me. Have you seen such a thing before?"

Adore Alyse paused. "Not exactly."

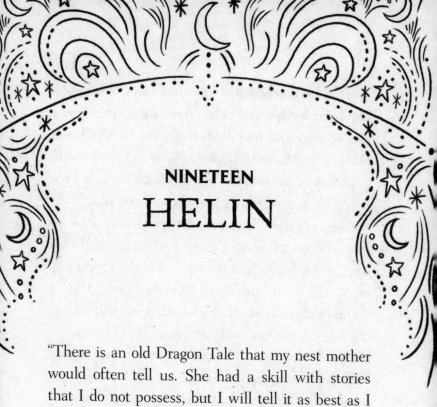

NINETEEN
HELIN

"There is an old Dragon Tale that my nest mother would often tell us. She had a skill with stories that I do not possess, but I will tell it as best as I remember," Adore Alyse said.

Paisley felt herself lean in, just as she used to when Mother or Father had told her and Dax stories before bed. She remembered the thrill of anticipation that ran through her as the story whisked her away on an adventure. Real-life adventures were filled with much peril and too much danger, she realized as she ran a finger over her stars and wished that the anxiety she now felt could be replaced with the excitement.

"In the beginning of the dark days, after Sabra had betrayed her sisters by trying to steal the Heart Stone, after she had been banished by all Dragon Walkers and forced to walk the world alone, after the Soul Sisters realized that the ambitions of Sabra had not been quelled in her banishment and they broke the heart of the world and scattered the four pieces to its corners, after the George had vanquished all of the Great Dragons and the shadow of their loss raced across the Earth, there was a young Dragon Walker named Helin whose touch allowed her to travel along the edge of the Veil and see the tracks of many.

"Helin was held in high esteem by her sisters. Her accuracy at predicting the track of a person was sought after by our foes as well as our friends.

"One such foe was a foe of yours, Paisley, the Dark Dragon, Sabra, our former sister and traitor to The Way of Anu. Sabra wanted to know what lay ahead of her in her long track.

"The Dark Dragon came to the private chambers of Helin and forced her to look into her track and tell her what she knew.

"The Dark Dragon was looking for the key to triumph in returning the Great Dragons to the world, but as Helin slipped along the tracks and found the Dark Dragon's future, she saw the former Dragon Walker's death.

"'You think yourself invincible,' Helin said, 'protected by your touch, but there is one who will end your track. A shadow of your sister's sister's sister will one day bear a child, both touched by dragon and starlight. This child will call the Great Dragons into the world and destroy you, fulfilling Anu's Great Unfolding of the Mechanism, usurping the George and ending his reign, and that of his Designer too.'

"The Dark Dragon was enraged by Helin's words. She wanted to be the one to restore the Great Dragons, to be the one to end the George and cease the Mechanism. Then she would rule by the side of the Great Dragons for ever. In her rage, Sabra struck down Helin, stabbing her in the heart. But as the Dark Dragon fled the Trove, life from the Veil flooded into Helin, and she returned to the world altered.

"It soon became known that when Helin had returned from the Veil she had brought some of it with her. Veil Touched, Helin found that she could manifest rips into the Veil. The breaches in the world were hard to control, and they caused much damage to our central trove, and indeed some of our sisters perished. Soon after, Helin disappeared into the west, never to be seen again.

"Some say she formed a rift and entered it, others that she is still alive, waiting for her time to take revenge on the Dark Dragon."

"But it's just a story, right?" Hal asked.

"Do you not have stories in the Northern Realms that hold the truth within them?" Adore Alyse asked, a small smile dancing on her lips as Hal got a wistful look on his face, then smiled, nodding.

"Yes, we have such stories, like the saga of the world bridge that was destroyed when the Mechanism was created."

Adore Alyse sighed. "I have always felt that much was lost when the Celestial Mechanism was created. Anu, for all her part in its creation, was aware of the harm too."

They were all silent for a moment, before Paisley asked, "What does the part in the story about 'touched by dragon and starlight' mean?"

"Well, many believe that this is the first mention of the Dragon Lord. The touch of the dragon is easy to divine; it refers to Dragon Touch; so this child, who is descended from one of the Dark Dragon's sisters, the remaining Soul Sisters, no doubt, will have Dragon Touch. But the child would also be touched by starlight, an archaic term used to refer to the George, for the George is indicated by the presence of the King Star in his track and thus his destiny is said to be touched by starlight. It is thought that this boy will call forth a Great Dragon, and when he does he will destroy the Dark Dragon, the Mechanism and the George.

"Could the Dragon Lord be a girl?" Odelia asked, looking solidly at Paisley.

Adore Alyse tilted her head to one side in contemplation. "I guess anything is possible; we live under strange stars. But no girl has ever been made George."

"Until now," Paisley said, and she lifted her sleeve to show her track: the black King Star sitting in the middle of the golden circle.

TWENTY

THE STARS OF WAR

The Dark Dragon was in her war room. The fire was lit and it flickered its warmth on to the large table in the middle of the room. The table held a scale model of the Northern Realms with small movable figures to denote the forces of the North and those of the George.

Joining the Dark Dragon around the table were the fallen Dragon Walker Lorena, the Mistress of War, Hector, and the Master of Stars, her old Mechanist advisor. The Dark Dragon reached out with a small hand and moved the forces of the Empire closer to the North.

"The stars are fortuitous; I have consulted the Mechanism and any decisive action you take now will be successful," the Master of Stars said. The Dark Dragon smiled, her face glowing in the light from the fire.

"What is it, Roach?" she snapped, not looking up from her plans as she sensed his appearance.

Roach walked towards the Dark Dragon, extended Paisley's star scroll to her, then took a large step back.

Being the bearer of bad news was always a dangerous task – more so when a dragon was involved.

Roach watched as the Dark Dragon read the scroll, her face becoming more and more still and tranquil as it glowed in the flickering of the fire. When she had finished reading it, she crumpled the parchment in her tiny hand and let out a scream of rage, knocked the model from the table, sending the forces of the North and the George to the floor in a thunderous crash.

"The Mechanism seeks to block my every track, but not this time. Paisley Fitzwilliam will not be the device that sees my demise, but I will be hers.

Where is she now?" She rounded on Roach, her face no longer calm and beautiful.

"In York, with the Dragon Walkers. I don't know where exactly," Roach lied as he heard his voice stammer and falter. "She removed her tracking cogroach." He realized in that moment that he was terrified of what the Dark Dragon might do to Paisley. It had been so long since he had felt anything for anyone other than himself that the realization shocked him.

"I know where she is likely to be," Lorena said. "There is a warehouse that the Dragon Brothers keep in York. They sometimes use it as a place of refuge."

The Dark Dragon paused, then turned towards the fireplace for a moment. When she turned back, she was calm once more. She gave Roach a sweet smile, and he felt the hairs on the back of his neck stand up. "Not to worry, Roach, this is not of your doing. The stars are beyond your control, but they will soon be under mine."

The Dark Dragon turned to Hector. "You will tell the George and his knights about this warehouse. Make sure that those who are loyal to you are part of the capture of the would-be George, and if her stars were to be put out, if there was some accident to end her track before her ascension, then that would please me greatly. If their tracks are not easily bent, then have Paisley delivered to me and I will put an end to her once and for all. With Paisley out of the way, all preparations will be made for the return of the Great Dragons."

Roach felt his insides squirm as Hector took his leave to halt his niece's track.

"I'll come with you," Roach said, his mind whirling.

"No, Roach. I have need of you," the Dark Dragon said. "Once Lorena and I have finalized the plans for war we need to pay a visit to the Alchesmith."

Roach deposited himself into a chair at the edge of the room. He had an uncomfortable feeling deep inside. He shifted in his seat as he watched Lorena restore the model to the table and the Dark Dragon plan out the attack on the Northern Realms. The chatter from the war council washed over him as his mind wandered towards Paisley, and he thought of how he could warn her, how he could tell her that the King's Men were coming for her. He had promised to keep them safe.

As he pondered, he heard a hissing from the tin in his pocket.

*

Paisley batted an arm in the air as a soft buzzing woke her. The mid-morning light was peeking in through the bottom of the heavy curtains.

The bells had stopped ringing, and she realized that she had heard the gentle buzzing before. "Cogroaches!" she called out as she sat bolt upright in bed, opening her eyes wide, and there it was, hovering just above her.

Paisley grabbed the pillow and batted it to one side as she leaped from the bed. Odelia entered the bedroom, slamming the door behind her, her toothbrush still in hand.

"What's wrong?" she asked, assessing the room. "You called out?"

"A cogroach!" Paisley said.

Odelia lifted an eyebrow. "Do you think Roach is close?" she asked.

"I don't know. I would have thought that he'd have taken my stars straight back to the Dark Dragon."

"Watch out, there it is," Odelia said as a second

cogroach joined the first, and then a third. They flew around the room, swooping close to Paisley and Odelia but never touching them.

Paisley grabbed a book from the small desk near the bed, knocking over a bottle of ink as she did. She cursed as she swung the book towards one of the cogroaches, hitting it across the room.

Odelia reached under her pillow and pulled out a whip, swinging it slowly around her head, then as a cogroach came close to her she flicked her wrist and struck it. It fell motionless to the ground and Paisley slammed the book down on it with a metallic crunch.

"Where's the other one?" Paisley asked as she looked about the room. She and Odelia were quiet as they listened for the whirl of the cogs. In the silence, Paisley heard the tiny metallic tap of the cogroach's legs scuttling over the desk.

The spilled ink now had a little trail of many tiny footsteps in it as the cogroach scurried across the table. Paisley took a step closer and tilted her head to one side. The line of inky footprints looked as if it spelt a word. "Run?" Paisley said as she read it.

Odelia was at her side, tilting her head to read the warning.

"Is Roach trying to tell us something?" she asked.

Paisley's eyes widened as she remembered his promise to help protect her friends.

"I think he is!" Paisley said in mild disbelief.

Odelia's face was grim as she fled from the room, her wings and nightdress streaming behind her.

Paisley pulled open the curtains, looking for a threat. If one was coming, it wasn't there yet.

She quickly crossed the hall and woke Hal, before dressing and grabbing her backpack and satchel with the dragon egg inside. Then she went in search of Odelia, finding her in the sitting room, with Adora Alyse and Rufus.

"I've sent out some of the brothers to watch for trouble. The city is full of knights; the Order of the Mechanists have called them in to help look for the new George," he said, with a knowing look in Paisley's direction that made her feel hot. She couldn't bear it if her second stars had put the Dragon Walkers in danger, not after all they had done to keep her safe.

"We need to leave. Some of the Taken that we freed are ill and weak; I had hoped they would have had more time to rest before we moved them." Adora Alyse looked anxious.

"If only the river wasn't frozen, we could have sent you away quickly and quietly," Rufus said. "But, as it is, we have two goods vans that we can use to smuggle you out of the city to the aerodoc. We have some influence there that we can use to gain safe passage."

Odelia nodded.

Adore Alyse was quiet as she considered for a moment. "Very well, let us move quickly; all the sick and vulnerable must be moved first."

"I will co-ordinate the brothers. We will not let this safehold fall without a fight," the Dragon Brother said, and something about the way he said it made Paisley worry.

TWENTY-ONE

THE KNIGHTS DRAW IN

The Brothers' Warehouse instantly became a hive of activity. Brother Rufus was joined by four other Dragon Brothers that Paisley hadn't met, and the younger brother who had delivered dinner the night before; they began organizing everyone.

Paisley quickly realized that the Dragon Brothers had a plan, and that this was something they had practised and prepared for. She knew what that felt like: Mother had always drilled them on what to do if the King's Men came calling, how to keep Dax safe, how they were to flee, if needed.

Paisley stood in the warehouse ready to leave, her

satchel over her shoulder, Odelia's bag in her hand, and Hal standing by her side.

"What can we do to help?" Hal asked a passing Dragon Brother.

"We're just securing the last of the Taken in the van, then we need to load the cases." He nodded towards a small stack of wooden boxes.

"We can do that," Paisley said, shirking off her backpack and making a bundle with Odelia's bag and cloak. Hal grabbed one end of a crate and together they carried it towards the large van that had been driven into the loading dock through the double doors at the front of the building.

The Taken were inside already.

Odelia jumped out of the back and turned to speak to CeCe, who was standing on the edge of the van. "You look after them. I'll see you at the aerodoc station. But if not, know that our tracks will cross again soon."

"Soon," CeCe said, and she embraced Odelia before moving deeper into the van. Paisley and Hal passed up the crate to a waiting Dragon Brother, who secured it in place.

"Are we going with them?" Hal asked.

"There's not enough room. The sick and the injured Taken need to be moved first, besides..." Odelia looked at Paisley.

"It's the George that they're after, I get it. I'd only put them in danger," Paisley realized, and she wished that she hadn't returned to the warehouse after getting her stars.

"What's in the boxes?" Hal asked as he and Paisley passed up the last one.

"Our most precious treasures," the Dragon Brother said.

"Gold, jewels?" Paisley asked.

"Information and intelligence," the Dragon Brother replied. "Each of these chests are booby-trapped to explode, should we need to stop them getting into the wrong hands."

Paisley was glad that she hadn't known that when she had been handling the wooden crates.

The Dragon Brother jumped down and Odelia closed the doors to the van as the last crate was loaded.

"Three of the Dragon Brothers, Adore Alyse, Cece and Never will go with the first van. We will go in the second with the remaining Dragon Brothers.

Both vans will take different routes. We will take a longer journey, drawing the knights away if we have to, giving the others time. All being well, the injured Taken should be safely at the aerodoc station before we arrive," Odelia told Paisley and Hal. Paisley nodded; she was glad that the others were going first, as she couldn't bear the thought of the Taken being found by the King's Men, being locked up and experimented on again. She gave a shiver.

"The Dragon Brothers are coming too?" Hal asked. "They are not going to stay and defend their position?"

"Their nest has been found and is soon to be breached. A dragon knows when to flee, but it does not desert without a fight, nor does it leave its spoils for others." Odelia's eyes flashed.

The first van left, and a second one backed into the warehouse, taking its place. Paisley and Hal began to help the Dragon Brothers load the second van, throwing in their backpacks. Paisley picked up her satchel with the egg safely tucked inside and slipped it over her head. "The King Scroll case!" She suddenly remembered the golden case that the Mechanist had given her in the cathedral. He'd said it was full of everything she needed to know.

Paisley ran off through the warehouse just as one of the brothers rushed by. "The King's Men are here!" he shouted.

Paisley looked around in a panic.

"Where?" she heard Odelia and Rufus ask in unison, as she ran up the stairs above them.

"Three patrols. One is taking up position on the bridge, the other is moving in from the opposite side," the brother called.

"Did they see the first van leave?" Odelia shouted to him.

"We don't think so," the Dragon Brother replied.

Rufus slammed one of the van doors closed. "We move now, while they are still trying to coordinate their forces!"

"But, Paisley!" she heard Odelia say as she slipped into the hidden space and ran as fast as she could, her satchel jostling around next to her.

The scroll tube was on the sofa where she had left it.

Paisley snatched it up, tucking it safely in her satchel as she ran back through the warehouse. As she descended the stairs, she could see Hal and Odelia standing in the back of the van, one door open, beckoning for her to run faster. She jumped, and the two of them grabbed her and pulled her in just as Brother Rufus drove the electrica van out of the loading dock. Hal lost his grip on the door as he pulled Paisley into the van, and it swung out, hitting the side of the van as it sharply exited the loading bay.

The three Dragon Brothers sat in the front cab while Paisley, Odelia and Hal tried to gain purchase in the back amongst the crates of treasure. As the truck turned on to the main road, Paisley, Hal and Odelia tumbled to the floor, the few loose crates that hadn't been secured following them. Paisley watched as one careered towards her; she rolled to the side just in time, pulling the egg in the satchel close to her. The crate pounded into the wall next to Paisley's head, and she sucked in a lungful of breath as she remembered what the brothers had said about booby traps.

Paisley pulled herself up to standing, leaning on the stationary crate.

"These crates are rigged to explode! We need to secure them before they accidentally blow us all up," Odelia called as she threw a length of rope to

Hal and they began to lasso the wayward crates to the van.

"Paisley, see if you can close the door," Hal called.

Paisley was next to the open door, looking out on to the street, and in the distance she could see something moving fast towards them. She reached for the door of the truck as it swung towards her, grabbing it just as the van turned on to another cobbled road, away from the warehouse, and as it did, a mighty explosion tore through the warehouse, blasting out the windows and igniting a massive fire. The booming blast wave took Paisley by surprise, and she toppled forward, holding on to the van door as it swung open and back on itself, hitting the side of the van and leaving Paisley dangling over the road.

Paisley kicked her legs, trying to get a hold of the lip on the door as she held on to the locking bar for dear life. Over her shoulder, she glimpsed the knights rushing towards the blazing warehouse, and from the bridge she saw three electricacycles driving towards them. Each one had two knights on it – one driving and one brandishing a lance.

Paisley's eyes widened as the door of the van began to swing back and the knights on the first electricacycle looked as if they were getting ready for target practice, levelling the lance in her direction and increasing their speed.

Paisley felt the tingle of electrica running through her as the Veil rift formed.

It hung above her, a small dark cloud less than an arm's reach away.

"Go away!" she shouted at it, struggling to hold on to the door. "I have enough to deal with!" A small part of the Veil cloud pulled away from the rest of it, and as the door swung open from the side of the van, the door made contact with the smaller rift, leaving a hole in the metal a hand's width from Paisley's head.

The knights on the electricacycle moved into view, and as Paisley's attention was caught by them, the larger rift went zipping through the air and sinking into the ground in front of the electricacycle. The road vanished, leaving behind a hole that the front wheel of the electricacycle fell into, sending the knights flying towards the ground. Behind them, the second electricacycle swerved and sped up to follow the brothers' van.

In all the excitement, Paisley lost her footing, her feet scrabbling for purchase as she clung to the bar.

The egg in the satchel felt heavy as the strap dug into her shoulder. The door kept bumping against the side of the van, as if trying to dislodge Paisley. She feared that it might succeed. "Help!" she yelled.

Odelia flew out of the van and swooped high into the sky, then around in an arc, coming behind the knights as the door of the van continued to swing and bang against the van, each time Paisley feeling her grip loosen.

Odelia swooped till she was flying just above the knights. She tapped the driver on the head, and as he looked up to see her, he lost control; the electricacycle tipped on to its side and skidded under the van as it made a tight turn, the knights tumbling from it before the cycle was crushed under the rear wheels, jolting Paisley as the momentum of the turn swung the door closed and threw her back into the van, where she landed on Hal, sending him sprawling.

Paisley pulled the satchel towards her and frantically shoved her hands inside, pulling out the egg and running her fingers over the surface to check for cracks.

Hall managed to stand up with one hand on

the van's interior side, the other rubbing his back. "Unlike people, dragon eggs are unbreakable from the outside!" he said.

Paisley jumped to her feet as she heard Odelia cry out.

The knight on the back of the remaining electricacycle had Odelia caught by the ankle with a long tether. Odelia had reached for her sword to cut herself free, and the knight on the electricacycle was starting to slow down and pull away from the van, taking Odelia with him.

Paisley couldn't help but think of a younger Odelia who had been taken by the King's Men and held captive, whose stars had been burned from her and who had been experimented on. She wasn't about to let that happen to her friend again.

"Quickly, help me!" Paisley called to Hal as she got behind one of the crates, cutting its bindings with her sword. The two of them pushed it off the van, where it landed on the cobbles with a *thud* and sat in the middle of the road.

"OK, not what I was expecting," Hal said.

"But the brothers said it was booby-trapped!" Paisley said, staring at the wooden box and willing something to happen. Then as the electricacycle reached the crate it exploded, sending the knights, the cycle and Odelia flying into the air.

Odelia regained her composure, hovering above them. She reached down and pulled the tether from her ankle, dropping it on to the wreck of the cycle as the knights moved about on the ground. She then flew gracefully to the van, catching the door and slamming it shut behind her.

"You OK back there?" Rufus called through the window in the back of the cab.

"We are now," Odelia said, and even in the dull light of the van, Paisley knew that Odelia had an eyebrow raised.

TWENTY-TWO
WITHIN ARM'S REACH

The Dark Dragon ascended the staircase to the forge and Roach followed close behind her. The heat of the furnace spilled down the steps, greeting them like a waterfall of warm air, getting hotter with every rising step. The Dark Dragon kept the deep red cloak wrapped over her shoulders.

At the top of the stairs, she held out her hand and Roach gave her the key.

As the door opened, the heat intensified. Roach pulled off his coat and slung it over a chair just inside the door, his shirt and waistcoat feeling tight as they began to cling to him, his breathing laboured as the hot air from the forge filled his lungs.

Corbett was working away, his sooty shirtsleeves rolled up around the top of his biceps, dragonhide gloves and an apron giving him protection from the flames and sparks as he hammered the glowing piece of metal that he held in a clamp. He loosened the metal and picked it up with the dragonhide gloves, the scent of fresh-made honeycomb filled the air, then the smell dissipated as Corbett plunged the metal and his gloved hand into a nearby vat of water, it hissed as a cloud of steam rolled over Corbett and he lifted the metal out.

Roach saw that it was no longer glowing red. Instead, it was the midnight black of nightsilver.

Roach gave a small cough and Corbett turned, finally realizing that they were there. He put the nightsilver on the workbench and pushed the goggles up on to the top of his head. He stopped the bellows and pulled a lever that opened the vents in the ceiling. The air instantly cooled by a few degrees, then settled at a level that was almost bearable.

Corbett kept his eyes fixed on the Dark Dragon, crossing his arms defiantly and staring at her with a look that spoke of both hatred and curiosity as she silently made her way over to the workbench and examined his work. Roach knew that the effects of the gift had worn off and was glad to see that Corbett's senses had returned.

Eight of the larger dragon spies stood on the benches, seven complete and one missing the wing that Corbett was just finishing.

The Dark Dragon stood still and gently tilted her head to one side. A fraction of a second later, all eight dragons mirrored her motion as she sent out her intention, the part of her that was bonded with the copperich coursing through the nightsilver and other metals of the dragons, making them move to her will. She smiled, her eyes bright and excited. The dragons all stretched their wings and leaped into the air, seven of them flying in circles around the room. Corbett just managed to reach out and save the eighth dragon before it crashed to the floor. He held it tight as it tried to escape his clutches and join its clockwork cousins.

The large dragon spies landed back on the workbench, and Corbett let the eighth one join the flock. They stood immobile again as the Dark Dragon turned her attention away from them.

"Excellent work, Mr Grubbins," the Dark Dragon said as she took a step closer to him. "Violetta was right to place her trust in you; your skill with Nightsilver is quite remarkable. I think you might be my best Alchesmith yet." She smiled sweetly. Roach knew that look, the childlike innocence and joy. He could see Corbett melting, being taken in, as the Dark Dragon's blood inside him stirred. She was so small and young, and when she wanted to, she could look quite helpless and vulnerable. That was when she was at her most dangerous, Roach had found.

"Is my arm ready?" she asked sweetly.

Corbett nodded and pulled off the dragonhide gloves. Then he plunged his hands under the tap to quickly wash them. Roach noticed that on his left forearm Corbett had a nasty cut, fresh and sore and ripe for infection amongst the dirt of the forge. Corbett dried his hands, tugging his dirty shirt sleeves down as he saw Roach looking.

"Here it is," Corbett told the Dark Dragon as he pulled back a sheet on the adjoining table.

Roach understood why Corbett had washed his hands. The arm was a thing of beauty, and Corbett took pride in his work.

It was made of hundreds, maybe even thousands, of interlocking metal scales, most made of nightsilver, a few of steel and some of copperich, which also edged most of the scales.

The Dark Dragon let out a sharp breath as Corbett lifted the arm and she reached out with her mind, flexing the fingers, then curling them into a fist. Each of the fingernails were tipped with a nightsilver point that retracted like a cat's claw as the fingers made a fist.

The Dark Dragon tossed back her cape, and the tunic underneath moulded around her shoulder and the top of the arm that had not been taken into the Veil.

Corbett held the nightsilver arm as he placed it on the Dark Dragon. As he held it in place, he instructed the Dark Dragon on the functionality of the arm he had made. "If you think about it tightening itself, it will."

The interlocking scales on the arm began to slide over each other, creating a tight seal between the arm and the Dark Dragon.

"The scales can also extend slightly. Think about stretching your arm out to reach the bottles on the shelf over there." He pointed to a shelf on the opposite side of the room, and the metal scales of the Dark Dragon's arm shifted, her clawed fingers reaching out, extending much further than those of her other arm.

She was delighted as she contracted her arm and ran her other hand over it, feeling the sleek scales, cold and powerful.

She then turned to the workbench and, balling her hand into a fist, she punched it, the solid oak splitting down the middle and sending the tools from the bench scattering to the floor. Then she crossed to the doorway and, extending her claws, she swiped at the stone that framed the doorway, cutting into it like butter and sending a massive chunk crashing to the floor.

She kneeled down and pressed her hand upon it, giggling as the solid rock burst into a fine splattering of dust and rubble.

"You have done well, Mr Grubbins. I am sorry to lose your service," she said as she wiped the chalk from her hand on to her cape and crossed to Corbett.

"You're letting me go? Just like that?" Corbett asked.

The Dark Dragon smiled sweetly. "Just like that."

Roach saw Corbett's shoulders relax.

"Well, once you have finished with my dragons, that is. When they are all done, Roach will release you."

"Thank you," Corbett said, and Roach winced at the hope in his voice.

The Dark Dragon walked towards the door, and Roach followed her. After the door had shut and the lock turned, she said to him, "You know what to do. Release him to the Veil as soon as he is done and ensure that his body is found so that dear, sweet Paisley knows what I have done to her friend. He will serve as a message of what I will do to all she cares about if she and her stars should stand in my way."

TWENTY-THREE
THE ARISTARCHUS

The brothers had stashed the van in a hangar on the far side of the aerodoc. The first van, now empty, was parked next to it, and the small aerocopter that the brothers housed in the hangar was gone.

Paisley sat in the back of the brothers' van, the doors open and her legs swinging restlessly back and forth as she waited for Odelia, Rufus and the others to return. It was only a matter of time before the King's Men would come for them here. The stars on her wrist tingled, and she pulled back her sleeve to look at them. She had put everyone in danger, she and her stars.

She pulled her sleeve down when she noticed Hal watching her. He jumped up into the back of the van and headed for his rucksack, rummaging inside. Then he sat next to her, handing her an apple and a small book.

"*The King Star: A Study of the Georges, from the First to the Present,*" Paisley read aloud.

"I found it on the bookshelf at the Brothers' Warehouse," Hal said between bites of his apple. "They had quite a lot of books on the George and his knights. I guess it is good to have as much knowledge about your enemy as possible. I read this one, you know, after your stars, and I thought it might come in handy for you."

"Thank you, that's very thoughtful of you," Paisley said as she began to flick through the book, taking a big bite of her apple. She paused on a page that showed the golden tube that the Mechanist had given her.

"Ah, *this* is helpful!" she said, and reached over, grabbing the tube and bringing it towards her. "I couldn't open it yesterday, but the book says that it is a puzzle tube." Paisley looked along the scroll case, then back to the book.

Hal leaned close and read over her shoulder. "Ah, yes, it said something about aligning the stars with those of the George. I wonder if they mean the stars on your wrist?"

"I doubt it. I mean, how would they know what my stars were before I'd got them in the schematica? And would it mean my first stars, or my second?"

Hal took the tube from her and looked over it. Paisley wished that Corbett was there; not only would he have loved the idea of the star puzzle, she was sure he would have solved it in no time.

"There are lots of stars on the tube, in between the swirls and dots and things," Hal said as he twisted the tube into the light.

"And yesterday I managed to get the casing to twist," Paisley said, taking it back off him and turning the tube. It consisted of many rings that could twist clockwise and anticlockwise.

"Look, this star here is black, just like your King Star," he said, pointing to a star in the middle of the tube. "Hold out your wrist."

Paisley hesitated for a second and then shirked back her sleeve. She and Hal looked back and forth from the tube to the stars on her wrist.

"That grouping of stars on the ring above the King Star looks exactly like this grouping on your wrist." He pointed to them and lined them up with the King Star.

"And if you draw a line from those," Paisley murmured, "through the King Star, on to the part from my first stars, it matches with these two stars on this ring here."

"Like a map," Hal said, his eyes wide as he smiled at Paisley.

"Exactly!"

As Hal twisted the last star into position, there was a resounding *click*. He passed the tube to Paisley, and she took it with a smile.

Despite all the fear that the King Star brought, this felt like a moment of adventure.

She held the two ends of the tube and gently pulled them apart.

Within were several tightly bound scrolls rolled inside one another. Paisley tipped them out and jumped down, and, using the floor of the van as a table, she unrolled the parchment and was surprised to see that it lay flat, as if it had never been rolled at all.

The first collection of parchment was bound

on one side with a golden thread, and on the front it said in Old Celtic, *The Contract of the George*. Paisley lifted that collection of papers and moved them to one side. Underneath was a series of loose blueprints, each one showing a lance. In the corner of the blueprint was a maker's mark, a date, and a series of numbers running in an ascending sequence, but with breaks and different starting points.

"There's a section on the lances in the book. Every George has one, and they all have to make theirs themselves – or with help," Hal added.

The last lot of papers was again written in Old Celtic and said, *The Treaty of the Celestial Mechanism*. Paisley moved this to sit on top of the contract, then rolled them both back up and put them in the tube.

She left the blueprints for the lances out and she and Hal looked over them, referring to the book and discussing them in turn until Odelia returned with a tall, athletic woman with short grey hair. She wore blue trousers and an aeronaut jacket with the insignia of the Imperial Aerocopter Fleet on its pocket. Below that was a name badge that read: Captain Hewitt.

Paisley rolled up the blueprints and stuffed them in the tube, closing it and twisting the stars to lock it again before putting it in her satchel alongside the dragon egg.

"Where are the brothers?" Hal asked, as both he and Paisley stared at the stranger.

"The brothers have bought passage to the Amerikas and we have found safe travel to Inverness with Captain Hewitt here," Odelia said, nodding towards the aeronaut captain. "We should arrive late this evening."

"Is this my cargo?" Captain Hewitt asked, her voice as big as she was. It bounced around the empty hangar.

"Yes, although the papers the brothers gave you say that you are carrying alchemical substances for the making of nightsilver."

"That they do," Captain Hewitt said with a smile, showing them a set of official-looking documents. "These are very fine indeed."

Odelia reached inside her cloak and pulled out a thick envelope. "I think you'll find that this will cover the cost of fuel, plus a little extra for your trouble."

Captain Hewitt took the envelope, felt its weight

and then placed it in the inside pocket of her jacket. "Shall we?" she said.

Paisley, Odelia and Hal gathered up their things, and Captain Hewitt led them all across the airfield to the awaiting aerocopter.

It was a small vessel, smaller than Paisley had been expecting. Its balloon was already filled, the propeller engines on either side idling, their low droning filling the air.

Paisley didn't know much about aerocopters, but this small cargo carrier was only a little larger than the passenger aerocopters that she had flown aboard to the floating boroughs above London. However, inside the aerocopter was a surprise: instead of the lounge-style seating and refreshment area she was used to, there was a large void, filled with crates of cargo that were secured to the metal structure of the aerocopter with large netting and thick ropes.

"She isn't exactly built for comfort," Captain Hewitt said, "but the *Aristarchus* is reliable and swift when she wants to be. She outran a Skywayman attack just last month, and since then I've installed precautions."

The way Captain Hewitt said "precautions"

reminded Paisley of the way that Odelia talked about the deadly fortifications of the Dragon Vaults.

"But she's carrying a lot of weight today, and with my legitimate cargo I'm only sanctioned to fly out of the way of other aerocopters. We'll be lucky if we reach Inverness by the small hours of tomorrow morning."

"What exactly are you carrying?" Paisley asked.

Captain Hewitt gave her a look. "You know, miss, there are some questions that are best not to be asked, and that right there is one of them."

Paisley felt her face flush as she found a space on the floor near a large crate marked *VOLATILE*. And as the *Aristarchus* lifted smoothly into the sky, she felt the stars on her wrist itch and the Veil scar on her chest grow cold.

She wondered if the most volatile thing on the aerocopter was actually her.

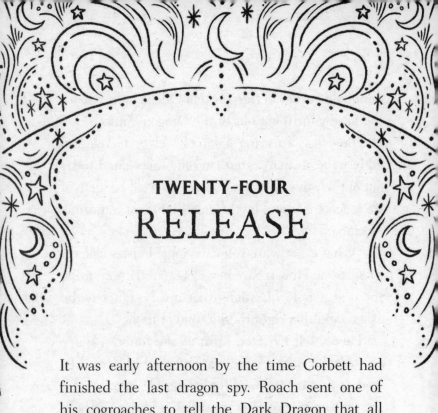

TWENTY-FOUR
RELEASE

It was early afternoon by the time Corbett had finished the last dragon spy. Roach sent one of his cogroaches to tell the Dark Dragon that all was finished, and half an hour later he watched as the inanimate dragons suddenly sparked into life, extending their wings and flying out through the window that he just had time to open before they would have smashed through it.

"So, I can go now?" Corbett asked, as he stood gaping at the open window.

Roach pulled the window shut and latched it. "Sure, grab your stuff."

Corbett had been poring over Russell Hertzsprung's journal. He closed it with a soft *thud* and placed it on the workbench before making his way to the mezzanine to collect his bag and blazer along with Roach's old coat.

Roach waited until Corbett was out of sight before he reached for the journal and placed it into his pocket. He was at the door when Corbett returned.

Locking the forge behind them and ushering him down the stairs, Roach felt uneasy. He knew what he had to do, but it didn't sit well with him.

Corbett got to the bottom of the staircase and looked from left to right. The sewers of Lower London lay in the darkness on either side. Corbett was so lost. Roach wondered if he could just leave him in the sewers, not killing him but not helping him – would that fulfil the promises he had given to both Paisley and to the Dark Dragon?

"This way," Roach said as he shone the electrica torch to the right. Corbett blindly followed the light.

The sewers seemed to contract; the time that Roach had been counting on to sort through his feelings seemed to fly by as all too soon he could feel fresh air on his face and the smell of London on the crisp breeze. He looked up at the ladder, then moved to one side. Corbett stared up and sighed, the soft electrica streetlights peeking through the holes in the manhole cover above, lighting the edge of freedom.

He placed one foot on the ladder and had made it up three rungs before Roach dragged him back down. Corbett hit the ground hard, his legs buckling as he slammed down in the dirt. Winded by the fall, he gasped as Roach jumped on top of him, pinning his arms down, holding him in place.

Roach held the electrica torch high above Corbett's head, shining the light on his wide eyes. He remembered Paisley's wide eyes from the chapel the night before, how scared she had been when her hand was trapped inside the schematica, with the bells ringing and the King Star forming on the ceiling, how he had felt bad about following her and stealing her stars, how he had promised her he'd protect Corbett to make amends.

Roach let out a frustrated cry and pushed himself up off of Corbett. He turned and kicked the wall of the sewer in frustration.

Corbett sat up, coughing and catching his breath.

"What was that about? I thought... Oh. She was never going to let me go, was she?" Corbett said, realization settling in.

"No. I was supposed to kill you, and to make sure that Paisley found out about it," Roach said.

"So why didn't you? I mean, I'm glad and all, but..."

"Paisley!" Roach said, his voice hard. "I ... I made her a promise."

"You? When? Did you tell her that you had taken me? Did you tell her what I was doing for the Dark Dragon?"

Roach shook his head. "No, that's your secret to keep or tell. She thought that you were home in Scotland. I think she's making her way to your family's forge to try and find you." A hint of bitterness crept into his voice and he swallowed it down. He wondered if anyone would care enough to go looking for him like that.

"That's a mighty big promise you made her, knowing that the Dark Dragon had me. What did she have to do for it?"

"She had to give me her destiny," Roach said.

"You must have heard the bells the other night – ringing in the King Star. They were for Paisley."

"Paisley!" Corbett's voice was full of disbelief. "Paisley's the next George? I was about to ask if that was possible, but this is Paisley, she seems to defy every star in the sky."

"Yep, she sure does, and if she's gonna have any chance of keeping her stars shining then she's gonna need all the help she can get. It won't just be the Dark Dragon coming for her. The George won't be happy about giving up his power, his stars, his track."

"He doesn't have much choice. If it's in his track, then..." Corbett's voice trailed off as he looked at Roach. "You know something."

Everyone knew that once a new George was appointed the old George soon began to plan his departure to the Veil. But something about the way the George had greedily swallowed the Dark Dragon's blood made Roach doubt that he would just hand over the Empire to Paisley; the Dark Dragon was definitely counting on that.

"Not for sure, but I do know that Paisley's going to need you, Corbett. The Dark Dragon is going to try to destroy her, but first she wants to make her suffer any way she can. Paisley will need all the friends she can get."

"And what about you, are you a friend or foe? Because I can't tell right now."

Roach took a long breath in. "To be honest, neither. I can't afford to be."

Corbett placed a hand on the ladder. "Will this bring me out in London? It doesn't lead to the Dark Dragon's throne room or something?"

"No, that's more to the west, you'll be fine." Roach reached inside his pocket and pulled out a small coin purse. It clinked as Roach passed it to Corbett. "Here, you'll need to keep out of sight. The Men of the Yard are looking for you, and you won't get far if they clock you, but you'll get nowhere without any money. If you hurry, you can get on the next train and be home by teatime. The ladder will bring you out behind King Star Station."

Corbett looked at the purse before tightening his fingers around it.

"And you'd best take this too; I think Russell would have wanted you to have it." He passed him Russell Hertzsprung's journal. "Now, there's something I need you to do for me." Roach saw the look that passed over Corbett's face, the distrust sliding back into place.

"What?" Corbett asked. "I'm not going to kill anyone or make anything else, not after she tried to double-cross me, and you might have done a few things that are right, but you're still on her side and I still don't trust you."

"Relax, it's nothing like that." Roach took a step closer to Corbett, his face illuminated by the faint glow from above. He cocked a half smile. "I want you to punch me right here." He pointed to his chin.

"What?"

"And don't be soft about it; I need it to look convincing."

"You want me to punch you?"

"Yes, how else did you get away?"

Roach saw Corbett take a big swallow, then watched as he raised his hand and hit him across the cheek.

"What was that? You slapped me. Honestly, my little sister could hit better than that."

"You have a sister?" Corbett asked.

"Had."

In the silence, Corbett's shoulders slumped.

Roach sighed. "Don't do that. Don't feel sorry for me. I don't need you to feel sorry for me. What I need is for you to hit me . . . *hard*."

There was no fight in Corbett's eyes as he made a fist and half-heartedly punched Roach in the cheek again.

"This is not going to work. You need to do it properly. I know how strong you are – working in the forge, hitting all that metal. You're holding out on me."

"Look, I'm sorry, but I don't want to, I—"

"I don't care if you don't want to. You owe me this. Don't you understand what might happen to me if she finds out that I just let you go? More than a punch to the face, I can tell you that for sure. So, you are going to punch me, and you are going to make it good because I swear to you if she realizes that I let you go, then whatever punishment she deals out to me I will deliver the same to you and your family, do you understand?"

Roach's voice was full of promises, and before he could pull in a breath, Corbett's blow landed square on his jaw, hitting him so hard that it sent his head ricocheting off the ladder with a metallic clunk that echoed down the sewers. He stood swaying for a moment as little stars burst into life.

Corbett's brow was low, his eyes stormy, his breathing fast and rough. Roach watched as his face transformed from anger to shame, and he felt guilty for goading Corbett into doing something he hadn't wanted to do.

"Thank you," Roach said as he lifted a hand to his head and felt warm blood where it had hit the ladder.

Corbett didn't reply, he just scampered up the ladder, bathing it in the light from the streetlamps above as he opened the manhole cover and ascended into the night.

As the manhole cover clanked back into place, Roach had an urge to rush up the ladder and go with Corbett. But he stayed and shook his head, the stars from his blow to the head fading, a sharp ache settling in.

It was in his track to save Clara, and if that meant walking in the shadow of the Dark Dragon and doing her bidding, then that was what he would do.

TWENTY-FIVE
THE FORGE
AT ORD

The night was full black when the *Aristarchus* made port just outside Inverness at a large delivery depot. When Odelia had told them their destination, Paisley had felt a little lurch, as if her track was nudging her forward, and she wasn't sure if it was comforting or something to rebel against. Either way, it took her a step closer to Dax, and she would soon see Corbett with his family just outside Inverness at Ord Forge.

He must be worried sick about them – they would be two days late meeting him there.

"It shouldn't be that hard for us to find the forge," Paisley told Odelia.

"I'm sure. I wonder what he found out about the Mechanism," Odelia said.

Paisley blushed a little; she hadn't given much thought to the broken Mechanism. There were so many other things pressing in on her and feeling more immediate that somehow the ruin of the Celestial Mechanism had faded away, despite how enormous that was.

"Do you think it *is* broken?" Hal asked, a hint of hope in his voice.

Odelia shrugged. "I'm not sure that it was working before, at least not for everyone, so if it is broken there will be many for whom it makes no difference, I'm sure."

When the *Aristarchus* landed, Captain Hewitt passed them on to a waiting delivery truck. The driver was taking the goods from the aerocopter into town, and on the way he would drop them as close to the road that led to the forge as he could.

The truck driver loaded the cargo along with Paisley, Odelia and Hal, and made his way along the snow-covered roads into town.

The day was closing, crisp and clear, and Paisley felt as if the cold was cutting its way into her bones.

The three of them sat in the back of the open-topped truck, huddled together for warmth.

Paisley stretched out her glove-covered finger and pointed to the comet as it blazed into view in the west, chasing the long set sun. "Oh, my stars, there it is," she said. "My mother's comet. Do you think it looks bigger and brighter than it did before?"

"A little, but that might just be because the night is darker here – no electrica lights or houses," Hal suggested.

Paisley shivered, not just from the cold any more, and Odelia stole a look about before she unfolded her wings and wrapped them around both Paisley and Hal.

Within moments, Paisley felt life rushing back into her hands and fingers as Odelia's magnificent dragonhide wings cut out the freezing-cold air and thawed them like a blanket that had been warmed by the fire.

Paisley felt herself nodding with sleep at the warmth and the gentle motion of the electrica truck, and she allowed the weariness of the last few days to seep in.

She snapped her eyes open as the truck came

to an abrupt halt and Odelia folded her wings back, the cold instantly reclaiming its hold on them. The driver pointed them in the direction of a snow-covered lane, and Paisley shivered as she slipped from the back of the truck, thanking the driver.

The snow was crisp and deep, the night darker now as large snow clouds had gathered, and although the old moon was waning, the light of the comet and the stars bounced off the snow, giving them enough to see by.

No sooner had they started walking than big clumps of fresh snow started falling. Hal took the lead. He broke off a branch of a nearby tree and used it as a walking stick, testing the depth of the snow ahead before proceeding.

Seeing Hal with the stick, his blond hair tousled in the starlight, made Paisley think of Dax. She hoped that Hal was being truthful when he said his father would not harm Dax, that he would be well cared for, but even so: just being separated from him was painful. Paisley and Dax had never spent longer than a day apart from one another. His loss felt as vast as the heavens above them.

They'd been walking through the snowstorm

for a little over half an hour, Paisley's feet turning into blocks of ice, when they caught their first sight of the forge through the mounting blizzard. It was nestled down in a natural dip in the landscape, a cosy-looking cottage with a twist of smoke rising out of its chimney and next to it the long building of the forge with three large chimneys, all dormant.

Paisley felt a little rush of warmth fill her: she realized she had missed Corbett more than she had appreciated. She began to quicken her pace and then run down the lane, kicking up huge flurries of snow as she went.

On the cottage door hung the most beautiful Small Turnings wreath Paisley had ever seen: a series of brass circles held together by steel and nightsilver cogs that slowly turned golden stars around the wreath. Paisley reached up on her tiptoes and knocked in the middle of the circle of metal, her knuckles so frozen she hardly felt them.

She stepped back and looked over at Odelia and Hal. The Forge was quiet and still. Paisley realized that it was late enough to be the next day and that Corbett and his family were probably all in bed, safely cocooned from the snow that was now falling so heavily that when Paisley turned back, she could hardly see down the lane they had travelled.

Paisley was just about to ask Odelia if she should knock again when a man opened the door.

He took up the whole doorway, his beard long and bushy, full of grey amongst the sandy strands. His hair was the same mixture of sand and grey, and wild with sleep. His eyes were wide with the worry of being roused from his bed in the dead of night.

He stood in silence, taking them in, and Paisley spoke tentatively. "Mr Grubbins?" she asked.

"Aye."

"We're friends of Corbett's. My name is Paisley Fitzwilliam, this is Odelia, and Hal. We were—"

But Paisley didn't get to say anything else because in that moment, Corbett's voice called out from inside the cottage.

"Paisley!"

And then he was there at the door, pushing his father aside and stepping out into the cold to throw his arms around her. "Paisley." He hugged her tight, and she felt how warm he was, and before she knew it, she was crying.

"We got held up, and by the time we were at the

station you were gone, and then we—" She looked over at Mr Grubbins. "Well, we're here now."

She pulled away from Corbett and looked at him. By the soft light streaming through the door, she could see that Corbett was a little worse for wear, a bruise on his jaw and small cuts on his face. "What happened to you?"

"It looks like you've had as interesting a journey as we have," Odelia said, her arms folded across her body. She fixed Corbett with one of her stares, then lifted an eyebrow and broke into a rare smile. "It is good to see you."

Corbett smiled. "Och, you missed me," he said, stepping towards Odelia and throwing his arms around her. She stood still for a second, then hugged him back.

"I wouldn't go that far," she said as they parted, her face back to being serious.

Hal reached out and shook Corbett's hand. "How long have you been home?" he asked.

"I arrived late this afternoon," Corbett said, his voice low, darting a look towards his father behind him.

"What! Why? How? We thought you had caught

the train as planned. . ." Paisley said, but she tapered off as she saw the meaningful look he was giving her.

"What's going on here?" a voice said as Corbett's mother joined his father. She looked like Corbett, thick glasses covering her inquisitive eyes, and behind her was a tall, muscular young man, with curly, sandy brown hair like his father. He was a little older than Corbett but with the same inquiring look.

"Mum, Dad, Norris, these are the friends I was telling you about."

"The girl who died, the Dragon Walker and the Krigare?" Corbett's dad said, looking at each of them in turn, as he took in the unlikely trio and then glanced at his son with a playful smile. "Our Corbett always did have a knack of making interesting friendships. Remember when you kept that box of toads under your bed one summer?

"Aye, Pa, but no one wants to hear about that right now! Paisley, Odelia and Hal – meet my parents, Judy and Robert, and my brother, Norris."

"Well, we're glad to meet you," Corbett's mother said. "But we'd be even gladder if we weren't letting all the warm out and all that snow in. Come on, Robert; let the bairns in."

The cottage was full of soft electrica light and two fires, one in the kitchen and another in the sitting room, where Mrs Grubbins led them all. Paisley slipped her backpack off and lifted the strap of her dragonhide satchel over her head. Her shoulder ached from the weight of the egg, and she held both the satchel and backpack in one hand so that she could massage it.

"Here." Corbett took the satchel and backpack from her. "What have you got in here, a dragon?" he asked with a chuckle.

Paisley shot a look at Hal that Corbett registered – he stopped laughing and placed the satchel gently on the floor by the window.

"Move it close to the fire," Paisley said, and Corbett picked up the satchel and did as she asked.

"I was only joking, but are you serious?" he whispered, his eyes wide. "Not the egg from the vault?!"

Paisley gave Corbett a serious look, and he paled a little as she shook her head and said, "I'll tell you everything later."

Paisley was getting warmer now, and she pulled her coat and scarf off, joining Hal and Odelia

259

warming their hands by the fire, bending life back into their fingers.

"I'll put the kettle on and find you something to eat," Mr Grubbins said, giving Corbett a pointed look. As his wife followed him into the pantry, Corbett also trailed after them, but Norris stayed by the door to the kitchen, watching each one of them keenly.

"I don't think we should have come here," Odelia whispered after they had spent a few minutes warming up by the fire.

Paisley sighed. "I know you and Corbett aren't the best of friends. . ."

"It's not that. We're putting his family in danger by being here."

Paisley felt a little jolt in her track. "It never even crossed my mind. Should we leave?"

"No need for that," Corbett said as he rejoined them. "You won't be putting them in any more danger than I am already,"

"What do you mean?"

"Well, the Dark Dragon is probably after me, and she knows all about my family and this place." He opened his arms and gestured to his home.

"I don't understand," Paisley said. "I mean, I know she's after us all, but why would she come here?"

"Because she's the reason I was delayed. She found me after I'd been to Greenwich Overhead, and was keeping me captive. Well, Roach was, actually, before he helped me escape."

"He helped you escape?" Odelia said.

"Yeah, he did." Corbett rubbed the back of his neck, and Paisley thought that he looked more than a little annoyed. "While I was being held, the Dark Dragon made me build her a new arm, from nightsilver and copperich."

Paisley shook her head. "Copper-what?"

"Look, sit down, I'll tell you everything."

Corbett's parents came in and filled the table with cold cuts, cheese, bread and current buns, then kept them supplied with tea and warm buttered crumpets. While they ate, Corbett told them what had happened from the moment that Roach and Lorena had captured him to when he had emerged back in the streets of Lower London, behind King Star Station just minutes before the train to Inverness left.

"I . . . I'm not sure I can come with you, to the north. The Dark Dragon, she threatened my family. And if she does come for them, I need to be here. I don't think I'd be able to live with myself if anything were to happen to them. I have to stay. I have to keep them safe, or at least try to. Besides . . . I don't mind letting you know, I'm a little scared. I thought I was going to lose my track when I saw her in her throne room. I thought I was gone for sure."

He looked earnestly at Paisley, and she nodded, feeling a lump form in her throat.

"Yes, yes of course. We get it. We totally understand." Paisley smiled at Corbett, but inside she felt as if she had just lost something important. She hadn't realized how much she had missed Corbett or how much she was counting on him, but she understood: she didn't want to put his track in any more danger, and she knew that he was trying to look after his family. After all, she was doing the same, for Dax.

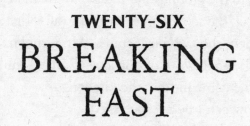

TWENTY-SIX

BREAKING FAST

It was late morning when Paisley woke, warm and comfortable, with a now unfamiliar feeling of safety. It soon evaporated as she woke up fully and all the fears and anxieties surrounding her rushed in.

She and Odelia were sharing Corbett's room, and he had bunked in with Norris, while Hal had taken the couch. But Odelia was not in the room.

Paisley washed and dressed, and when she pulled open the curtains, she saw Odelia and Hal fighting in the deep, snow-covered yard outside, practising their sword skills.

Odelia bested Hal, knocking him smoothly into

the snow and taking his sword from him. Hal lay there for a moment, shaking his head, laughing in good humour. Then he swiped with his leg, knocking Odelia to the ground, and the two of them began to wrestle in the snow. Paisley turned away with a smile.

When she got downstairs, Mr Grubbins was serving up a big pot of porridge. Corbett smiled at her as he came in from the kitchen.

"How can I help?" she asked.

"Here, lay the table." He passed her four bowls. "It snowed pretty hard last night, and a big drift has come in off the neighbouring field. Norris is out clearing it now, and Mum's working in the forge."

Just then, a gust of cold filled the room as Odelia and Hal came in, their cheeks flushed and noses cold. Mr Grubbins put a bowl of cream on the table and a jar of mixed nuts, seeds and dried berries. Then he fetched a large pot of tea for them all.

"Are you not joining us, Mr Grubbins?" Paisley asked.

"No, lass, I had best go and help Norris with the clearing – I reckon it might take us a day or more to shift all that snow before anyone can leave. But you lot tuck in."

Paisley bit her lip as she nodded – another day at least before they could get on their way to Dax. Corbett dished up large ladles full of steaming porridge into each of their bowls, then Paisley plopped a big dollop of cream on top, followed by some honey and the mixture from the jar.

She put a spoonful in her mouth and let out a large "Umm" of appreciation. Hal and Odelia loaded their porridge and did the same.

"This is the best porridge I have ever had!" Hal said.

"If I was only allowed to eat one thing for the rest of my life, it would be this!" Odelia added.

Corbett smiled. "I'll be sure to tell my dad – he'll be dead chuffed with that."

"Corbett, if we're going to be stuck here for a day or two, can you help me to make something – in the forge?" Paisley asked.

"I can try. What do you need?" Corbett asked.

"I'll tell you once we're in the forge," Paisley said with a look towards Hal and Odelia. She reached down beside her and pulled up her satchel, placing it on the table. "But first, I have to tell you a few things." She stood up and opened the satchel, reaching inside to pull out the egg. It was as big as Paisley's head now, and the once-polished black surface of the egg was now a dull, matt-flecked grey.

"Is that the egg that Dax found in the trove?" Corbett asked in wonder as he took off his glasses and rubbed them on his jumper before placing them back on and blinking at the egg.

"Yes, it is," Paisley said, extending the egg towards Corbett.

He lifted his hands into an eager cup and Paisley gently placed the egg into his care, watching as his face lit up.

"It's so heavy, and warm – really, really warm, like a hot-water bottle."

"Hal says that it was fired by a dragon's breath," Paisley said. "We think it happened at the observatory when Lorena burned Mother's watch with her Dragon Touch; the egg got caught up in the blaze."

"Do you think Doc Langley was right – that this is a Great Dragon egg?"

Hal nodded, his mouth full of porridge.

"We think so," Odelia said as she looked at the egg, a shadow of a smile on her lips.

"Corbett, you never told us what you found out about the Mechanism," Paisley said as she scooped up another spoonful of porridge.

Corbett put down his spoon and wiped his mouth on his napkin. "Well, I wasn't able to find out as much as I would have liked. But there is definitely something going on, and the Celestial Physicists were all in a quandary. I told them what had happened – well, most of it. I told them that Violetta hadn't died when they thought she had, that the experiment was performed again. But they didn't believe me; they said I was delusional from grief, and they wouldn't let me into the observatory or the laboratories. However, I did manage to get a copy of the data on all known objects, including the comet. It's out of date now, but it's still in my journal. I haven't had time to look at it all yet, but I will as soon as I have an astrojournal to compare the coordinates to the expected values."

Paisley let out a long breath. She felt responsible for what might be happening with the Celestial Mechanism, but had no idea how to fix it.

"I'm sorry to interrupt; this is all very interesting,

and if I was at all a fan of the Celestial Mechanism, I'd be quite worried," said Hal. "But as it is, I am not, so can I have some more porridge?"

Paisley smirked, Odelia gave Hal her best disapproving eyebrow, and Corbett flustered, "Yes, yes, of course," as he invited Hal to help himself from the pot.

*

There was no cheery breakfast with friends for Roach as he sat opposite the Dark Dragon onboard Hector's private aerocopter.

It was a snug little waxwing copter, speedy and light, good for small distances. A little less comfortable for the journey that was ahead of them, but it was more discreet than public transport, especially when travelling with Lorena and her fallen Dragon Walkers.

"We'll be taking off in a few moments," Hector said as he settled down next to the Dark Dragon.

She tossed back her long hair and sat still and small in the large chair. "And how many times will we need to stop to refuel?" she asked.

"Twice: once in Nottingham, then Durham – where

we'll stay the night, then up to Dundee to meet the George and his army."

"And do you feel confident that the George has everything under control?" she asked Hector.

"If not the George, then those around him. I have many who are loyal to me working as his closest advisors, and even with Arch Architect Harman worried about the missing George and the fact that she is a girl, I feel I have enough influence among the knights to ensure that all goes to plan."

"Have you told the Arch Architect that Paisley is the George?" Roach asked, and he registered the small flinch the Dark Dragon made, the bulging vein in her neck belying her otherwise calm exterior.

"I have not. That is information that only we know for now," Hector said.

Roach nodded. "Well, us and the Chief Designer," he added.

"The Master of Stars assures me that the new George will never take the throne. He said that Paisley's King Star was tainted by a disturbance in the Mechanism. I see this as a sign that she will be destroyed, and soon," the Dark Dragon said with a cruel smile.

Roach felt a lump rise in his throat, and when the air steward came around with fresh croissants shortly after take-off, he declined, finding that the lump had stuck fast.

TWENTY-SEVEN
FORGING FRIENDSHIPS

Corbett opened the small wicket door that sat in the larger double doors of the forge. Paisley ducked a little as she followed him in; the snow had started to fall again and Paisley shook the clumps from her hair as the warmth of the room instantly started to melt them. The pit was still glowing from the work Corbett's mother had been doing that morning. She, along with Odelia and Hal, had gone to help Norris and Mr Grubbins clear the road to try and get ahead of the new snowfall.

Paisley placed her dragonhide satchel on a nearby workbench and unbuttoned her coat.

"There's something important I need to tell you about, Corbett," she said, starting to pull up her sleeve to reveal her stars. "I'm the new George." She tried to keep her voice flat, but she could hear the wobble of excited fear that had crept in.

"He was telling the truth, then!" Corbett said as he took a step closer and gazed at Paisley's stars. "Roach said that you had been bestowed with the King Star, but I didn't really know if he was lying or not. I heard the bells ringing the night before last, but not for a moment did I think that they were for you." He looked at her in awe. "What does this mean? I mean, I know what it means: it means you're the George, you're . . . oh my stars, you're the George! Should I bow? Should I call you Your Georgeness?"

Paisley shook her head, her cheeks reddened from awkwardness as much as from the heat of the forge. Once people knew about the King Star, they wouldn't look at her in the same way; except maybe Odelia and Hal, they had never treated her any different, and neither had Roach. She blushed even more as she thought of him.

She was sure that although Dax would think it was exciting, he'd still treat her the same. She hoped that Corbett just needed a bit of time to get used to it. She was, after all, still getting used to it herself.

Paisley reached inside her satchel, her hand brushing against the dragon egg as she pulled out the golden tube that the young Mechanist had given her. She ran her hands along the now-familiar tube and deftly twisted each of the sections into place, lining up her stars until it clicked open.

She felt a little thrill as she tipped out the blueprints, smoothing them out on the workbench. She looked at the image on the blueprint, feeling the importance of what she was about to do.

"I need a lance," she said. "The scriptures are quite clear; they say that *I* need to forge it, or at least help." She ran her hand over the blueprint of the lance, and the old Celtic scripture that surrounded it. "There's one more important thing," Paisley said.

"More important than being the George and needing a lance?" Corbett asked.

Paisley retold the Dragon Walker tale that Adore Alyse had told them about Helin, and the prophecy that she had given the Dark Dragon about the end of her track.

"Let me get this straight: Helin predicted that

the Dark Dragon would be killed by someone who was descended from one of the Soul Sisters and bestowed with the King Star."

Paisley nodded.

"Wow!" Corbett said. "That's a lot for your wee track to hold."

Paisley shifted uncomfortably and began to fiddle with the blueprints. "It sure is, but I think that maybe with this lance I might be able to destroy the Dark Dragon, vanquish her, just as the original George did the Great Dragons."

"What makes you think that?" Corbett asked as his finger was busy tracing under the Old Celtic scripture as he read.

"There's an important bit on the last page – or the first, I'm not sure of the order, it has the oldest date on it," she said, flipping through the blueprints. "Ascalon, the lance of the First George. There are marked differences in all seven of the iterations of the lance design in the tube. They slowly move away from being functional to decorative, and here –" she pointed to a section that looked like a void in the internal workings of the lance – "this part here disappears completely in later versions."

"What do you think the void was for?" Corbett asked as he looked over the blueprint.

"A power supply of some kind. Well, not some kind, the scripture is clear about what was to be placed here." She pointed to the text and Corbett read it.

"It says that the lance contained a large fire diamond. Look, there's a drawing of it here." He pointed to the image of the black gem stones.

Paisley smiled. "I saw that drawing too and couldn't help but think of how much it looked like..."

"Part of the Heart Stone," he said, his voice full of wonder.

Paisley nodded. "So we need to get to Dax, and we need to retrieve the Heart Stone, and when we do, I need a lance to place it in, because this bit here" – Paisley flipped over the blueprint to show some analytical writing on the back – "tells you how the tip of the lance can open something like the Veil rifts, and how the early Georges used it to vanquish all of the Great Dragons, sending them into the Veil."

Corbett's voice rose a notch as he excitedly said, "Remember Doc Langley told us how they had found very few remains of the Great Dragons? This must be why! They were never killed, they were quite literally forced into the Veil!"

Paisley nodded. "Exactly."

"But wait," Corbett said. "When Dax told us the tale of the Soul Sisters, he said that the Heart Stone had been broken after the Purge."

"Did he?" Paisley said, thinking hard to remember the tale. "I guess all stories and tales have a little bit of flex in them as they are retold. Like the Dragon Touched Boy." She pulled up her sleeve again. "Maybe he is actually a Star Touched Girl." Paisley said.

"Aye, quite possibly, but one thing that rings true is the power of this lance, especially if powered by part of the Heart Stone. I can see how it would be a game changer when it came to facing the Dark Dragon, and I have an idea about something else that will give you an edge."

Corbett pulled a small, battered journal from his inside coat pocket.

"When I was with her . . . the Dark Dragon, and I made her arm for her, I learned how to forge a new metal, copperich."

"You mentioned that last night," Odelia said. "What exactly is it?"

"Paisley, do you remember when we were on top of the roof of your house and Roach had sent his cogroach beetles after us?" Paisley nodded; she wasn't likely to forget that, ever. "Well, remember how in the crushed ones there was a strange, coppery-coloured wire that was attached to all of the moving parts of the cogroach? Well, that was the copperich; that was the part that allowed Roach to control them with his . . . I don't know, thoughts, intentions, desires."

Corbett placed the journal down on the desk and placed a hand reverently upon it.

"This journal was written by Russell Hertzsprung. I think he might have been the greatest ever Alchesmith, a genius. He was very secretive, but his work was the best, and the price reflected that. About twenty years ago he disappeared, and it was said that he had cut himself off from the world as he searched for the Unseen Metals of the Mechanism – the metals that the Chief Designer forged the Celestial Mechanism with. Alchesmiths have been looking for them since for ever. But to actively search for them is frowned upon because only the Chief Designer can make them.

"But even if it isn't one of the Unseen, he found something, and it's remarkable."

Corbett flipped open the journal and pulled out two thin metal wires. They were similar to the metal that Paisley remembered from the cogroaches.

"I learned how to make copperich from Russel Hertzsprung's notes. It would seem that when he disappeared, he was actually taken by the Dark Dragon."

"Where is this Alchesmith now?" Hal asked.

"His track has ended," Corbett said, his hand resting on the journal. "But his discoveries are still going strong."

Paisley thought of her mother and how her discoveries and the repercussions of the turning of her track, and all her actions upon it, were still being felt in the Mechanism. Sometimes a small cog turns many tracks, and Paisley sensed that Russell Hertzsprung's discoveries, like her mother's, would prompt the turning of other tracks.

Corbett pointed to one of the copperich wires. "This one was made from Roach's blood, and this one from the Dark Dragon's. Just like with nightsilver, there are small differences in the quality of the metal. The marrying of the host and the metal transfers something of their nature, but where the nightsilver seems to entangle a person's strength, courage and determination, copperich connects to their deep intentions and motivations – it allows the host to control the conduct of the item that the metal is attached to."

"Remarkable. May I?" Paisley asked before she lifted both of the copperich strands into the air and twisted them in the light.

Paisley saw that the strand that belonged to Roach was a little deeper in colour than the one that belonged to the Dark Dragon. It was duller too, whereas the Dark Dragon's strand shone with an extra lustre.

Corbett hurried over to a dark corner of the workshop and bent down, rummaging around in a box before bringing out a knotted bundle of fabric.

"The copperich is made from a special strain of copper ore only found in Amerika – there's a map in the journal. And it is mined via a process called phytoleeching." He unwrapped the fabric to show the toadstools.

"The fungus draws the copper ore from the ground and purifies it," he said, turning over a toadstool to show the soft copper gills. "This is all that was left of Hertzsprung's store. I snatched it when Roach came for me."

Paisley picked up one of the toadstools and twisted it in her hand to catch the light. The glow from the forge reflected a twinkle of starlike copper sprinkles scattered across the paper-thin copper gills.

The toadstool felt incredibly cold, and after a few moments, Paisley's fingers had turned numb.

"It's so cold!" she said.

Corbett nodded. "I have no idea why, it's almost like the toadstool sucks the warmth out of you – maybe it has something to do with the photoleeching process. I think we should use some of this ore to make some copperich for your lance, connecting you with it on a deeper level."

He pointed to the blueprint from the first George's lance. "We'll make this one, with a few modifications, and leave a gap for the Heart Stone."

"I wonder if you could marry part of a Heart Stone to a metal?" Paisley wondered.

"Umm … maybe?" Corbett replied as he continued to pore over the blueprints for the lance, his concentration already on the task at hand.

Paisley picked up the book that Hal had given her on the George's turning to a page that showed the first George vanquishing a dragon with his lance. Was she ready to do that to the Dark Dragon? Paisley took a deep breath. If it meant saving Dax, or her friends, then yes, she was.

TWENTY-EIGHT

NÆSS

Paisley watched as Corbett got straight to work on making a new blueprint.

"Norris is always better at this than I am – his blueprints are so rich and detailed. I think they're even better than Mum's, but don't tell her I said that."

As soon as Corbett had finished with his plans, he collected all the material he needed.

"Just one more thing we need," he said to Paisley.

"Um ... yes, and how do we get my blood out?" she asked, her palms feeling a little sweaty.

"Och, that bit's easy, just put your hand in here."

Paisley warily eyed a machine that looked a little like the schematica. She nervously extended her right hand.

"Do you trust me?" Corbett asked.

Paisley looked at him and smiled. "Yes, completely." And she placed her hand in the machine. It closed just as the schematica had done, trapping her arm in place. For a moment she remembered being in the Mechster at York, the bells ringing all around her as she was trapped under the shining light of the King Star, and panic filled her, so she focused on taking deep breaths.

She felt a sharp scratch on the back of her hand and closed her eyes, remembering Roach trying to prise the machine open to free her, his jaw clenching as he worked her sword back and forth between the blades that trapped her in place. Then she remembered how he had tied his handkerchief around her bleeding arm.

The handkerchief was in her pocket; she had kept it, and thinking of it and him made her feel confused. She opened her eyes as the machine let her go and she saw Corbett joyfully displaying a small glass phial of her blood. The confused feelings over Roach fell into anger as she remembered that he had held Corbett captive and tried to end his track, even after he had promised to protect him. Yes, he had helped Corbett to escape in the end, but she was sure he was only doing so for his own best interests and not hers or Corbett's. She felt a fool for believing him and wouldn't make that mistake again.

Corbett labelled the blood with Paisley's name and put it into a pouch with three other small phials.

"Whose blood is in those?" she asked.

"This one is Roach's." He held it up to the light; it was almost empty. "I found it amongst Russell Hertzsprung's things. This one is mine." He held up a half-full phial. "And this one belongs to the Dark Dragon." The phial was almost half full too. Paisley resisted the urge to grab it and smash it on the floor. He leaned over with a mischievous grin. "I didn't use all of it when I was making her arm," he said. "I swapped it for someone else's. I made the copperich with hers so that she could control the arm, but not the nightsilver."

"That was brave, Corbett. If she'd found out!" Paisley gave a little shudder. "But it was definitely the right thing to do," she said as she thought of what strength the nightsilver would have if entangled with the Dark Dragon's blood.

"Whose blood did you use?" she asked.

"Mine," he said with a bold smile, lifting his shirtsleeve and showing the cut on his arm. "I think she would have killed me herself if she'd realized," Corbett said.

Paisley had to agree with him, and hoped that the Dark Dragon would never find out.

*

By early evening the lane to the main road was clear and Norris had ventured into town to get some of the supplies that they needed for their journey north.

Paisley and Corbett called it a day in the forge. There was still some way to go before the lance was finished, but they were both weary; Paisley felt as if her arms would never stop aching after all the hammering and toil. Mrs Grubbins had drawn her a nice, hot bath, and after she had washed, she sat by the fire wrapped in a blanket, letting her hair dry while she sipped milky tea and listened to Norris.

"The whole of town is buzzing with the news of war," he told them. "The George is serious; he says that the Northmen tried to kill him and that they and the Dragon Walkers have been plotting against him. All travel to the floating boroughs has been suspended, and it says in the *King's Herald* that the floating boroughs are actually giant warships that are going to obliterate Lower London!"

Odelia rolled her eyes and let out a *humph* of frustration as she reached for the paper that Norris held out.

"Are you sure about going to the Northern Realms?" Norris asked. "It sounds like there's a whole load of trouble heading that way."

Paisley looked from Hal and Odelia to Corbett. She nodded. "Yes, we're sure. If trouble is heading that way, it's best that we get there before it does."

"I thought you might say something like that," Norris said with a shake of his head and a small, sad smile. "I met Fergus – he's a good pal of mine, works on a merchant vessel carrying cargo to the Northern Realms. He says that he was sure his captain won't mind the three of you onboard, but it will cost a fair bit."

Paisley looked at Odelia, who said, "We will have enough to cover the fare and to get the remaining supplies we need. A dragon is never far from gold."

"That's good. Fergus says that the boat leaves Dundee with the eleven o'clock evening tide the day after tomorrow. It's then two and a half days' sailing in good weather."

"There's a small aerocopter that leaves that morning from Inverness to Dundee," Hal said, consulting another piece of parchment.

"That will give us enough time to finish in the forge," Corbett said.

Paisley looked at Odelia, who nodded. "This sounds like a good plan. We will soon be reunited with Dax." Odelia smiled, but Paisley felt a small electrica prickle run down her spine and wondered if this was the right track for them to be taking.

*

The next morning, Hal and Odelia joined Paisley and Corbett in the forge as they finished crafting the lance.

Paisley lifted it from the bench, and felt a thrill of excitement run through her. She turned the lance and held it vertically. Fully extended, it was taller than Paisley by an arm's length. The whole thing was forged from nightsilver, black and strong, the copperich entwined within, the intricate twists of the metal curling and flowing in complicated patterns.

The tip was sharpened to a deadly point. The modified design had various hand grips running along the shaft of the lance; one at the very end with a cuff that flared out to protect Paisley's hand as soon as she gripped it, and another two in the middle that responded as soon as she grabbed the lance and twisted it horizontally. She instinctively moved the lance as if she were fighting, and the cuffed end shifted to form another deadly point. And as she turned and thrust the other end forward, the point split open into a dangerous trident of sharp edges.

"The copperich is responding to your intentions. It senses the way that you want to fight, and it moves the lance, reshaping it to help you," Corbett said. "It's remarkable."

The lance felt so smooth and agile in Paisley's hands, she swung it through the air and twisted it in high arcs.

It had been hard work forging it, and Paisley felt as if she had put in more than just her blood to make it.

She passed the lance to Odelia, and as she did the shaft became impossibly smooth, with no grips for her hands, and all the barbs and edges folded in on themselves, leaving only rounded ends. Odelia raised an eyebrow.

Paisley smiled and looked over at Corbett. She could tell he was bursting with pride: the copperich was responding in a way that was exciting and beyond what Paisley ever thought was possible.

Odelia balanced the lance on one finger, checking the weight before inspecting it closely.

Paisley turned to Hal. "We should name it," she said. "All the Georges in the past have named their lances, and I should do the same. How do you do it in the North – name your weapons and tools, I mean?"

Hal looked thoughtfully at Paisley. "It is a very personal and complicated thing, naming a weapon or a tool. Some name them in praise of the makers, some in thanks to the wood or the metal that they are made of. Some name them after the season, others after a loved one they have lost. Personally, I like when things have new names, something that is uniquely theirs, but I'm not very good at thinking them up."

Paisley thought hard about what she wanted to achieve with the lance, to bring back order and unity, to mend all that had been broken, to reclaim that which had been lost.

"Næss," she said.

Hal nodded. "That is a good, strong Old Celtic name. Was there not a warrior named Næss who disguised herself as a knight and fought in the Great War, before the Empire, before the George?"

Paisley nodded. "Mother told me her story often. Her stars said that she was to lead, and despite the obstacles in her way, she found a way to live up to the promise of her track. Not only was she victorious, but when the fighting was done, she set up the peace treaties between the Old Clans. Of course, that was all broken in time with the coming of the George, but each clan living in unity and without the fear of war was a wonderful idea, and something I hope is in the track of us all. But for now, war is coming, and I could do with a little of Næss's wisdom by my side."

Odelia passed the lance to Hal. He held it horizontally and told Paisley to kneel.

"We have many customs and traditions that we follow in the Northern Realms. A lot of them focus on who we are and the choices that we make. This is how we use the naming of a thing to set our intention, to show the world what we plan to do, and to hold ourselves accountable. The way that we name a tool shows those around us how we are going to use it, and, Paisley, you have selected a name for your lance that tells everyone that you intend to use Næss to bring order and peace, even if the lance itself is used for war." Hal spoke solemnly as he held the lance above Paisley's head. Then, in Old Celtic, he blessed the making of the weapon, thanking Corbett's and Paisley's skill and hard work and named it Næss, bidding it to be strong and to protect Paisley as she showed who she was to the world.

He then lowered Næss, and Paisley grasped it in both hands. Then she used her intention, thinking of what she wanted from Næss in a deliberate way, and the lance began to shift and move and fold in on itself until it was no longer than Paisley's outstretched hand and only a little thicker than it had been at its full length.

Hal gave a short laugh. "That is very impressive!" He hit Corbett on the back. "When this is all over, I wonder if you would make me a weapon?"

Corbett nodded. "It would be my honour."

Paisley stowed Næss in her inside pocket. She could feel its warmth against her chest, and not only that, but she also realized that she was aware of the lance, as if a small part of her attention now resided within the black metal and all she had to do was reach for it with her mind and it would spring into action.

TWENTY-NINE

GOODBYE, CORBETT

That evening, as she packed the canvas backpack with the things that Odelia gave her, Paisley felt a melancholy set in. She had enjoyed her time with Corbett's family, and the forge had felt like a small harbour of safety, but now she was about to go out into the storm. As she thought about it, she worried that Dax was in a small ship all on his own, weathering the waves, and she felt guilty for wanting to cling to the warmth and homeliness that she had found over the past few days.

The evening meal was a subdued affair. Hal had helped Mr Grubbins to cook, and the food was as comforting as it had always been since they had arrived, but the conversation was less cheery. Paisley felt herself withdraw especially from Corbett. She'd just got him back, and now they were to part again.

She tried to avoid talking about the journey that she, Hal and Odelia were about to take without him, but it dominated the conversation as well as her thoughts.

"I journeyed to the Northern Realms once, when I was a girl," Corbett's mother told them. "Now we get some beautiful nights here, with the sky as dark as nightsilver and the stars so bright and clear you can almost hear them guiding you along on your track. But up there in the North, the sky sings in colours that I only ever dream of. The *Norrsken*, they call it. Well, I'm sure you're used to it, Hal: it hangs from the sky like great swathes of delicate material, green and purple and pink and blue; it shimmers and sways as if attached to the skirts of a dancer who is skipping and twisting along the tracks of the Celestial Mechanism.

"My pa had taken his telescope with him to see the stars, but what we saw was so much better. I felt so free and brave and powerful sitting in that cold wind while the sky danced for me.

"It's a shame you won't get to see it; you would have loved it," she said, turning to face Corbett, who nodded and gave a tight smile. "You got your grandpa's love of the stars, as well as his sense of duty and loyalty. He was so excited the day you got your stars, and they said that you would come to understand the nature of the Celestial Mechanism better than anyone in it; he'd always been fascinated by that type of thing, and I like to think the two of you had some common stars in that regard. I'm not sure that you got any of my stars of excitement for adventure. But I understand why you don't want to go north." She leaned over and kissed Corbett on the forehead, and he gave his mother a hug.

Paisley felt her chest tighten, and she missed her mother more than ever.

Sleep took a long time to come to Paisley, and when it did, she dreamed that she was dancing on the unseen tracks of the Mechanism with the planet far below her. Trailing from her skirt was a diaphanous material that changed colour: green and purple, pink and blue.

And just as she felt she was flying along the tracks, the material caught and snagged, holding her in place. Then she felt herself being pulled back, and, as she looked over her shoulder, she saw the sweet face of the Dark Dragon holding on to the material and pulling hard. Paisley fell from the Mechanism and woke with a jolt.

It was early in the morning, too early for the sun to have risen. Paisley gently lifted Odelia's wing from where it had wrapped itself around her and pulled on her socks before draping a blanket over her shoulders and tiptoeing down the stairs.

She slipped past Hal, asleep on the sofa, his snores light, his face smooth, save for the scar that ran over the hollow of his eye socket. Paisley made her way into the dining room. The fire there was all grey embers. She stirred them, and a small glow burst into life. Paisley built a little pyramid of kindling around it that soon caught, burning hot enough for some smaller logs to be added. In no time at all the room was warm and she was sitting, thinking about the journey ahead of her and how even after she had found Dax, they wouldn't be safe, not till the Dark Dragon was destroyed and the Celestial Mechanism fixed.

Paisley felt a little itch along her back where the

Veil scar was; it twitched with electrica and worry. A second later she heard footsteps and looked up to see Corbett.

"I thought I heard you tiptoeing out of your room to come down here," he said.

Paisley smiled. "You wouldn't have heard anything if it had been Odelia and not me."

"True. Are you worried about crossing the sea to the Northern Realms?" he asked.

"Yes, and what I'll find when I get there."

"Dax will be fine. Hal promised that his father would look after him, and although I never thought I'd say this, I trust the Krigare."

"I know," Paisley said. "I trust him too. And I'm not worried about Dax. I mean, I am, he's alone in a strange place and he must be so scared. And I don't want to think about what might happen to him if they discover his Dragon Touch. But what I'm worried about more is that by going to him and taking him with me, I might be putting him in more danger."

"You can't see what's along your track, Paisley. You need to trust in your stars, listen to your heart, and act with your head."

"I just want to do the right thing. Not just for

Dax but for my parents too, and now —" she pulled her arm from the blanket, her golden stars shining around the black King Star — "now I feel like I have to do what is right for *everyone*, and I'm not sure I know what that is because, honestly, Corbett, I don't want my stars. They feel so full and bright that I can hardly see myself or feel what is right any more. It's all too much, and I don't want the responsibility." Tears streamed down Paisley's cheeks.

Corbett shifted closer to Paisley on the hearth rug, and he threw an arm around her and squeezed her to him.

Paisley felt more than her shoulders tighten as she hugged in close to Corbett.

"I'm scared," she told him.

"I know a thing or two about being scared. I've never been brave and fearless like you and Odelia. And you know what, it's OK to be scared. It's OK not to have all the answers, and it's OK to fail."

Paisley nodded and wiped her tears on the edge of the blanket. "I don't understand why the Chief Designer chose me," she said, shaking her head.

Corbett pulled back and looked at her. "Really? I do! Paisley, you are the kindest, bravest, smartest person I know. You're selfless and strong, and you have a heart as big as a dragon! If there was ever anyone who could stop the Dark Dragon, it is you, Paisley Fitzwilliam, the girl who came back from the Veil, the girl walking about with a Great Dragon egg in her bag, the girl with the King Star, the girl who is destined to save us all."

Knowing that Corbett believed in her filled Paisley with a rush of strength and determination. She grasped his hand and gave it a squeeze before kissing his cheek. "Thank you, Corbett. It will give me something to hope for, knowing that you are here with your family and that one day I will return, and I'll bring Dax, and I'll tell you everything that happened, and Dax will talk over me, and we will laugh, and Odelia will scowl at us, because she'll be here too, and Hal. And when I tell you all the scary bits that are going to happen, it will be OK because I'll be here, and you'll be here, and you'll know that we got through them. And we will get through them because I'll know that I need to come and tell you everything that happened."

*

The goodbyes were hard. Mr and Mrs Grubbins hugged each of them, and Mr Grubbins gave Hal a jar full of the spiced nuts and berries that he loved so much, as well as a few handwritten family recipes bound up in a dragonhide pouch. Mrs Grubbins gave Odelia a small knife with a sharp blade and a beautiful handle. "It's not nightsilver, but it's the next best thing," she told her.

And Corbett pulled off the nightsilver bangle from his wrist and gave it to Paisley. "Here, this way a little bit of me will get to go on the adventure with you." He looked over at his parents, standing side by side and smiling. Then he hugged Paisley and she held him so tightly, slipping the bangle on to her wrist to sit amongst her stars.

Norris helped her climb up into the back of the flat-bed electrica truck. She tried to smile cheerfully as she waved goodbye to Corbett and his parents, but as soon as they had travelled around the bend in the track, she let her hand drop – and her tears.

THIRTY
INVERNESS

The aerodoc station was near the centre of town. It was built from soft grey stone that in the falling wet snow darkened to the grey-blue tones of the ocean that they were soon to travel across. But first they needed to get to Dundee, and before that they had to pick up the last of their supplies.

Paisley could feel that Odelia was on edge as they made their way from shop to shop, her keen eyes taking in everyone that they passed and looking around for trouble: the news of war and the missing George were dominating the papers now, but that didn't mean that no one was looking for the three of them, or that their photograms weren't being circulated by the King's Men.

Paisley had got used to the relaxed Odelia of the past few days, so seeing her like this – full of tension and constantly cautious – made Paisley feel a little sad.

Paisley remembered what Odelia had said about her passion for dancing and realized that over the past few days she had glimpsed a side of Odelia that would have blossomed if she had been left to twirl and leap.

When they had finished collecting all the items on the list, they sat in the little café at the aerodoc station and drank hot chocolate and ate warm fruit buns covered in butter.

Hal was on his third when he looked up through the window and his face went white, his single eye wide as he tracked the movements of someone as they walked down the street beyond.

Paisley made to turn her head to see whom he was looking at, but he shot a hand out to stay her.

"The King's Men are here," he said in a casual tone as he wiped his mouth with his napkin.

"Are they coming this way?" Odelia asked. She had positioned herself with a clear view of the door and the stairs up to the second level, but not the window. Between the two of them they could see danger before it saw them; Paisley also realized that they had steered her to a seat between them, so she would be less exposed, protected.

Odelia smiled to the waitress and asked for the bill as Hal and Paisley quickly but smoothly gathered their belongings.

Odelia shook some coins from her purse, then led the way. Instead of going out of the door and into the street, she led them up the stairs, through the upstairs parlour, and then into the ladies' toilet. Hal locked the door behind them as they all squeezed in.

It was a small room with a sash window closed tight against winter, fresh-fallen snow pushing itself up against the glass. Beyond was the flat roof of the kitchen below, and behind and to the right was the landing zone of the aerodoc station where two aerocopters were anchored.

Odelia pulled open the window, the cold wind snapping in at them.

"Which copter is ours?" Paisley asked.

"The smaller one to the right," Hal said. "I asked when I bought the tickets."

The aerocopter was the one furthest away from them.

"How long before it leaves?" Paisley asked.

"About fifteen minutes."

Odelia knocked the snow away with her backpack before lowering it out of the window and on to the roof.

"We need somewhere to hide till then," Odelia said.

"What about that maintenance hangar?" Paisley asked, pointing to a building in the distance.

"What about the copter?" Hal said.

"We will head for the hangar," Odelia decided as she grabbed the top of the window and smoothly jumped through feet-first, landing on the thick blanket of snow with a light bump.

Paisley threw her backpack down to Odelia, then checked that the dragon egg was safely nestled in her satchel before she swung her legs outside. She was sitting on the window seal when she heard a loud knock at the door.

Hal gave her a push and she let out a small yelp as she fell into Odelia's arms.

Both she and Odelia heard Hal raise the pitch

of his voice and call out, "This room is occupied!" His backpack dropped to the floor as the loud knock came again.

"One moment, please!" he called in the high tone again, before dropping from the window and landing in front of Paisley.

He was holding a long, thin cord that was attached to the window. He gave it a tug and the window closed with a *thud*. He then quickly tied the cord around one of the small metal chimneys that popped out from the roof, the rope securing the window closed.

Odelia had already scooped up Hal's backpack and thrown it on to the ground at the back of the café. Paisley followed her and threw her backpack too, before dropping to her hands and knees, looking back up at the window they had just escaped from. She pushed her satchel behind her, feeling the egg shift about, as Hal skidded over the edge of the roof and jumped down beside Odelia. Paisley lowered herself off the edge just as she saw the door smash open and a flash of red – undoubtedly the King's Men.

She snatched up her backpack and ran

after Odelia and Hal, who were heading for the maintenance shed.

"Wait!" Paisley called. "Wait, I think they can see us!"

But Odelia and Hal continued running, kicking up snow as they headed for the maintenance hangar. As soon as they were there, they slid open one side of the huge doors until there was just enough room for them to squeeze inside.

Odelia and Hal slipped out of view and Paisley followed them, pushing the door closed behind her.

Inside was an aerocopter, its balloon deflated and its body propped up on scaffolding. It was cold and dull in the building, but Paisley could see her hot breath forming small white clouds.

"Odelia! Hal!" she called out.

"Over here!" Hal called back, and then she saw them both climbing a ladder at the back of the building.

Paisley adjusted the straps on her backpack and pushed the satchel to a more comfortable position before she climbed up the ladders: one, two, then another that led up to a hatch in the roof.

"They saw us. They'll be here any minute," Paisley said as she joined Odelia and Hal on the roof.

"Good," Hal said, as he reached down and pulled up the ladder that she had just climbed up. Then he closed the hatch and pulled the ladder over it, jamming it shut.

"What now?" Paisley asked. The roof of the maintenance shed was much higher than the roof on the back of the café. *Higher than the roof back home*, she thought, and remembered how Roach had fallen from it and she had tried to save him, breaking his fall.

Odelia had discarded her thick, fur-lined cloak. She held her arms open to Paisley. "Quickly, I'm going to fly you over there to those trees that flank the aerodoc. You'll need to cut a way through the fence and then run for the aerocopter."

Paisley nodded as she wrapped her arms around Odelia's neck and hugged her close. Odelia lifted them both into the air, the snow whipping at their faces and Paisley hoping that the dark storm clouds behind were enough to disguise them.

They landed smoothly by a small copse of trees beyond the perimeter fence of the aerodoc station.

"Hal and I will meet you onboard the copter. Get a seat at the back, near the emergency exit, with a clear view of the door, if you can," Odelia said before she ascended into the sky again.

Paisley quickly moved through the trees. Here the snow had drifted into knee-high piles, and once or twice she lost her footing and found herself with a face full of snow.

When she reached the thick metal fence that encased the aerodoc, she stopped and reached inside her pocket for Næss.

As she held her arm out straight, the lance snapped into action, extending to its full length with the deadly point aiming up.

Paisley twisted the lance and ran the point along the bars once above her head and then again at ankle height. On the second pass, each of the bars dominoed in the direction of the lance and fell silently to the snow.

Paisley smiled, and the lance retracted into being a small nightsilver baton once more.

Before she stepped through the opening, she looked back. There was no sign of Odelia and Hal.

The clock on the station began to toll noon; the copter would leave at five past the hour.

Paisley hastened to the aerocopter, sticking to

the shadows of the fence and then skirting along the building and joining the short line of passengers.

She kept looking to the sky for Hal and Odelia, but they were nowhere to be seen. She hoped that they were in the trees and would soon be beside her.

As she neared the front of the queue, she plunged her hand in her pocket for her ticket, then showed it to the inspector and hastened up the gangplank. Onboard, she picked her seat according to Odelia's instructions, with a good view of the woods and the platform beyond the open door. This way she could see Odelia and Hal coming, but, also, she could see any of the King's Men too.

Paisley kept her attention on the outside, and suddenly Hal and Odelia were there, as if they had just dropped from the sky. Hal was holding both backpacks and presenting the inspector with their tickets while Odelia shrugged on her cloak.

They smiled as they entered the aerocopter, their cheeks flushing as the warmth of the cabin hit them.

Odelia sat opposite her and Hal next to her.

"What kept you?" Paisley asked. "Hal wasn't trying to be gallant again, was he?"

"No," Odelia said with a look at Hal. "Nothing

at all like that. We made it, that's all that matters," she added with a small smile, and Paisley looked between the two of them.

The inspector blew his whistle and the cabin crew moved to secure the door. Just then there was a commotion outside, and Paisley's heart sank: the King's Men, she was sure of it! She made to grab her bag, but Hal shot out a hand and stopped her. "Is that Corbett?" he asked, and Paisley pushed her face against the porthole. It was Corbett!

He was arguing with the inspector and thrusting a ticket at him, but the gangway was already withdrawing into the copter. Corbett took a few steps back, then ran and jumped for it . . . just making it!

Paisley laughed as he scampered up the retracting gangway and into the copter, the cabin staff cheering him on, clapping him on the back in good humour, and the inspector on the platform shaking his fist after him.

"Corbett!" Paisley was on her feet, her smile so big it hurt.

Corbett beamed as he walked towards them and hugged Paisley over the table. "You changed your mind," she said.

"Well, my parents helped with that. They said that if it was in my track to be part of something great, who was I to shy away from it and defy my stars?"

He then slid into the seat beside Odelia. "I'm glad that you decided to join us," the Dragon Walker said.

"Well, you know what us scientists are like, always up for death-defying adventures!"

THIRTY-ONE

THE THINGS WE DO FOR LOVE

Roach walked close beside the Dark Dragon as they made their way up the staircase of the Quayside Hotel, Hector and Lorena following. Somewhere in the hotel, checking the perimeter for any threats, were Lorena's band of fellow fallen Dragon Walker sisters, a small but deadly force, all answering to Lorena and all supporting the Dark Dragon's cause.

The Dark Dragon and her entourage entered a large suite of rooms, richly carpeted and elegantly decorated. She took off her coat and flexed her nightsilver arm.

"Was there any news at the desk?" she asked.

Hector was removing his coat and stamping the cold from his boots on to the thick carpet. "Yes, Your Darkness, there were several messages. The King's Men have had a sighting of Paisley and her friends in Inverness. They had them in their sights but lost them. It would seem that Corbett Grubbins was there too, so he must have managed to make his way home after escaping from Roach! His parents own a forge just outside the city; the knights have gone to investigate."

Roach felt everyone's eyes on him and he self-consciously rubbed at his jaw; the pale bruise where Corbett had hit him still smarted. He crossed to the window and looked out at the people coming and going on the main thoroughfare while Hector continued talking:

"It's good that they are closing in on her. The Mechanists won't like it, but I have given instructions that once captured, she and her friends are to be turned over to me, by authority of the George, of course. Speaking of which, the combined army of the King's Men will be here tomorrow morning, and the ships arrive the day after to take us to the Northern Realms. The George will be here this evening, and I expect there will be some pomp and ceremony around his arrival and our departure."

Lorena shifted in her seat on the velvet couch. "Do you think that we might have been more successful with a smaller party? If the aim is to reclaim the stone and capture the boy, then I could go ahead with my Dark Dragon Walkers and secure both with little fuss, I am sure."

The Dark Dragon stood up, her dark hair falling like a shadow down her back. She wore a black double-breasted military jacket similar to the dress uniform of the King's Men, but with the addition of two long tails at the back; it had red buttons and piping, and her black dragonhide trousers and boots made her look like a small child playing at knights.

"The time for stealth has passed," she said. "I have it on good authority that after Roach took Soul Fire, the Northern Realms' defences were increased. I need the stone back: with Soul Fire and the quarter that Violetta's family had, that's half of the Heart Stone. Of the two parts left, one resides in the vaults of the Dragon Walkers in the empires to the East, and the other will be found in the Amerikas. It lies in the lost grave of the last Great Dragon, Endedógor, along with an old adversary under the gaze of another fallen foe. We will travel to the Amerikas and find the hidden grave as soon as we have successfully completed our mission in the North. Of course, once all four parts of the heart are reunited, I will be in control of the single most powerful source of electrica energy in the Mechanism."

The Dark Dragon smiled in a way that made Roach shudder. "Now that Paisley is the George Ascending, I will need leverage over her more than ever. And using someone she loves, using Dax, is still the best way of controlling her.

"Besides, I want Paisley and the Northern Realm to suffer. I want them to fear my shadow. I want them to know how powerful I am, that I summoned the Great Dragon and that I will use it to destroy everyone who stands in my way. Defeating the North is the next step to achieving my desire. The George is the pawn that I will use to do that."

"And when do you think the comet . . . I mean, *the dragon* will arrive?" asked Hector. "When will the Veil be opened? When can I be reunited with my brother?"

Roach flinched at the hope and want in Hector's voice, but couldn't help but lean forward, eager to hear when the Dark Dragon would fulfil her promises to Hector, and to him. He wondered whether he had the same pleading in his voice when he spoke of getting Clara back?

Roach turned his gaze from Hector and saw the pitying look the Dark Dragon was giving him, which made him think of Corbett and the sympathetic look he had given Roach. "*She was never going to let me go,*" Corbett had told Roach, and he wondered if she was never going to let him go either.

Roach felt his chest clench as he turned his full attention to the window again, and as he did, his breath caught.

Paisley was walking along from the quay, heading towards the hotel! Behind her was Odelia and Hal, and next to her was Corbett Grubbins.

Roach stood ramrod straight as his mind raced. After a moment of indecision, he made for the door.

"Where are you going? I have not given you leave," the Dark Dragon said, and Roach could hear the danger in her voice.

He gave a small bow. "Forgive me, I thought I'd check on your luggage, and the other rooms n'all," he said.

The Dark Dragon looked around as if she had just remembered her belongings were not there. "Yes, go, and be sure they are careful with my trunks. And see if there is a message from the Master of Stars. I am vexed that he would not make the journey. I will still need his consultation of the Mechanism to ensure that all goes to plan, that the stars still outline my triumph."

Roach gave another small bow and left. He hastened through the corridor, his head and heart wheeling. His head was full of the Dark Dragon's plans of bringing back the Great Dragons, of opening the Veil, of everlasting tracks all under her control – and the thought of Clara. His heart was torn between what he knew would happen if the Dark Dragon succeeded and what he knew wouldn't happen if she didn't.

As he reached the staircase, he saw the porters bringing up the Dark Dragon's luggage. He moved to one side to let them pass and then carried on down to the main foyer, where he saw Paisley and the others being led towards the dining room, Paisley trailing behind, adjusting the strap on her satchel.

The group had their backs to him as he raced

down the stairs and jumped the last few, grabbing Paisley's arm.

As she turned, her face shifted from surprise to anger. She opened her mouth and he quickly hushed her, stepping in close and putting his mouth to her ear to say, "She's here!"

Paisley pulled back, her large blue eyes wide, her jaw set.

Roach could feel a tingle of electrica in the air and felt himself getting a little hot. Paisley grabbed the front of Roach's jacket and pulled him off to a small alcove under the twisting staircase.

"You betrayed me!" she hissed in an angry whisper. "I told you to protect my friends, to protect Corbett. I gave you my stars in exchange, and you kept him captive, and forced him to make her an arm, and then – then you tried to kill him, even though you promised!"

Roach rubbed his jaw again. "But I didn't, did I? And anyway, I think you'll find that it was the other way around. Corbett did this." He pointed to the bruise on his chin. "And this." He lifted his hair to show the healing cut on his head from where he had struck the ladder.

"You're impossible!" Paisley hissed.

"Look, we don't have time for this. She's here, and so is your uncle."

Roach watched as Paisley's face lost all its fury and she looked around, as if she was about to see Hector and couldn't quite work out if she wanted to or not.

"Where are they?"

"In the Dark Dragon's suite – it overlooks the quay. I saw you coming and thought I should warn you."

"Why should I believe you?" She was all seriousness, her voice a soft whisper.

Roach felt uncomfortable; he swallowed and looked about. "I don't know," he lied. He knew the way he felt when he was near Paisley: she seemed to bring out all that shone in his track, and just the thought of her made him wish that his stars were different.

"Why is she here? You must know the answer to that one?"

Roach opened his mouth to answer, but out of the corner of his eye, something caught his attention. A small, deep, dark rift had appeared just to the left of Paisley. He grabbed her and swung her behind him, placing himself between her and the rift.

"It's just like the ones from the observatory!" he said, shock and fear in his voice. He remembered what the rifts were capable of.

"It's OK," Paisley said. "It's just a little one, and I think I've got a handle on it."

Roach looked around at her.

"This one seems easier to control than the others have been," she added.

"You can control them?" Roach asked slowly.

"I'm trying to," she said.

"I ain't seen any since that night... I thought they had something to do with the machine, but..." He turned and looked at her, then gave a lopsided smile as he shook his head. "You are always full of surprises, Paisley Fitzwilliam." He gave a small laugh and saw that her cheeks went pink and the Veil rift became a little smaller.

"The Dark Dragon is here to make war on the Northern Realms. The George has raised an army. She convinced him that the North are to blame for the comet, that they captured your mother, forcing her to perform her experiment before killing her, and that they meant to kill him too. The George is going to make war with the Northern Realms so that she can use his forces to get a hold of the Heart Stone ... and your brother. She wants to hurt you, Paisley, or use you and control you to get what she wants, especially now she knows about your stars." He looked at her earnestly, hoping that she could feel how important this was to him, how much he needed her to leave. "Come on." He pulled on her arm and led away towards the staff area of the hotel. "I've got to get you out of here."

She tugged her arm free. "Not without my friends," she said, turning back.

Roach looked at her, then up, as if he could see through the ceiling and all the rooms above. "She'll wonder where I've got to. If she comes looking and finds you ..."

"Then go back to her. I'll get the others and we'll leave or ... you could come with us?"

"Why would you want me to come with you? I'm not on your side, Paisley. I'm against you; I'm with her."

A small smile danced around Paisley's lips. "If that were true, then why are you here?"

Roach felt as if his insides were being pulled in every direction.

"I ... I don't know, Paisley. I know my stars, I can see my track clearly, I know what I must do, but every time I ... you, you, Paisley Fitzwilliam, it's as if my track twists towards you and away from my stars, just like your mother forced the comet to twist from its track." Roach took a step towards Paisley, looking at her earnestly. "I'm going now," he said, feeling his heart pounding in his chest. "The Army of the George arrive tomorrow, and we set sail for the Northern Realms the day after. If you can get ahead of us, do, but Paisley: she will be coming for you. And so will I."

He left her standing at the back of the foyer and made for the stairs, taking them two at a time. His foot struck each one a little harder than was necessary.

He put his hand inside one of his pockets and pulled out the small picture. There was Clara, smiling at him; she was all that mattered.

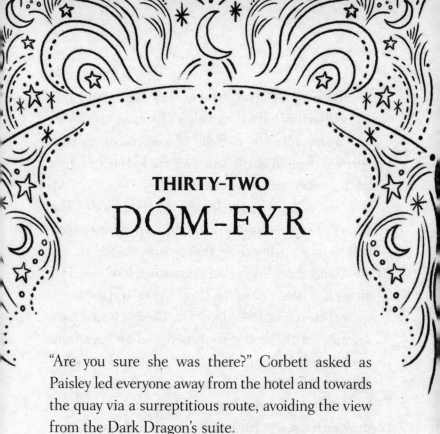

THIRTY-TWO
DÓM-FYR

"Are you sure she was there?" Corbett asked as Paisley led everyone away from the hotel and towards the quay via a surreptitious route, avoiding the view from the Dark Dragon's suite.

"I'm sure of it. I told you, I saw Roach," Paisley said as she took a left down an alley that she thought would allow them to double back on themselves.

Corbett gave a little shudder. "I know we're up against her, but I will happily live all my days if I know I never have to see her again. She gives me the creeps," he said, looking a little pale.

Hal was suddenly by Paisley's side. "And this army is setting sail for my father's lands in two days?"

Paisley gave an *uh-huh* of agreement as they reached the end of the lane and she led them across a busy street and down another alley.

"We will be ready for them," Hal said. "The Warriors of the Northern Realms and the Krigare will form a mighty force that is sure to stop them." He sounded confident, but Paisley was less sure. Her father had been one of the King's Men, and she knew what their training was like. The George would have summoned the best swordsmen and archers from every order of knights to join the combined army and fight for Albion, the Empire and the George.

At the end of the lane, Paisley came to a stop as she saw the sea in front of her. They had come out at the far end of the quay. They started walking towards where a large ship named *The Sea Jack* was docked.

"I don't like it," Corbett said, looking up. "There's too much turmoil about. Even the sky is fretful." Troubled grey clouds hung boldly as the setting sun made it look as though the sky was filling with blood. "A doomfire if ever I saw one," Corbett said, shaking his head at the clouds.

"A doomfire?" Paisley asked.

"Aye, a portend of doom, a sign that something mighty and ferocious is on its way. 'Ye best beware of a doomfire sky, hold close all that's dear till the morn does cry.' Have you never heard the warning?"

"Oh, wait, a Dóm-Fyr, in old Celtic! Yes, I've heard of it, an old superstition: the red light from the sky is supposed to affect your stars, or track, or something," Paisley said, looking up into the burning sky. It looked powerful and full of strife, but it was glorious too. It reminded her a little of Odelia, or Mother – the look they sometimes got in their eyes. Beautiful and fierce.

Corbett led the way up the gangplank and shook hands with a young, stocky man, about the same age as Norris. Corbett introduced Fergus to them all, and Paisley shook his hand. His skin felt as rough as stormy waves, but his presence felt like a calm sea.

"It's a bigger boat than I was expecting," Paisley told him as she looked about the large vessel.

"*The Sea Jack* is a goods vessel, mostly, but we dinnea often take passengers," Fergus told them. "The berths are small and the cooking is only half bad, but the fare is cheap," he said.

And with that, Odelia paid for their passage.

Fergus led them around the deck to a thick metal door and then into the ship. The metal floor and stairs clanked as they followed him, each footstep echoing through the large vessel. Paisley took in the cold grey of the metal. *The Sea Jack* was more machine than ship, it felt to her: no luxury, all function.

Fergus showed them to their berths, two bunkbeds squeezed in with just a small gap between them. Paisley stuck her head in the door; it was smaller than the carriage on the train had been. "Sorry, we're a full ship tonight. There's trouble brewing. You probably heard that the George is going to make war with the Northern Realms." He paused and looked at them.

"Oh, aye, we've heard a bit about that," Corbett said, and Paisley saw Hal grin at him.

"Well, lots of people are trying to get home, or just escape the King's Men for their own reasons, if you catch my drift!" Fergus added with a wink and a tap of his nose.

Paisley's nerves jolted as Fergus looked in her direction. She tugged down her sleeve, making sure her stars were covered, but he was looking beyond Paisley at a shady-looking man with faded Krigare marks who was entering the cabin next door to theirs. The man looked them all up and down, his eyes lingering on first Hal and then Odelia.

After he closed his door, Fergus lowered his voice. "He's a Skywayman, wanted by the George, so be sure not to cross him. You know what those types are like – ruthless fighters." Paisley almost laughed as she saw Odelia raise a single eyebrow. Fergus didn't know the meaning of ruthless if Odelia was not his marker for it.

"It's going to be a choppy crossing; there's a storm coming in. So if I were you, I'd batten down and get some sleep whilst you can."

Fergus was right about the storm. The doomfire sky was fulfilling its promise. Just after midnight, the waves started churning, and the boat began to rise high and then hang in the air before crashing back down to meet the water.

Odelia sat bolt upright in her lower bunk, her back against the wall. "I do not like the sea," she declared as the boat crashed down again. "I am a creature of the air, and all of this water is troubling."

However, it was more trouble to Corbett than it was to Odelia. No sooner had he settled down in his top bunk again than he was rushing off to be sick.

Only Hal was content, sleeping soundly.

Paisley went to sit next to Odelia, slipping from her bunk opposite. She brought the dragon egg with her, cradling it in her lap, feeling its warmth. It had grown again and was now too big to fit back in her satchel. Paisley had a strange feeling that she should keep it close to her. Maybe it was the storm, but the little dragon was tapping away at the inside of the shell. She crossed her legs and put the egg on her lap, then held Odelia's hand.

"It will be all right; the storm will pass, and we will soon be there," Paisley whispered.

Odelia took a deep breath, and Paisley knew that she was using all of her self-control not to be sick.

"Yes, give me a breeze or a gust or a gale and I will ride it with ease, but these waves have me wishing for land – glorious, firm, unmoving land – and once on it we will soon be reunited with Dax," Odelia said.

"Do you think he is all right? I can't help but feel that he is in danger."

"Listen to your instincts. If you think that he is in danger, then he probably is."

"That's not very reassuring," Paisley said as a flash of lightning lit up the world beyond the porthole, and for a brief second she could see the dark waves, high and terrifying. She looked away.

"Would you rather I lie to you, Your Georgeness?"

Paisley realized that Odelia was more blunt than normal when struggling not to be sick. Thunder rumbled angrily above them.

"No, you know I wouldn't. It's just that . . . he's my responsibility, and I feel as if I've let him down as it is. So to think that something terrible might happen to him and that I wasn't there to save him. . ."

Paisley suddenly thought of Roach and his sister being taken by the Men of the Yard, and how he must have felt to know that there was nothing he could do to stop them, nothing he could do to save her from the Veil. And she remembered what he had said to her when they were in the Mechster, of how all that he did for the Dark Dragon was to get his sister back. She wondered: would she do the same, to save Dax?

"When we are reunited with the Dragon Lord, it will be a joyous thing," Odelia said.

"Do you still think that Dax is going to lead us all to freedom?" Paisley asked.

"I do, I think that he is Malgol, and so are you, together," Odelia said. "The Unknown Unfolding works in complicated ways, and I do not believe that he or you will do what needs to be done alone. Your stars will help him, and his you. And I feel that all our tracks have a part to play – mine, Hal's, Corbett's, even the Dark Dragon's. Everything and everyone in the Celestial Mechanism is connected. We cannot see how, and we do not know why, but that is not for us to wonder about.

"Think of this. If Adore Marea had not been captured by the King's Men and we had not been delayed from reaching the station, the King's Men would not have stopped the train, we would not have fled to York, I would not have been reunited with my brothers and sisters, you would not have received the King Star when you did, we would not have been introduced to Captain Hewitt, she would not have taken us to Inverness, we would not have been reunited with Corbett, and his brother's friend would not have found us passage on this ship.

"Think of all the cogs that needed to turn, all the

tracks that needed to loop, all the stars that needed to align in order for us to be sitting on this miserable ship, miles from land, being tossed about by a storm."

Paisley laughed. "Yes, I think it was all worth it."

"It will be, Paisley. It will be. Anu will make sure of it."

Corbett returned from the bathroom and collapsed on Paisley's bunk. "I think the storm's getting worse," he mumbled into the quilt, face down.

"Sometimes a track gets rough before it smooths out again," Paisley said automatically as she lifted the dragon egg up to look at it. The tap, tap, tapping from inside was persistent, but it had just made a different sound.

She twisted the egg around in her hand, feeling its surface, and as she did her fingers felt a crack in the shell.

"Oh no! I think it's hatching!" Paisley said, holding the egg a little away from herself.

Hal smoothly dropped from the bunk above.

"I thought you were asleep!" Corbett said as he struggled to prop himself up on his arms to see the egg.

"A warrior never truly sleeps," Odelia said, her voice stern as she remained bolt upright, resolute that she would not be sick. Another flash of light filled up the cabin, followed by a menacing, deep rumble that shook through the boat like a dragon's roar.

The electrica light in the cabin was dull, and Paisley felt as if she and the egg were in a cosy cave of some kind, the soft bunk beneath her and Odelia to the side.

Hal moved and sat on the edge of the bunk opposite, beside Corbett. "Let me see," he said as he leaned over, peering at the egg.

Paisley rotated it towards Hal to show him the crack, and as she did the dragon tapped again, making it a little bigger and lifting the shell.

"Oh!" Paisley giggled in surprise.

"That's it, little one," Hal said, before looking up at Paisley, his blue eye twinkling as he smiled. The dragon tapped again and the tiny crack extended across half of the shell. Then a small piece flew off and hit Corbett as he lay still on the bed, mesmerized by the hatching dragon as the boat continued to heave up and down.

Paisley turned the egg back towards her and looked in the hole. A flash of lightning lit up the room and she could see a small red eye looking back at her; it flickered with all the colours of a fire. Paisley smiled and lifted a hand to try and prise the shell open.

"Don't, let her do it herself. It will make her stronger," Hal said. "We have a saying in the Northern Realms: 'let sleeping dragons lie and hatching dragons try'."

Paisley's face was close to the egg. She saw every push from within, every effort that the dragon was making to break free into the world.

She stroked the shell, feeling the small bumps and lines under her fingers. She whispered to the dragon, "That's right. Keep going. You can do this. The world . . . well, it's not ready for you. You're going to cause a bit of a commotion. And things are going to be tough. But just because something is difficult and others stand in your way, it doesn't mean that you shouldn't do it. It doesn't mean that it's not important. I'm not sure if dragons get a track, or if the stars will sing out your destiny when you finally hatch, but we'll be in the Northern Realms soon and none of that really matters much to them. They care more about what you do and say than your stars. I used to think that they were wrong, that they were limiting themselves by not embracing their paths in life, but maybe it's everyone who's been following their stars who are trapped." Paisley felt the stars on her wrist prickle, as if they had heard her.

The egg was still, and Paisley wondered if the dragon had been listening to what she said, listening and wondering and feeling a little fearful, just as she did. "Don't worry, little one, you won't be alone. We have a lot to do, you and I, but we have Corbett and Odelia. They'll be with us, and Hal, if he wants to, and soon we'll have Dax, and he is just going to be so excited to see you, almost as excited as I'm going to be to see him."

Paisley smiled and pushed away a tear as she looked up, remembering that the others were there.

Paisley coughed to clear her throat. "Um ... I don't think it will take her long to hatch," she said, and looked back down at the egg.

"We know," Odelia said, sidling up to Paisley. She extended a finger and ran it over the little cracks in the shell.

"In the North, once a dragon decides to hatch, they are pretty quick about it," Hal said. "This little dragon has done everything fast."

"Will it need anything, when it hatches?" Corbett asked. "A blanket? Food? A cage, maybe?"

"No cages!" Odelia said.

Hal nodded and looked at Odelia. "A blanket is a good idea, treasure is better, but as for food, the dragon would have eaten the remains of the egg sac before she hatches, so she won't need to eat straight away."

"And when she does, what will she eat?" Corbett persisted, and Paisley knew that he was thinking of the tales of the Great Dragons eating knights!

Hal shrugged. "She's a Great Dragon, so I can't say for sure, but the dragons of the North mostly eat grass and vegetables."

Corbett looked at him incredulously. "Grass and vegetables?"

Hal nodded with a smile, his scar puckering as it pushed up his eyepatch. "Yep, they also like fruit and nuts and berries too. I could give her some from the jar!" he said with a smile.

The dragon egg cracked again, and this time it

split in two, the top of the shell falling beside Paisley to reveal the baby dragon nestled within the golden insides of the egg. She stretched up and extended her neck towards Paisley. Her scales were a soft grey, darkening as they travelled down her body. The top of her head had two little horns that reminded Paisley of CeCe. The spines that ran along her back in two peaks looked like tiny mountain ranges and were topped with red, as were the edges of her wings. As she stretched up, the dragon placed the red claw at the end of one wing on the edge of the broken shell, then pulled herself up and forward, her other wing unfolding. Paisley held the egg in one hand and extended her other; the dragon shifted its wings to her hand. Paisley felt a small scratch as the dragon's claw gained purchase and she moved from the egg on to Paisley's hand, then into her arms.

Paisley needed both of her hands to hold the dragon; she was about the same size as a cat. Her tail twisted around Paisley's wrist, anchoring her in place, and when Paisley looked down, she saw that the barb of the dragon's tail was sitting among her stars, pointing towards the black King Star in the centre.

The baby dragon then shifted, pushing herself up

on to her legs and extending her wings as she stood upright. She gave a small, high-pitched squark, then snuggled down into Paisley's arms and folded her wings back in.

"Her wings are just like yours, Odelia! I mean, smaller and a different colour, but the same shape." Paisley looked at the Dragon Walker, then around at Corbett and Hal. They were all staring, mesmerized by the baby dragon, their faces full of wonder.

Paisley smiled at them all as another flash of lightning lit the room and a peal of thunder rung out.

The dragon stirred and opened one eye briefly . . . then closed it again.

"Is she supposed to sleep? Shouldn't she be flying about? Should we feed her?" Paisley asked Hal.

He smiled. "She's fine. She will sleep a lot, and as she sleeps, she will grow. It will be a few days before she finds her wings. I had best go see if I can find her some food for when she wakes; hungry dragons are no fun at all. Besides, I don't want her to eat all my nuts, seeds and berries," he said with a smile. As he stood up, another lightning flash filled the room and Paisley thought she saw a flicker of movement through the porthole in the door to the cabin. She shifted the blanket from the bunk around her and the dragon, hiding it from view.

"How long will she sleep?" Corbett asked.

Hal shrugged. "One thing I will tell you: don't wake her, wait for her to wake on her own. There is a reason why we let sleeping dragons lie, and it's best not to find out why, even with a baby dragon."

Hal walked towards the door, then stopped. "What are you going to name her, Paisley?"

Paisley looked up at Hal, her eyes wide; she hadn't given it much thought. She looked back down at the little dragon, who stirred and again opened one bright-red eye lazily before closing it again. "We shall call her Dóm-Fyr. Dóm for short!"

"Ah, the doomfire sky. Well, she's bound to be mighty and ferocious!" Corbett said.

Odelia reached over and stroked the velvet scales on the dragon's back as she slumbered. "Dóm. I like it, a good strong name. She'll need that for what is to come."

Paisley hugged the sleeping dragon closer.

THIRTY-THREE

BEYOND THE CURVE

Paisley wasn't sure when the storm had passed, but it was late morning the next day when Corbett stirred and woke her.

The first thing she did was reach for the dragon ... but she wasn't there! Paisley shot out of bed, hitting her head on the bunk above. "Dóm!"

"It's OK, she's here," Hal said, and Paisley turned to face Hal on the top bunk, rubbing her head and watching as Hal extended some cauliflower to Dóm. She sniffed it first, then took a big bite. Her double row of teeth were sharp and bright.

"She likes spinach and broccoli too; I haven't tried offering her the green beans yet."

"Did you find any turnips?" Odelia asked from her bed on the bunk behind Paisley.

"No," Hal answered.

"Good," Odelia answered as she rolled over and pulled the covers over her head. Paisley smiled as she remembered what Hal had said about Sterk-Natt and her love of turnips.

Dóm finished eating, then made her way over to Paisley, pausing at the edge of the bunk as Paisley raised a hand and Dóm scampered up her arm to curl herself around Paisley's neck. Her scales were soft and she felt warm; her rhythmic breathing was soothing.

"We need to keep her out of sight," Corbett warned.

"I've been thinking about that," Paisley said, and she lifted her dragonhide satchel; it was empty now, so she snatched up a soft fur scarf and stuffed it into the bag, lining the bottom and sides with it like a pocket. Then she picked up the two halves of the hatched egg's shell, marvelling at the lustre of the gold inside them.

"Is it real gold?" she asked. Both Corbett and Hal replied at the same time – Corbett with a "No", Hal with a "Yes".

"It's dragon's gold," Hal said. "It looks like gold, probably tastes and smells like gold too, but it's not *real* gold, no."

"I see," Paisley said, and she put the shell in her backpack instead of the satchel. "Do we have any treasure?" she asked as she pulled off a gold necklace she was wearing. Dóm looked up, following the necklace with her eyes as Paisley added it to the bag.

Paisley looked down at her wrist but kept Corbett's Nightsilver bangle on, thinking that she really ought to give it back to him now that he was coming with her.

"Why do you need treasure?" Corbett asked as he took off his watch and handed it to Paisley.

"I'm making a nest for her, in my satchel. Hal said that dragons like to nest on treasure." She turned to Hal, who smiled and nodded.

"Here." He handed her a gold ring from the little finger on his left hand. "But I'm going to need that back; it has my Krigare seal on it."

Paisley popped it in the bag.

"What about you, Odelia?" Hal asked.

Odelia grunted and rolled out of bed. She stuffed a hand into her pocket and pulled out a pouch which she upended into the bag: it was full of gold ingots, pearls, rubies, diamonds, sapphires and emeralds. Then she pulled out a bigger pouch full of gold, silver and bronze coins and poured them in too. Paisley's mouth opened wide in surprise, Corbett's eyes bulged and Dóm made her way down from Paisley's neck and into the satchel, where she began to shift and sort and organize the treasure.

"Wow! Odelia, where did you get all of that?" Corbett asked.

"A dragon is never far from treasure," Odelia said with a knowing look, and Paisley got the sense that there was more where that had come from.

*

Paisley was tired the next day, and when Dóm slumbered so did she. The sea was calmer but still churned, and with every lurch of the boat Paisley imagined that their progress was two waves forward, one back. Her thoughts pressed in on her and she felt stifled in the small cabin.

That night the seas were calm, but Paisley was restless.

She got up and dressed, wrapping herself in layers of the cold-weather clothes they had brought with them from Inverness. She slipped her satchel over her head and went up on to the deck of the boat.

Paisley looked up into the sky, and as her eyes adjusted, she realized that she was not surrounded by a dark, empty nothingness but by the light of a million trillion stars, each one casting the fate of the world below it.

Her mind was full of the stars that she had seen in the Mechster at York, and how she had marvelled at their beauty. She realized now that she had been foolish: those stars were small and pale and weak in comparison to the vista before her.

She wondered which of the brilliant points of light had marked out her King Star.

She sighed just as a falling star streaked across the heavens, and she said a small word for the owners of the lost star, hoping that their track was strong enough to carry on without it. And she made a wish, in case the star was hers.

As she made her way around the ship, she saw Corbett; he too was wrapped in his winter furs, his glasses glinting in the light from the stars, a small telescope in his hand as he wrote in his journal. He saw her and waved.

"Couldn't sleep?" Corbett asked.

"Not really," Paisley replied.

"Me neither. I was out here tracking the comet, but it set a long while ago now." He pointed to the west and Paisley was glad not to see it.

The two of them began to slowly walk around the deck of the boat. It was empty, but above, on the high bridge, there was a soft light and the silhouette of the crew as they steered the ship.

When they were on the other side of the deck, Corbett pointed to a patch of light on the horizon.

"Do you know what that is?" he asked.

Paisley shrugged. "Electrica lights, I assume? But what's making them?" She saw nothing but the blackness of the sea under the soft glow.

"That'll be Västerut Hamn, the port that Hal said we're heading for. It's sitting just beyond the horizon."

"Beyond the horizon."

"Aye, just out of sight over the curve of the Earth,

344

so we can't see the land yet, but we can see the light that the port town gives off."

"Ha, so we know it's there, even though we can't see it."

"Aye, a little like our tracks. We know they're there, we can see the effects that they have, but we have no way of looking at them properly or knowing for sure what they have in store – save our destinies, that is."

"Yes, apart from them," Paisley said with a light chuckle.

Corbett began to fidget, then turned to Paisley and said, "You do know that at some point you won't be able to escape your stars any more, Paisley. You'll have to become the George."

Paisley shrugged. "I know, it's just that I like to think that I'm in control of my own track and that I turn my own cogs. Sure, I also want to know where I'm heading. I want to see that glow beyond the horizon and know that it means something is waiting for me; I think we all do. But I want to have the freedom to choose what colour that glow is, what is making it . . . and to walk away from it, if I want."

Corbett nodded. "I understand. I didn't before,

but I'm starting to get it." He hugged himself and stamped his feet on the deck.

They stood for a while more watching the constant glow, then heard a banging as a door behind them opened and the Skywayman from the neighbouring berth stepped out on to the deck. He looked over at Corbett and Paisley and stared at her satchel; she instinctively pulled it towards her, and as he stood in the doorway with the lights from behind highlighting his silhouette, she remembered that the night before, when Dóm-Fyr had hatched, she had seen something move outside the pothole of the door. Someone had been standing at the door as the lightning flashed. Not someone, but the Skywayman.

"Let's go," Paisley said to Corbett as she stared down the Skywayman. He moved aside for them, walking towards the railing, where he paused and looked over his shoulder at her again.

Paisley swiftly made her way back to their cabin, Corbett trailing along behind her.

She'd seen the greedy look on the man's face before and feared for her dragon.

THIRTY-FOUR

THE NORTHERN REALMS

Hal practically bounced off the boat and bid them all follow him away from the dock and up into the town. He had washed off the make-up that Odelia had given him and braided his hair. He was once again wearing his Krigare uniform, and Paisley felt that he looked much more comfortable as he led them through the port town.

She glanced around, checking for any signs of the Skywayman as they made their way through the pretty port, but he seemed to have vanished. She had not shared her suspicions with the others, but she was sure he had seen Dóm and wondered if he knew that she was a Great Dragon. As she followed Hal up the slope towards the village, she held her satchel close against her body. Dóm slept soundly on her nest of treasure, guarding Paisley's King Scroll that was tucked alongside the little dragon. The satchel felt solid and she supported it underneath with one arm as she walked. Soon, she would need to find something bigger to transport Dóm in.

The buildings were made of wood and had been painted in all the colours of the sea: blue-green, grey-purple, off-white, and all the colours in between. The streets were dusted in snow; it collected in between the hard grey stone cobbles of the road and clung to the salt-scattered sidewalks.

Hal led them towards an impressive building at the top of a long slope that led all the way down to the port. Hal explained that it was the customs house, where all the trade brought in on the ships was dealt with and taxed; it was also where the Baron of Västerut Hamn lived and worked, and where the Krigare stationed to guard the port resided.

Amongst the business premises along the steep street, they also passed a small Mechanist Chapel, the wooden side of the building ornately carved in a style similar to the stone buildings Paisley was used to seeing in London, but also uniquely its own.

"You have Mechanists in the North?"

Hal rolled his eyes. "Some believe in the blueprints. We get a lot of foreigners in the ports, and they bring their beliefs with them. True Northmen see the restrictions of the Celestial Mechanism, how it cut us off from our homelands across the stars, and from our autonomy – but we do not deny that it is there, that it influences our lives with its prison of intention."

Paisley was startled by Hal's last words; for most of her life, she had wanted the certainty of a track. But now that she had experienced the impact that her track had on her, she too was starting to feel like it was more of a prison than a freedom.

"The whole place looks very civilized," Corbett whispered to Paisley as he moved aside for a lady to pass.

"*Tak skal du ha!*" she said in thanks.

"What did you expect, that we all lived in caves and huts and fought each other in the street?" Hal asked, having clearly overheard.

Corbett blushed a little and Paisley wondered

if he was an avid reader of the *Herald*; after all, she too had believed that the Northern Realms were full of trackless ruffians out to steal from the Empire ... until she'd got to know Hal, that was. She too blushed as she remembered all her previous misgivings.

The doors of the custom house were thrown open, and Hal walked straight in and over to the secretary seated behind a large wooden desk. He told the man who he was. There was a brief pause. Hal walked back to Paisley. "Sorry, can I have my ring back?"

"Now?" Paisley asked as she started to unbuckle the straps on her satchel.

She put in her hand and soothed Dóm as she stirred. Then she felt under the dragon for the ring, hooked it on her finger and slowly pulled it out ... but Dóm wasn't so eager to give the ring back. Paisley yelped as she felt the dragon's teeth sink into her knuckle. Her hand bleeding, blood dripping over the ring, she passed it to Hal.

"That wasn't kind!" she whispered into the bag.

Dóm gnashed her teeth at Paisley.

"Hush, or someone will hear you!"

Odelia reached into her cloak and pulled out a large diamond which she popped into Paisley's satchel. Seconds later, a low, soft purr of a grumble came from the bag, and the little dragon settled back down. Odelia smiled in satisfaction as Paisley reached into her pocket and pulled out Roach's handkerchief, wrapping it around her finger.

"Let me guess," she whispered to Odelia. "Never take a dragon's treasure!"

Odelia nodded. "Not if you want to live, or at least avoid injury."

Hal went back to the desk and presented the ring to the secretary, and suddenly a large commotion broke out as the man leaped up and shook Hal's hand, then bowed several times and called to a colleague as he passed. Hal looked back at Paisley and the others and rolled his eye a little before smiling at them.

Within moments, a host of people were escorting them into a large room full of beautifully woven colourful tapestries and strong functional furniture. A man who was obviously the Baron of Västerut Hamn greeted Hal and offered him a horn full of honey-coloured liquid. Paisley found herself being offered one too, and as Hal called *"Schol!"* and drained the cup, Paisley did the same, her eyes bulging as the sweet liquid burned the back of her throat.

Odelia finished hers with a satisfying lick of her lips, and Corbett almost sprayed his all over the polished floor as he started coughing.

Paisley patted him on the back and asked the young man who took the cup if they could have a glass of water. The man looked at her funny, so she asked again, this time in Old Celtic, and he nodded and went off to find some water.

Paisley watched as many people came and spoke to Hal, and he politely spoke to them in Norse. The language was close to the Old Celtic of the Empire that she had been taught at school and she could make out the odd word, like *war* and *preparation*. Every now and then, Hal looked as if he was a little frustrated, but this would pass and his good humour quickly returned.

Eventually, Hal broke away from the knot of officials around him and came over to where Paisley, Odelia and Corbett had been seated. "Good news! My eldest brother, Magna, was betrothed while I was away; I thought it was likely to happen. The bad news is that the threat of war has only just reached my father. He is, however, taking things very seriously and has called all the Barons to an assembly – including the Baron of Västerut Hamn. He was just preparing to leave. Magna and my older sister, Linnea, are raising our land armies, and my little sisters, Thea, whom you might remember from the observatory on her green dragon, and Stina, are organizing the Krieger. My father's keep is a few hours' flight from here, but we will have to make do with other transportation, as dragon-back is out of the question."

"However, we have the next best thing: wolves!" said a large man as he strode over to them. He was Kristoff, the Baron of Västerut Hamn, and Paisley felt intimidated by his size.

"Did you say wolves?" Corbett asked.

"Yes, the sledges are being readied now," Kristoff said.

"Sledges!"

Hal laughed. "Yes, Corbett, sledges. You two will love them," he said, smiling at Paisley and Odelia.

Hal was not wrong. Paisley sat low in the sledge,

surrounded by thick, warm furs, Odelia behind her, and their backpack stowed further back, Dóm safely tucked in the satchel resting in her lap. The dragon was sleeping soundly, and Paisley remembered what Hal had said about sleeping and growing.

A young girl named Alva stood on the back of the sledge, steering her pack of wolves through the snow.

In the sledge behind them rode Hal and Corbett, and Alva's mother, Mya, stood behind them, reins in hand, controlling her wolves. Kristoff rode his own sledge, and inside sat his closest advisor, an old woman named Lena.

The sledges moved swiftly as the wolves ran, their powerful legs pulling them across the snow. The blades of the sledge created no resistance, cutting through the snow as if it were icing on a cake.

Paisley and Odelia were sat only a few inches from the ground, and the world whooshed past them in a flash of harsh white, soft brown, and vivid green as they sped through a thick woodland of enormous fir trees. The cold wind hit Paisley's smiling face, and she delighted in the sensation.

"Flying is still best," Odelia told Paisley as she

leaned a little forward and spoke into her ear. "But I could get used to the thrill of gliding through the snow."

Paisley agreed, and her heart trilled every time they rounded a bend or went down a slope. And when the wolves climbed up an incline, she marvelled at their agility and strength and the way that they moved as one together, graceful and powerful.

"How do they control them like that?" Paisley asked.

Odelia pointed to the wolf at the front of the pack. "You see that one? She is the Alpha. Where she goes, the rest follow. A little like you!"

Paisley was startled and twisted to see Odelia's face; the Dragon Walker smiled at her, then returned to watching the world speed past.

Was she really like that? Paisley wondered, and as she did, she saw Alva tug the reins to the left, and the lead wolf veered that way.

If Paisley was the lead wolf, then who controlled the reins? The Chief Designer via the track she followed? Or Anu and with her Unknown Unfolding?

Paisley wondered if the wolf ever thought about breaking free and leading her pack where she wished, or even leaving them behind and escaping her responsibility altogether.

The sun had just dipped over the horizon when they finished crossing a large expanse of open country, the woodland far behind them and the wolves beginning to tire. But as the light dimmed, so Paisley could see a soft glow of electrica light in the distance. She realized that Hal's father's keep was close, just as with the lights at sea, and so was Dax.

Even wrapped in all the furs, the inactivity of sitting in the sledge had made her limbs cold and stiff. But she could feel the heat returning to her as she thought about her brother.

By the time the wolves crossed through the first gate into the walled citadel, Paisley felt ready to leap out of the sledge and run to each and every house looking for Dax, if needed.

Alva and Mya pulled the wolves to a stop near a tavern, and Paisley eagerly stepped from the furs and into the cold night.

"Which way?" she asked Hal as she pulled her satchel open and checked on Dóm as she slept.

Before answering, he thanked Alva and Mya

and gestured that they, Kristoff and Lena, should follow them. He pointed in the direction of a long wooden building raised on a slope. This building looked older, less formal and grand than Paisley was expecting, more like a barn than a king's castle.

Paisley edged in that direction, and Hal called after her: "Wait up! I know you are eager, but there are traditions that need to be upheld. I have to visit with the Seer first and have my return marked in the *Book of Travellers*, and then my deeds must be recorded, and runes cast, new tattoos bestowed. . ."

"Hal, I need to see my brother!" Paisley could hear the pleading in her voice.

"Well, I guess all of that can wait. This *could* be classed as a diplomatic emergency." He smiled and his eye twinkled.

"Thank you." Paisley turned and carried on in the direction of the longhouse.

"Besides, if they catch sight of Odelia, someone might try to arrest us," Hal said.

"Arrest me! I'd like to see them try," Odelia said with a raised eyebrow.

"You know, I think I would like to see that too,"

Hal said with a laugh. "Dragon Walkers are not always welcome in the Northern Realms; there are some Barons of the North who still remember that it was the Great Dragon Anu who forged the tracks and broke the bridge to the realm beyond and stopped our ancestors from visiting."

"That is nothing more than a Northern Tale," Odelia said haughtily.

"I am amazed at how a story can be nothing but a Northern or even Dragon Tale to one person and sacred scripture to another," Hal said with a cheeky sideways glance at Odelia, who looked a little flummoxed.

Paisley noticed that Hal was the only person who had this effect on Odelia. With everyone else she was as strong as nightsilver, but with him she was ever so slightly yielding, like copperich.

"What's this about a bridge?" Corbett asked, but he never got to find out because then they were at the longhouse, and the doors flew open as they approached, as if someone inside had been looking out for them.

Inside was one very long hall, full of merrymaking. There was music playing and a great mix of people, all ages together, all talking and laughing as they ate and drank and danced.

Paisley pulled off her gloves and stuffed them in her pocket, then let her backpack slip from one shoulder, and unbuttoned her coat under her satchel strap as she moved into the hall, following Hal.

A large man greeted Hal with a hearty handshake, then a hug. He said something to Hal in Norse, and Hal replied in Old Celtic, "It is good to be alive! Here, allow me to introduce my friends. This is Corbett, he is a scientist from the Empire of Albion. Paisley too is from the Empire, and she is . . . well, she is quite complicated, actually. And this is Odelia. There is absolutely nothing complicated about her except that she is a Dragon Walker. I would give my life to protect hers . . . and that of my other companions, so let it be known that no one is to cause any trouble for my guests." Hal fixed the man with a serious look. "Odelia, Paisley, Corbett, this is Kurt, he is my father's Justice, and will ensure that you are well looked after while you stay with us."

Kurt nodded a head towards them as they each said hello. "You join us on a special evening; we are celebrating the triumphs of the trials and welcoming the new Krigare," Kurt said. "Come, drink, eat, be merry, for who cares what troubles tomorrow might hand to us? This evening offers us joy."

Then Hal let out a merry laugh, and led them through the gathering.

The large wooden columns that supported the roof of the hall were covered in intricate carvings and coloured in white and red paint. Between the columns, high up in the rafters, hung great banners of greenery, the sweet smell of pine sap filling the air along with the smoky smell of seasoned wood and spiced meats cooking.

Hal pushed through the crowd, then suddenly someone yelled and ran towards him: a young girl with white-gold hair that flew behind her. She leaped at Hal, and he caught her and twisted her high in the air. Paisley recognized her as Thea, the Krigare who had ridden the green dragon during the fight at the observatory.

Thea hugged Hal close and then punched him in the shoulder as he put her down and she began telling him off.

People were gathering around and laughing at Hal as his little sister shouted at him. She then turned and shouted at them, and they soon piped down. Thea was small, but she was mighty, and Paisley could see that as the leader of the Krigare she was respected.

Paisley saw Dax just before he turned and saw her. He was sitting at a long table near the thrones. He was wearing the uniform of the Krigare, and as he turned to face her, she saw an ice-blue tattoo running up the side of his neck.

"Dax!" she yelled, and ran to him, pushing her satchel on to her back. He leaped on to the bench, his brace-less leg propelling him on to the table. He knocked over food and drink as people shouted, and then he leaped towards her, and she was there to catch him.

She held him tight, and her knees buckled, and she sobbed on to his shoulder as he wept on to hers, and for a few moments the two of them were all that mattered in the universe; everything else fell away.

Then Paisley pulled back and held his face in her hands and looked at him, before kissing his cheeks, and his forehead, and he smiled and laughed and told her to stop, but she didn't care, and she knew that he didn't mean it.

"What's happened to you? Your leg – you have no brace!" Worry flashed over her face.

"It's all right, Paisley, honestly! Everything is fine! But I'm so glad you're here. I missed you more than you'll ever know." And he was hugging her again, and she thought that they might melt into each other as intricately as the blood and metal of nightsilver, never to be parted.

Slowly, Paisley became aware of all the other people in the room. The hall was a little quieter than it had been; some had ceased their merriment to watch Paisley and Dax's reunion.

Odelia was beside them. She bowed to Dax: "My Lord, I am very glad—"

Dax suddenly leaped at her, and, while still holding Paisley, he pulled Odelia in for a hug too.

Paisley kissed the top of Dax's head, then looked up to see that Corbett and Hal had joined the three of them in the mass embrace.

Paisley felt as if she were in the centre of all of them, and never wanted them to be parted.

THIRTY-FIVE

DRAGONS, DESTINY AND DR MICKLE MICHAELSON

Paisley, Odelia and Corbett were invited to sit at the top table, where Dax and Thea sat, and, as they drank and ate, Hal and his younger sisters lowered their heads and talked in hushed voices about battle plans.

Paisley was sitting next to Hal and could tell the serious nature of what the siblings were saying, and even if she didn't know how to speak their language, every now and again a word similar to Olde Celtic cropped up and she could piece a few things together.

But Paisley found it hard to think of the battle

that was coming. She kept looking at Dax and smiling. She was so happy she thought she might burst.

"What have you been doing?" Corbett asked, gesturing towards the ice mark on Dax's neck.

"I became a Krigare! Can you believe it? There was a trial, and things I had to do, and at times I thought I couldn't do them, but I did, and being a Krigare is brilliant. But my plan had been to get my own dragon, and then leave and come and find you, but I don't need to do that now because you're here!"

"And what about your. . ." Paisley looked down at Dax's leg.

"Oh, Paisley, it's the best thing ever!" He lowered his voice. "It doesn't hurt any more. I don't have to pretend."

"Did you tell them?" Paisley looked about anxiously.

Dax shook his head. "No, but they don't ask about it, and they don't really care that I walk funny or that my leg twists and turns differently to others; they just accept it as part of me, and I don't have to explain. Thea says that a person's worth is measured by what they do and how they live their life."

Corbett gave a little *ha*. "Well, that is easy for her to say: her father is a king and she is head of the Krigare!"

"She had to earn that, just as Hal did. In fact, no one else in Hal and Thea's family has ever been head of the Krigare."

"Well, they might not have got to be head of the Krigare, but I'm sure his older sister will rule the Northern Realms. They have a strange way of passing things between families rather than letting their stars decide."

Dax nodded. "Yes, they do. It is a bit weird, but it's not necessarily the eldest child who gets to rule. They test the siblings who want to take charge of the country, to decide who is most suitable. Hal and Thea's father, King Harken, was the second youngest of all his brothers and sisters. And his mother, who ruled before him, was not the eldest either."

Paisley thought it was a fascinating way of choosing who governed a country and was interested in the way that they still kept it in one family. But she felt a little unsure about it; it was not at all like the George, who was appointed by the Chief Designer and could be born anywhere in the Mechanism. But if the Empire had the same system as the Northern Realms, then Paisley would never have been given the King Star, and although that would have been a lot less to bear . . . a small part of her was also a little upset about the idea of not being the George, and she was surprised by that.

Paisley tugged down her tunic sleeve, conscious of her stars. She was wondering when the best time would be to tell Dax about her track when, out of the corner of her eye, she spied Doc Langley. Paisley sprang to her feet as he made his way towards her, and when they met, he threw his arms around her and hugged her close. "I am mighty pleased to see you, Paisley Fitzwilliam."

"And I you, Doc. There's something I need to show you," she said, and led him back to Dax and her satchel. Then she pulled them all to a quiet corner of the hall where no one could see or hear them.

Doc Langley gasped as she opened the satchel and showed him the sleeping dragon inside.

Dax peered inside, his eyes growing large. "Is that my dragon, from the egg?" he asked.

"I have never in all my days. . ." Doc reached out

a finger and stroked the soft, grey-dappled scales.

"This is Dóm-Fyr," Paisley said proudly.

"What a perfect name," Doc Langley cooed.

"I need you both to help me keep her safe and hidden. There's a war coming, and we can't afford for the Dark Dragon to get her hands on Dóm."

"She's coming here, that savage little girl?"

Paisley nodded at Doc.

Dax said, "I know that when you saw the egg, Doc, you said that the dragon inside would be a Great Dragon, but I didn't really believe you. But . . . she is so different from the northern dragons, I can tell just by looking at her. She really is a Great Dragon, isn't she?" Paisley and Doc Langley nodded in unison as Paisley secured the satchel once more.

"You know, I already have a dragon, Paisley! It comes with the job," Dax said, motioning to his uniform. "I don't think Stark-Natt would be too impressed if I got another – you really shouldn't make a dragon angry, so I think Dóm-Fyr should be your dragon."

"Oh, I don't think it works like that, Dax, but thanks. I think," Paisley said, nudging her brother as he smiled at her.

Paisley wasn't sure that anyone ever owned a dragon, especially a Great Dragon, and was just about to tell Dax so when some music struck up, loud and rousing. A few people started to dance, and Paisley saw Hal rise from his chair. Paisley realized what he was going to do the moment before he did it.

He crossed to where Odelia was standing. As ever, she was on the alert, looking for trouble. Paisley smiled; she doubted that Odelia had expected trouble to have such an engaging smile or persuasive tongue.

Paisley watched as Hal and Odelia moved gracefully around the hall. Odelia still had her cloak on, and as she spun and twirled, Paisley could see the edges of her wings peek out from the bottom of the fabric. Odelia's face looked just as serene as it did when she was fighting. But even as she stepped and twisted around, her wings were held down by the coat.

Paisley wondered if Odelia – or any of them – would ever be free of their stars.

*

The next morning, Paisley woke with Odelia's wing pulled over her, and it took a moment for her to realize where she was. For a horrible second, she thought she had only dreamed of seeing Dax.

She shot out of bed, and Odelia followed her, pulling her curving sword from under her pillow, ready to face the danger in the room.

Paisley threw her arms up. "It's OK, I just need to see Dax. Sorry, I didn't mean to startle you." Paisley was already pulling on her warm clothes and was surprised at how accustomed she had already become to wearing trousers, and what London society would have said if they'd seen her.

"I'll come with you," Odelia said.

Dóm-Fyr let out a little *squark* as she sat on the chest of drawers next to the bed, and Paisley held out a hand to her. She climbed up her arm and nestled around Paisley's neck.

"I guess you want to come too!" she said. Paisley picked up the satchel with Dóm's treasure nest in it. It was heavier than before, and when she looked inside, she saw a gold letter opener and a silver candlestick in there. "Hey, you can't just take treasure like that! You have to earn it, or have it gifted to you – we don't take what isn't ours," she scolded Dóm as she removed the candlestick and letter opener. Dóm gave Paisley a quizzical look and hissed at her.

"And don't start any of that either," Paisley said. "Come on, in your nest with you." The little dragon tried to flap from Paisley's shoulder, half gliding, half falling into her arms, then crawled to the open satchel, where she curled up, her head facing away from Paisley.

Odelia watched with interest.

"What?" Paisley said.

Odelia shrugged. "I think that little dragon likes you. She didn't try to attack you for stealing her treasure, like last time, so I think that's a good sign."

A short while later, Paisley and Odelia were walking through the halls of the keep, with Dóm quietly snoring amongst the treasure in the satchel. Unlike the castles of the George, the rulers of the Northern Realms had built their strongholds out of many connecting buildings. Paisley wondered if the whole citadel might be connected in such a way, and if it were possible to travel to every building without setting foot outside. She and Odelia weaved their way around the connected dwellings and finally came to the great hall that they had been in the previous night.

There they found Hal. He was holding the jar of spiced nuts and berries that Corbett's father had given him and was talking to a lady about them.

He caught sight of them and gave the jar over, then came to join Odelia and Paisley. "She's going to see if she can make some from the ingredients in our store," he said with a smile.

"Do you know where Dax is?" Paisley asked. She didn't expect to sound as anxious as she did, but after only just finding him, she could feel herself becoming tense, not knowing where he was.

"He'll be in the training grounds," Hal said confidently. "I'm going there to meet with Thea. Come, I'll show you the way."

Hal led them out of the hall and into the snow-scraped street, where they walked around the hall to a small gate in a wall, which opened up on to a large area of open ground. At the far end, Paisley could see a group of dragons. And up in the sky there was another small group, but with riders. She instantly knew that one of the riders was Dax.

Hal pointed up to the deep blue dragon, its bronze-coloured horns and talons glinting in the crisp sunlight. "There's my Sterk-Natt, although she is not mine any more. She will do well by Dax," he said, and Paisley could hear the sadness in his voice. Hal would never ride a dragon again. The dragons of the Krigare had many young riders in their lifetimes, but it was always the same: as soon as a Krigare reached the age of maturity, the dragon would turn on them and not let them ride them. It was plain to see that Hal had loved his dragon, and being a Krigare, flying on her back and feeling the rush as he soared through the sky. Something he had loved so much was gone from him for ever, and now he had to find who he was without it.

Odelia shook off her coat and extended her wings; in two short flaps she was soaring towards Dax. She hovered in the air and spoke to him. Then she darted off, and Dax and Sterk-Natt chased her, the other Krigares soon realizing that a game of chase was happening, and joining in.

The dragons were strong and powerful, and they flew at terrifying speeds as they chased Odelia. But she swooped and pivoted and turned and soared through the air with a dexterity the dragons couldn't match.

"She looks like she's dancing! I've never seen

anyone as strong and graceful," Hal said, his face upturned, watching Odelia's every move.

"She is remarkable," Paisley said.

Paisley felt a nudging in the satchel and looked down to see Dóm pushing her way out of the bag. It wouldn't be too long before it would be too small to contain her. The dragons above her were strong, but Dóm was a Great Dragon and one day she would make these northern dragons look small and insignificant by comparison. Paisley looked around to check they were alone. The Krigare above were occupied with their game and only she and Hal stood in the large open training grounds. Paisley reached in and pulled the baby dragon out, resting her on the top of the low wooden fence that ran around the perimeter of the training grounds. Dóm looked up at the dragons, her head twisting from side to side as she took in their every move. Then she stood tall and flapped her wings, trying to fly and falling to the hard ground with a *squark* before climbing up Paisley's legs and making her way back to the top of the fence to try again.

"She's a stubborn one," Hal said.

Dóm soon tired from trying and falling; each time she had put a bit more effort in, moving closer to her goal of staying airborne. Paisley put her back in the bag to sleep, stroking the soft spines on her back as she slumbered.

After almost an hour of out-flying the dragons, Odelia made for the ground and Dax and the others followed.

As the dragons were led away to their nests, Odelia flew over to Paisley and Hal, her eyes shining from the exertion and her raised spirits. "Dax is just seeing to Sterk-Natt. He said he would meet us in the library."

Paisley might have known; you could never keep Dax from a library, and it would appear that the same was true of Corbett. She, Odelia and Hal found him poring over some treatises of Celestial Mechanics in the corner of the library.

"What are you looking at?" Paisley asked, as Odelia and Hal went to sit on the couches that were arranged around the large fire pit in the middle of the room.

"The Celestial Mechanism," he said, and he pulled out his journal from under a pile of books and opened it to a page full of data. "Before Roach took me, I managed to get all the current data that the Celestial Physicists of Greenwich Overhead had on the objects of the Mechanism – including the comet." He flipped to another page of data. "I've been plotting out where everything should be in the Mechanism, and where everything is."

He pulled two sheets of paper towards him, each with the tracks of the celestial objects drawn out, and Paisley could instantly see that not only was everything in a different place to where it should be, but their tracks had shifted too – only slightly, but she knew well enough that even the smallest change could have huge ramifications. She ran her hand over the diagrams.

"We really did break it," she said solemnly as she looked around at the others.

"But that's not the worst bit. I mean, it's bad, but it's stable: everything is in a slightly different position but will keep turning, I think. It's Comet Wolstenholme we need to worry about. I managed to measure its position when we were at the forge, and again on the ship, and here last night. And, even taking into account my change of position … it's heading straight for us."

The room was silent.

"When you say straight for us. . ."

"The Earth, it's going to hit the Earth."

"And what will it do when it does?" Odelia asked. She and Hal had stopped talking and were making their way over to the table. Odelia's face was grave.

Corbett pushed his glasses up his nose. "To be honest I'm not completely sure. It depends on how fast it's travelling and where it hits, but potentially we could all be destroyed, or worse."

"What is worse than being destroyed?" Hal asked.

"A great many things," Odelia said.

"How much time do we have?" Paisley asked.

"I'd need to do a few more calculations to be sure, but . . . not long enough?"

"Long enough for us to build another machine and nudge it away?" Paisley asked.

Corbett shook his head. "Your mother and I worked on that machine for almost a year. At my best guess, we have weeks before the comet hits us. Even with a team of Alchesmiths working nonstop, I'm not sure we could make it in time, and besides, do you remember what I told you about the nightsilver itself? I still believe that your mother's blood had something to do with the machine working, and we'll never be able to make the same nightsilver without her."

Everyone was silent for a long minute.

"So what do we do? How do we fix it?" Hal said.

"I don't know," Corbett said with an exasperated shrug. "I'm just an apprentice, there is so much about Celestial Physics that I don't know about and don't understand. We need help."

"We should ask Doc Langley!" Paisley said. "He might know someone in the Order of Right Turnings who can help us?"

"Good idea," Corbett said. "We should find him right away."

"No," Odelia said firmly. "This is all strange and disturbing, and I am sure that if Anu wishes us to fix it then she will present us with a way to do so, but right now there is a more immediate barrier in our way – or, at least there will be by tomorrow. The Dark Dragon is coming, she is bringing the full fighting force of the George, and we know what she wants. We can't let her have it. If we don't think of a way to keep Dax and the Heart Stone safe, then there will be no use trying to stop the comet because the Dark Dragon would have won and she will destroy everything anyway."

"Of course, you're right," Paisley said, remembering something her father had often said: *We need to get through the battle if we are to win the war. One thing at a time.* And to her it felt that there were too many things, and that time was running out.

"Let's look at our immediate threat: how do we keep Dax and the Heart Stone away from the Dark Dragon, and how do we defeat the army of the George?" Hal asked.

They started talking through strategies, Odelia and Hal formulating most of them, Corbett jotting them down, and Paisley offering help where she could.

Someone delivered some sweet hot tea to the library for them, and shortly after Dax arrived with Thea and a short boy with long dark braids and a round face. Paisley smiled: Dax looked so smart in his Krigare uniform. He had always dreamed of being one of the Dragon Riders of the North, and now he was one he could hardly conceal his pride.

He hugged Paisley when he got close to the knot of sofas and chairs that they had fallen into, arranged around the large fire pit.

"Paisley, this is Brom, Brom Michaelson. And you already know Thea. They're my friends," Dax said with a smile.

Paisley said hello. Then something tugged in her memory. "Brom, you wouldn't happen to know a Dr Mickle Michaelson, would you? He's a Celestial Physicist, and he was a friend of our mother's?"

"Yes, that's my grandfather," Brom said with an earnest look. Paisley got the impression that he was a cautious lad, and something about his manner reminded her a little of Corbett's sensible attitude.

"Is he here?" Corbett asked.

Brom shook his head. "No, he has an observatory a few hours' ride away, further north, inside the Constant Circle."

Paisley looked at Corbett. She could tell he was back to thinking about the broken Celestial Mechanism and Comet Wolstenholme, but Odelia was right on two counts: it looked as if Anu had provided them with a lead on the comet conundrum, and that there were other things more pressing that needed attention first.

"Dax, there are a few things I need to tell you,"

Paisley said, and she began to explain to him about the Veil Touch and how she was beginning to control it, and then she told him about her second stars.

His eyes bulged. "*You're* the George Ascending!" he said, then a huge smile filled his face. "I don't believe it!" She pulled up her sleeve and showed him her stars. "You *are* going to be the George!"

"Yes, but I ran away and the King's Men are looking for me because I did, and they are under the Dark Dragon's control, and ... well, because I'm supposed to be sitting in a castle somewhere, I expect."

"Well, you are sitting in a castle," Hal said. "Just not the one you are meant to be in."

Then she told Dax all about Corbett's findings, about the comet and the Celestial Mechanism, and she could tell that he was more scared of this than he had been of the news that the Dark Dragon was after him.

"Do you think we could meet with your grandfather, Brom?" Paisley asked. "He might be able to help. Besides, we should tell him the truth about what happened to our mother."

She extended a hand to Dax, and he took it and

squeezed it. They hadn't spoken about Mother, or Uncle Hector, or all they had lost, but each of them carried the load. And now that they were together, they could share their grief.

Paisley led Dax away from the others to a quiet corner of the library. They sat next to each other on a window seat looking out on to the training grounds. They both knew what needed to be said, but neither wanted to say it.

Paisley took in a deep breath. "We were loved, Dax, by Mother and Father. We were lucky to have had parents like them."

Dax nodded and said, "Uh-huh," his voice thick with emotion already.

"We're still loved; we have each other, and friends, and we still have their love. We can still remember what it was like to be loved by Mother: warm and safe and unconditional. She loved us no matter what. She loved us fiercely and bravely and without limits." Paisley smiled as she remembered what it felt like to be loved like that.

"It . . . it still doesn't feel real," Dax said. "I know it is; I saw her lying on the floor, and at first it felt like I couldn't stop seeing her like that. But now . . . now I can see her differently. I remember her coming down the stairs at home, full of excitement and ready to teach us something. I wish I'd been more interested in some of the things she wanted to share with me, you know, the science stuff."

"Yeah, I know," Paisley said with a smile. "I hear her voice in my head sometimes. It's comforting to know that I have those memories of her, and I think we both knew her so well that we can work out what she would say to us whenever we need her."

"Like right now?"

"Like right now." Paisley squeezed Dax's hand.

"She'd tell us that she loves us."

"And she'd tell us to keep each other safe."

"She'd tell us not to give up and not to back away from danger. To be brave!"

"Yes, but she'd tell us to be smart about it, to use our strengths."

"And to trust in ourselves and our friends."

"She'd tell us that sometimes a track is full of steep turnings, and that just because something is hard or scary or difficult it doesn't mean that it can't be done."

"She'd tell us to do all that we could to stop the

Dark Dragon from winning, wouldn't she?"

"Yes, Dax, she would. She did. That was her last request of us, to stick together and to keep each other and the world safe from the Dark Dragon."

Dax looked up at Paisley, his eyes red with drying tears. "We loved her just as much as she loved us, and here in the Northern Realms they show the way they feel about people by the deeds that they do. I think we need to show how much we still love her by making sure that we keep our promise and do as she asked."

Paisley hugged her brother close and kissed the top of his head. "I agree. Let's show the world how much we loved our mother by saving it from the Dark Dragon."

THIRTY-SIX

THE ARMY OF ALBION

Roach stood on the deck of the George's principal warship and watched as the joint army of the King's Men began moving from the makeshift barracks they had assembled on the harbour of Dundee and started to load the ships. He'd marvelled at their trained precision. Each knight was dressed in the colours of their order, standards flying, coats of arms shining on their winter uniforms.

Along with the knights, the army was mostly made up of squires: boys as young as Roach, some a little younger, all dressed in the same uniforms, coloured to match their order, but without the knights' embellishments of rank and distinction. Roach watched them as they conveyed arms, the nightsilver weapons. Each had to be unloaded from the aerocopters and electrica trucks and placed on one of the three ships that were a small part of the naval forces of the George.

The Dark Dragon stood on the deck next to Hector a little away from Roach.

"I have a mind to make you stay in Albion, Hector," she said, her voice light and soft in the cold morning air. Her small hands clenched the railing in front of her, one gloved, the other the deafening black of nightsilver. "There is still no news on Paisley, and I do not want her reaching her brother before I do. She is your niece, after all; you might have more success in finding her."

Roach stayed perfectly still, his face impassive, but inside he felt his heart rate rise a notch as he thought of Paisley. By now she would be with Dax, and if they had any sense they would flee to safety; but he knew Paisley.

"I can stay, Your Darkness, if that is what you bid of me," Hector said as he lowered his head like a scorned puppy. "But to be honest, if there is anyone in the Empire that Paisley is most likely to hide away from, it would be me. After all, I had a hand in sending both of her parents to the Veil."

The Dark Dragon sighed and turned to face Hector. "No, you must come with us and be my emissary with the George, and more importantly his men. None of them will understand or respect me, even though I could break them so easily. I will have to have faith that the stars will not aid Paisley." There was a metallic crunching sound, and when the Dark Dragon removed her nightsilver hand from the railing of the ship's deck, the thick pipe had been crushed.

"Where is the George?" the Dark Dragon asked.

"In his quarters. No doubt he is tired after the full military parade from the aerodoc," Hector said with a roll of his eyes. Roach recalled the parade, the way the George had sat on his charge, nightsilver armour on and lance in hand as he led knights from all of his orders towards war.

"No doubt!" the Dark Dragon said.

"Would you like me to escort you to your quarters? Lorena and your Dark Dragon Walkers are securing them now."

"No, I think it is about time that I was reacquainted with the George. It has been many turnings since I last saw him in person," the Dark Dragon said with a radiant smile.

Roach followed along behind the Dark Dragon as she walked beside Hector, inspecting the forces of the George all primed for war and ready to do the Dark Dragon's bidding, even if they didn't realize that their tracks were bent towards her stars. Roach saw the hordes of nightsilver-tipped arrows and watched as every knight's personal squire unloaded a suite of nightsilver armour.

Along with the horses, there were war engines – great machines that could knock down walls and storm fortresses – and on the deck of each ship sat a small aerocopter, the balloons deflated and limp.

As he wandered through the weapons of war, Roach wondered if the upcoming destruction would be worth it. Then he thought of Clara.

He was still thinking of his sister as Hector spoke to the guards and gained access to the George.

The George was standing at a table that held a model of the northern realms, all the known towns and roads, citadels and keeps were presented in realistic if somewhat miniature detail, similar to the one the Dark Dragon had used to plan the invasion that the George was about to execute for her.

The First Knights from the Orders of Exploration, Justice, Valour and Conquest were all advising the George, moving small toy knights around the model, and Roach felt his stomach clench. Was it all just a game to them?

The George looked up as Hector coughed. Then his eyes fell on the Dark Dragon and a shadow of recognition passed over his face, and he shifted from one foot to the other before waving a hand at his First Knights.

"Gentlemen, there are one or two urgent points that I must discuss with Lord Hector. Please, leave us."

The knights filed past Hector, the Dark Dragon, and Roach.

The room was quiet for a long moment before the George moved forward and stood in front of the Dark Dragon.

"You ... you haven't changed at all," he said to her, his voice full of intrigue as he tilted his head to one side to get a better look at the Dark Dragon. "I met you when I was a child; the old George that my stars replaced was there, and you told me about the gift. He told me that if I wanted to live a long and powerful track, I should always do as you command, and accept your gift when given. He told me that you were the star that lit the track of the George. But tell me: how is it that you look exactly the same as you did then? You know, there are paintings of you in all of my palaces, paintings that go way, way back to the first George, and yet you are still the same. Your dress and hairstyle changes to fit the time, but you . . . you do not," he said, reaching up and touching his own cheek. Roach noticed that his hair had begun to soot and there were deep wrinkles forming around his tired-looking eyes. "My turnings creep across my body, but your turnings don't even see you, do they?"

The Dark Dragon smiled sweetly. "Some things never alter, while others pass so quickly it is as if they never even were. When you have lived as long as I have, you come to notice the slow changes of life, the long rhythms, the rise and fall. I have watched many Georges rise, and many fall."

The George stood up straight. "Are you here

because there is a new George Ascending? Are you here to tell me that I am no longer needed?"

The Dark Dragon looked at him with a sincere expression. "Far from it. You are most valuable to me and to the Empire," she said.

The George relaxed a little, looking pleased with himself.

"I am here because it is important that we work together to stop the Northern Realms and their barbaric ways. For too long they have rejected the way of the Chief Designer; for too long they have mocked you and the Empire. I am here because I was with the first George when he banished the first Great Dragon from the Mechanism, and it is my destiny to be with the last George when the Great Dragons return."

Anxiety alighted upon the George's face. "So, it is true what they say in the *Herald*: that the comet is not a comet after all, that it is a Great Dragon?"

The Dark Dragon tilted her head to one side. "You don't need to worry about that," she said sweetly. "All you need to worry about is crushing the Northern Realms and upholding the path the Chief Designer has given you. Of course, I will use my stars to assist you in any way I can."

Roach set his jaw as he listened to the way that the Dark Dragon manipulated the George, how she wove a narrative full of half-truths and played on his fears and beliefs, just as she did with all of those around her. To cement the George's cooperation, she pulled a small phial of her blood from her pocket and held it out.

He looked at it greedily.

"A small gift for you," she said, and the George stepped forward and took it from her, holding it tightly in his hand. "Hector will give you advice on how this battle will be fought. Look to him and you will receive my guidance."

With that, the Dark Dragon turned and walked past Roach, making for the door with Hector following her. As Roach turned to leave, he saw the George unstopping the phial and holding it to his lips.

Roach felt sick as he followed the Dark Dragon back through the ship, past the knights and squires whose tracks were bent towards battle . . . and for what? For whom?

He clung to the thought of Clara, pushing her face to the front of his mind over the next day and a half. Whenever he met a young squire or knight and thought about their chances in the battle, he thought of his sister. And when he stood on the bridge of the ship and watched as the King's Men aimed and fired the catapults on the deck at the port village of Västerut Hamn, he thought of her even more, and tried not to listen to the way her little voice crept into his head, questioning his actions and pleading with him to stop.

"So it has begun," the Dark Dragon said as she stood in her quarters and looked over the maps of the Northern Realms. "And everything is going to plan." An explosion rocked the boat slightly. Roach looked out of the window to see that one of the catapults had found its mark. The flaming incendiary device had hit the buildings dotted around the harbour, setting them ablaze.

"I still don't understand why we are burning the place down?" he said.

"Because I can, and I want to show them that." The Dark Dragon's voice was sweet and light. "These people, their lands, their lives, they are not only expendable: they are worthless. All that matters is the Heart Stone and Dax. When my dragon arrives,

I shall use its breath to cleanse the unworthy; we are just hastening their departure to the Veil. Roach, do you have the plans for the Northern King's keep?" she asked, her small hand outstretched and expectant.

Roach put a hand into his inner pocket and pulled out a folded square of paper.

The Dark Dragon snatched it from him and smoothed it, placing the hand-drawn floor plan of the keep on top of a cartographer's version.

Roach pointed at one part of it. "This is where they kept the Heart Stone before, in a power processing plant to the east of the Keep. I very much doubt it will be there now."

The Dark Dragon was scouring the rudimentary lines of the plan.

"Where do you think they will be hiding it?" Roach asked. "It could be anywhere."

"It doesn't matter where; all that matters is that Lorena and her Dark Dragon Walkers gain access to the right person."

Lorena took a step closer to the Dark Dragon. "We will not fail you. Mayme is able to manipulate the minds of those she is close to; all we have to do is find someone who will know where the Heart Stone is, and she will tease the information from them."

Roach shuddered as he remembered meeting Mayme at the Dragon Vault on Kensington Above and how she had made him see things that were not there.

"Yes, you are right, Lorena. My Dark Dragon Walkers have many talents, and I should use them all to my advantage. When the battle at the King's Keep begins, you will find me my prize by whatever means is necessary. Roach, you have studied these people, and you know those close to the King. Go with Lorena and find them easy prey."

Roach gave a nod of consent. He pictured Dax scared and vulnerable, with Lorena and her Dark Dragon Walkers hunting him down, and wondered if he would help to deliver him from or to the Dark Dragon.

He felt as if something inside of him had shifted since he had helped to capture Dax at the Natural History Museum, since the battle at the Greenwich Observatory. And not for the first time, he gave thought to the idea that when Violetta's machine moved the comet that night, it also moved his track.

THIRTY-SEVEN

THE SHAPE OF THINGS TO COME

Hal's father, King Harken, called his war council. The Northern Barons had come from all over the Northern Realms and now filled the hall that Paisley realized was the hub of not only the community at the castle keep, but also the whole of the Northern Realms. All the important moments that filtered down to the lives of the everyday men, women and children happened in this hall around the large fire, under the hanging sprays of greenery. There was something honest and homely about that, which Paisley connected with deeply.

The men and women who held the position of

Baron in their realms all had an equal place around the fire as they voiced their opinions to King Harken.

One of the lords from the west, Baron Viggo, who had arrived with a large battalion of men and women, was telling the assembly of how strong they were and how many archers they had. Hal and Thea were taking it in turns to translate to Paisley and the others.

Then the double doors to the hall swung out, and a young girl dressed in the dragonhide leathers of the Krigare stumbled in, her uniform charred, the side of her face blistered and bleeding.

"Your Highness! The Army of Albion has bested Västerut Hamn. Baron Kristoff has fallen, and his remaining troops are on their way here – as are the foreign invaders!"

"What of the people?" King Harken asked.

"Most had already fled to safety over the land, some by sea, before the tyrants of Albion dared to darken our shores."

"Baron Viggo, your people are from the lands to the West of Västerut Hamn, and Baron Gunnel, yours from the East. Will you both send word to your Krigare to look out for the people of Västerut Hamn and keep them until we are able to guarantee the safety of their home?"

There was movement from within the assembly as the Barons dealt with their missives and others began to talk amongst themselves.

Hal leaned over to his father and Paisley heard him say, "Once this council breaks, can I speak with you? It is urgent and important."

King Harken nodded, then stood. The room fell quiet once more. "We had hoped for more time to plan, but, as ever, the Mechanism has turned against us in its continued endeavour to thwart us. The Army of Albion is half a day away as the wolf runs, and we have much to do. They will be with us as night falls, and, if that is the case, we must be on our guard. The dark hides many terrors, and we will be one of them. We will rise against our enemy, and we will defeat them on the battlefield as the sun rises on our lands and we push these invaders from it!"

The gathered barons hailed the King as he left the hall.

"Come." Hal beckoned to Paisley and the others, and they followed him through the door that his father and his closest advisors had left through. Beyond was a large room similar to the sitting room at Paisley's home, with a warm fire and large couches, but to one side was a large desk littered with papers, and next to it hung King Harken's dragonhide uniform.

The advisors all collected around the fire, sitting in the sofas and conversing in Norse.

"What is it, Hal?" King Harken asked as he paced behind a large desk full of battle plans. "Have you and your friends decided to join us, to fight by our side? I hoped that you might lead one of the battalions alongside your older brother and sisters."

Paisley watched as Hal shook his head. "No, Father, I'm afraid that we have another calling in this war."

King Harken stopped his pacing and gave Hal a disappointing look. "Leave us. This is a matter for a father, not a king," he called to his advisors, and they filed out, closing the door behind them.

"Hal, what is this about? I know that your time in the lands of our enemies must have been ... difficult, but I did not expect you to run from a battle. If anything, I would have thought your time amongst our foe would have seen you eager to join your fellows in combat," King Harken said. "Before you left to regain the stolen Soul Fire you would have leaped at the chance to prove yourself, to add to your marks and let your deeds show the world the brave, fierce warrior that I know you are."

Hal placed his hands on the edge of his father's desk and leaned forward. "Father, I am still the Hal you know. I am asking you to trust me on this. I am asking to sit out on this battle so that I might help to win the war."

King Harken stood up straighter and fixed Hal with a serious look. "Is this about the dragon tales that you told me, about this Dark Dragon, this Unknown Unfolding—"

"Father, I told you, these things are as real as the tales we have of the world bridge. I have seen this Dark Dragon with my own eyes."

"But these are still not our concerns, they are the business of the Dragon Walkers and the Empire of Albion." Harken nodded first at Odelia and then at Paisley. "What do we care if she calls forth the Great Dragons and breaks the Mechanism? I am disappointed in you, Hal."

Paisley watched as Hal lowered his head and bit his lip.

"She doesn't want to break the Mechanism," Paisley told King Harken. She could hear the edge in her voice, sharp like a nightsilver blade. "She wishes to dominate it, to control it, to bend it to her will. She wants power and will use the Mechanism to get it if she can. We believe that the Heart Stone is the key to this, and by protecting it we will be protecting your people from greater suffering. You worry that Hal is not acting nobly. You know your son, you know how important it is to him to have your approval to fight alongside you for your people, and yet he is choosing the harder track. And he is asking for your support, your blessing."

King Harken looked at Paisley, his clear blue eyes steady. "I hear the wisdom in what you say regarding Hal." He turned to his son. "I still do not believe that the actions of this Dark Dragon are of any concern to us, or indeed that she is who she claims to be. But you have always done me proud as both a father and a king."

King Harken crossed to a large safe in the wall and from it he removed a small wooden box, which he handed to Hal.

"Here is Soul Fire, or was. It has grown and

changed so much since it was stolen that when we tried to reconnect it to our electrica grid, the sub station failed. Mickle Michaelson wanted to take it for laboratory experimentation, but here it is, your Heart Stone, or whatever you call it. Guard it well, son. I hope it is worth it."

Paisley felt so desperately sad for Hal, who reached out and took the wooden box, then stood tall and looked King Harken in the eye.

"I love you, Father, and although you cannot see it just now, I promise that I will prove my worth to you again. And as my king, you have my promise that I will prove you wrong."

"I hope that you do, on both counts, Hal," King Harken said.

THIRTY-EIGHT

THE BATTLE OF KING'S KEEP

Paisley stood next to Odelia on the top of the stone curtain wall that surrounded the building of the keep. Below them to the left, fortifications were being added to the wooden doors. Paisley looked out across the open ground that led to the forest. Soon this would become a battleground. Her eyes focused on the small, raised mound to the right of where she stood, and she let out a long, warm breath, the air fogging around her like smoke from a dragon.

The cold, dull morning had crept in along with the King's Men, who, during the night, had encircled the castle keep. Paisley looked over at the Army of

Albion, their war machines glistening in front of the command tents that they had erected close to the wood. Paisley realized that the large open land that lay between the low-lying wood and the keep was an excellent strategic defence: any attack would need to break cover and make its way out into the open.

Soon it would be flooded with knights racing to do battle.

"I find it hard to think that my stars say that one day these men will do as I command, but not yet, for now they are my enemy. How can that be?"

Odelia gave a shrug. "The world of men is a peculiar one. I know nothing of the way the Empire constructs its loyalties, if it has any," she said. "But war is something that I know a thing or two about, and the only loyal companions in battle are your sisters and the Veil."

Odelia gave Paisley such a look of genuine affection and understanding that she knew she and Odelia had transcended the realm of friendship and entered into a deeper sistership than any blood could have arranged.

"Do you think Dóm will be all right?" Paisley asked as she looked over at the large stone building that sat upon the entrance to the underground dragons' nests.

"Doc will look after her," Odelia said. "She'll be safe there, and when we are victorious you will claim her again. Come, we should get back to the others." She led the way along the ramparts, where the archers were setting their stores of arrows, and down the staircases that hugged the stone-walled fortifications.

They walked through the streets of the keep, quiet and still. Paisley glanced up and saw the Krigare circling above, the dark outlines of their swooping dragons as they guarded the castle keep below.

Odelia led the way into the great hall, which had been cleared, with all the tables stacked to one side. There was a small door to the left of the hall, hidden behind a tapestry, that led down to the stronghold.

As they reached it, a series of horns blasted above from outside. Paisley looked at Odelia: it had begun. She slipped into the safety of the room and Hal bolted the heavy door. The safe room was a fraction of the size of the hall above and was built as more of a storeroom than a place for people to hide in.

The walls were lined with shelves and on them sat crates full of precious items that had been in the hall above. Paisley went over to a pile of rolled tapestries that had hung on the walls of the great hall. She felt like a coward. People were fighting, and here she was, hidden away. She could tell that the others felt the same.

Corbett gave a small smile. "You have to remember, Paisley, that your stars are bigger than this one battle. We're all relying on you to win the war."

She felt the gravity of what he said hit her as she heard the first cries from above.

She looked over at Dax, expecting him to be scared, to come and cling to her arm, but instead he stood his ground, his dragon leg twisting out, covered in the Krigare uniform made of dragonhide, the same small interlocking dark scales that covered his leg. He held a sword, much larger than the one he had kept inside his cane, and he looked up at the rafters thoughtfully. He had grown so much, so quickly – the loss of Mother, the betrayal of Uncle Hector, the separation from Paisley, and becoming a Krigare had all pressed down on him and changed him in ways that made Paisley both sad and proud to see. She had been expecting to find her little brother, and that he would need her to take care of him, but Dax was growing to meet the struggles of his track and he no longer needed her to carry him along; they could walk side by side instead.

The battle raged on. Odelia and Hal took it in turns to pace, and every time someone ran into the great hall, or they heard a crash or a cry, they all stopped and looked up.

"Protect Dax, keep the stone safe, save the world from the Dark Dragon." Paisley said this to herself over and over again.

"Hal, why don't we place the Heart Stone inside Næss?" Odelia suddenly said. "It will keep it safe, and if the Dark Dragon does find us, Paisley can us the power of the stone to defeat her."

"That's a great idea," Hal said. He heaved down one of the crates, then rummaged around before pulling out the wooden box. He opened the lid to reveal the Heart Stone, the red glow lighting his face from below. Paisley gave a sharp intake of breath as she saw it, glowing red with a soft pulse as the stone beat in a long, gentle rhythm. She remembered seeing it at the observatory just after the Dark Dragon had combined the two lifeless parts of the Heart Stone and was struck by the same impression as now: that the stone was pumping like one half of a human heart.

Paisley kept her eyes on the Heart Stone as she reached into her pocket and drew out Næss. She thought about extending the lance and opening the compartment that Corbett had forged for the stone, just as in the original blueprints.

"Wow!" Dax said. "Where did you get that? Can I have one?"

"Corbett made it," Paisley said, and Corbett blushed with pride.

But when Hal tried to place the Heart Stone inside, it wouldn't fit. The gap was too small.

"But I made it to the specifications?" Corbett said.

"Ah, but this stone is made of two parts of the Heart, and I guess the original lance would have only housed one quarter of the original Heart Stone," Paisley said.

"Of course." Corbett shook his head.

"Wait – I'll think about making the compartment bigger."

Paisley concentrated hard on trying to make the space in the lance expand. She pictured it in her mind and sent out her intention till she felt her eyes cross and her temples ache, but there wasn't enough dexterity in the metal.

"It's no good, sorry," Paisley said as she shrank Næss down again, placing it in her pocket as Hal took the Heart Stone back.

Corbett sat on the floor, scribbling in his journal, trying to find a new design for the lance. He was looking up at the ceiling for inspiration when all of a sudden he stood up and started taking big long sniffs of air.

"Do you want a handkerchief?" Odelia said.

"Can't you smell that? It's fire."

Odelia sniffed. "I can't smell anything," she said.

"I can." Hal was looking up at the rafters, and the hall above it. "It is a common attack strategy; we have the water from the well, so we have a plan for such things." He sounded confident, but within a few minutes they could all smell the burning, and soft tendrils of grey smoke had started to seep down from the hall above.

"We should be safe here," Hal said. "There is a fire break between the hall and this stronghold. Although the hall may not survive if the fire is extensive. It is a shame; the hall has been here for as long as the Northern Realms have had a king. . ."

Paisley could see that he was torn, and how difficult if must be for him to hear his home being attacked, and to know that his whole family was in danger and there was nothing he could do to help them because he had given his word to help her. If it were her, and Dax was out there, she wasn't sure that she could stay put. But he stayed. He paced around, and flinched at every noise, his face growing more and more grave, but he stayed.

It was during one of his pacing fits when there was a pounding on the stronghold door.

"Hal! Hal, it's Magna! Let me in!" Hal moved to the door and opened it for his older brother before Odelia could stop him.

Paisley threw Dax behind her and pulled her lance out – it instantly sprang to its full height.

Magna was standing in the door; his eye was

swollen, and lip was bleeding. "Hal!" he shouted as Lorena hit him from behind. Magna crumpled to the ground in the doorway, making it impossible to then close the door.

Hal stepped out of the stronghold, sword drawn and Odelia beside him at once as Lorena surged forward, a group of five Dark Dragon Walkers close behind her in the narrow passageway.

And with them, Roach, lingering at the back.

Paisley locked eyes with him. How could he keep dancing the line between helping her and standing against her?

Hal and Odelia began beating Lorena back as her Dark Dragon Walkers tried to surge forward.

Paisley made Næss into a deadly point as Dax stepped out from beside her, sword drawn. Paisley grabbed his arm, and he turned to face her. "I can fight, Paisley. I can hold my own," he said as Hal and Odelia made ground on Lorena, pushing her forces back along the narrow passage. Corbett had dived behind them and was trying to drag Magna into the stronghold.

"I know you can," Paisley said. "But you shouldn't have to."

"I know. But we've had to deal with a lot that we ought not to have. This –" he lifted his sword – "is just another thing we have to deal with."

Paisley looked at Dax. "Together," she said.

He nodded. "Together."

And she let go of his arm and they both rushed forward, Dax helping Corbett pull Magna to safety and Paisley joining Hal and Odelia fighting just outside the doorway.

"Retreat and bolt the door!" Hal yelled as soon as Corbett and Dax had Magna in the stronghold.

Lorena breathed into her hand and threw a blazing ball of fire over their heads and into the room, striking the tapestries from the hall. Smoke billowed behind them, making their retreat impossible.

"The Heart Stone!" Paisley called, and Hal ran back into the smoking-room past Dax and Corbett, who were now carrying Magna out, both coughing as black smoke rolled from the safe room. Hal emerged with the rock in his hand as Odelia headed the charge, Paisley beside her as Lorena and her forces moved backwards up the stairs, away from Paisley and Odelia, and the wall of black smoke behind them. Exiting into the great hall, Lorena and her

Dark Dragon Walkers took up attack positions in an arc around the doorway, trapping Paisley and the others as the roof of the hall blazed.

Behind her, Paisley heard Hal close the door down to the safe room.

"We need to get out of here!" Hal called as he stood by her side, sword drawn and pulled the neck of his tunic up over his mouth to protect himself from the smoke. Paisley followed his lead as he stuffed the Heart Stone into his pocket for safekeeping. "There's a door to the left!"

They pushed forward, and Corbett and Dax made their way towards the door, carrying the still-disorientated Magna.

Paisley realized they were penned in as Lorena and the other Dragon Walkers closed the arc around them.

Lorena looked up, opened her mouth, and blew out a great gust of fire. It hit the roof and began to burn ferociously.

Paisley had hardly realized that the electrica was pinching the air until she saw the rift form behind one of the Dragon Walkers.

"Paisley!" Odelia called to her as she fought. She had seen the rift too. "Don't let go of it!"

Paisley swung her lance at one of the Dark Dragon Walkers, sending her toppling to the ground. Paisley could feel the rift and was trying to keep a hold of it, but couldn't help feeding it with all her worries and fear. The bigger it got, the more it pulled against her.

One of the Dark Dragon Walkers saw it too late and yelled as the rift swallowed her. The shock made Paisley lose hold of the rift, and it flew off through one of the elaborately carved columns and up through the ceiling. A burning beam fell from the rafters, bringing half of the roof down with it, trapping another of the Dragon Walkers and cutting off Dax, Corbett and Magna from Paisley and the others.

"Make for the door!" Paisley yelled to Dax and Corbett. "We'll find you!"

Paisley locked eyes with Dax and gave him a small nod as he helped drag Magna out of the hall and into the fresh air of the courtyard beyond.

She heard both him and Corbett coughing and yelling for help.

Another crack filled the air as another section of roof fell. This time it hit Roach, covering him as well as Hal and the Dragon Walker he had been fighting.

Odelia yelled as she flapped her wings, lifting

herself off the ground and using both of her feet to kick the Dragon Walker she was battling across the room. The Dark Dragon Walker hit her head on the wall of the hall, then fell into a heap on the floor. Odelia began pulling the debris off Hal.

The two remaining Dark Dragon Walkers focused on Paisley as Lorena suddenly rose from under the roof wreckage, the section that had separated Paisley from Dax.

As she fought, Paisley saw Lorena's charred and burned skin slowly healing thanks to her Dragon Touch. She cast Paisley a wicked smile before making for the door that Corbett and Dax had left through.

"No!" Paisley yelled.

The rift formed instantly, and without thinking about it, Paisley twisted her lance and sliced the rift in two; then she pushed each of the rifts towards the Dark Dragon Walkers. One of the Dragon Walkers smoothly bent backwards as the rift moved over her and headed for the rear wall of the hall, while the other Dragon Walker turned and ran the veil rift slowly stalking her as it grew smaller the further it got from Paisley.

Paisley pulled her attention back, and as she did the two pieces of the rip reformed and disappeared. In her head, Paisley could hear Never's voice: *"You are in control, you are safe, you are calm, you have the power to master the Veil rift."*

Paisley looked about: all of the Dark Dragon Walkers were down or had fled.

"Odelia!" Paisley yelled across the burning room.

"Go, save Dax!" Odelia called back as she continued to lift the burning wreckage off of Hal.

Paisley hesitated. There was no way she could get to Odelia, but she could get to Dax and Corbett. She pulled down her tunic the moment that she stepped outside, the fresh air sticking in her lungs and making her cough.

"Dax!" she tried to yell as she coughed and spluttered, stumbling across the courtyard and towards a hole in the curtain wall where the stones of the wall had been broken in and littered the ground. On the other side, she could see the retreating war machine that had knocked the wall in. Through the breach flooded a small group of knights. The fighters of the North raced towards the incoming knights, trying to keep them at bay. There she saw Magna and Corbett, lying on the ground, both unconscious.

"Corbett!" She shook him. "Corbett, where's Dax?"

Corbett's glasses were broken, and blood trickled down the side of his head. Paisley let him fall back against Magna as she heard Dax yell, "Paisley!"

She whipped her head round and there he was. Lorena had him bound and slung over her shoulders as she climbed over the rubble of the wall. Knights were streaming into the keep, their nightsilver armour gleaming as the fighters of the North battled to keep them back. Two knights had seen her and were heading in her direction, swords raised.

Paisley ran full pelt towards them, towards the breach in the wall, reaching out her hand: Næss shifted so that the lance became double-headed. Paisley dropped to her knees, her inertia and the smooth scales of her dragonhide trousers sending her gliding over the frozen earth. She held out Næss horizontally, the lance instantly growing longer and thinner, catching the nightsilver armour leg casing and sending the knights tumbling to their knees with howls of pain.

Paisley jumped back up to her feet and carried on running, swinging Næss up high into the face of a knight as he lunged towards her; slicing his nightsilver helmet in two, she brought the lance down on the top of his head, knocking him out.

Then Næss was a smooth pole and Paisley dug it into the ground at the foot of the rockslide in the breach. Næss was yielding as it bent under Paisley's weight and then catapulted her over the heads of the knights climbing into the keep.

Her feet pointing towards the sky, Næss in her hand, her eyes to the heavens, Paisley glimpsed the rift that hovered above her, following her as she hit the ground and continued running.

Lorena was ahead, making for a rise in the land just beyond the keep that reminded Paisley of the burial mounds of the Georges. On top of the mound stood the Dark Dragon. Around the tiny figure flew a flock of mechanical dragons that attacked anyone who got too close to her.

As Paisley ran, she heard a familiar *squark,* and as she looked to her left, she saw Dóm-Fyr flying alongside her.

"How did you. . .? What are you doing?" she

called to the little dragon, who squawked again and flew around Paisley as she ran.

"Dóm, this is serious business!" Paisley yelled to the dragon as she swung Næss out at a knight who lunged at her. The little dragon swooped down on him, opened her mouth and shot a blast of fire that caught his tunic alight.

The knight dropped to the ground, rolling around, as Paisley and Dóm continued towards the mound, the Veil cloud hovering above Paisley, her dragon flying by her side.

Paisley reached to her belt, and from it she pulled the throwing stars that Odelia had given her. Back in the forge Corbett had covered them with some of the leftover copperich and nightsilver from the lance.

Paisley knew instinctively what to do. She glanced up at the Veil rift above her, and it was as if a new understanding had formed between Paisley and the Veil. She launched one of the throwing stars high into the rift above her, and then thought about it flying off to hit one of the mechanical dragons; as she did, the star flew out of the rift, shrouded in a dark nebulous static, as if part of the Veil cloud had attached itself to the star. It flew further than Paisley would have ever been able to throw it herself, and hit one of the cogwork dragons, striking straight through it, absorbing its nightsilver casing.

It dropped to the ground, and the Dark Dragon looked over at Paisley.

Dóm squawked as Paisley locked eyes with the Dark Dragon, then twisted to the left, avoiding the swing of a knight's sword and striking him with her lance before tossing another star up into the rift. This time the star fell towards the ground, and Paisley swung Næss, hitting the star with the lance and sending it straight into another of the mechanical dragons.

Lorena had reached the mound now and had placed Dax on the ground near the Dark Dragon.

Paisley used the throwing stars to take out another of the mechanical dragons, and then she was at the foot of the mound, running up with Dóm gliding a little ahead of her.

Lorena took a deep breath and blew a circle of fire around her, Dax, and the Dark Dragon.

Paisley hesitated mid-stride as Dóm flew straight through the flames and over to Dax. Næss, knowing what to do, shifted to become the pole again so that

Paisley could vault the flames and get to Dax too. As she came through the flames, she kicked out, hitting Lorena square on the chest and sending her flying out of the ring of fire, landing in a crumpled heap on the other side of the mound.

Paisley twisted Næss around in her hand, the lance splitting to become a trident. The Dark Dragon reached for Dax, ripping his bonds with her nightsilver fingers and pulling him up to stand. Dóm flew around her, squawking and shooting small licks of fire in her direction.

"How cute. Did the Northerners give you your own dragon?" the Dark Dragon said as she lifted her nightsilver hand and grabbed Dóm out of the sky, throwing her to the ground with a *thud*.

The little dragon lay still, and Paisley and Dax both shouted in unison.

Paisley surged forward, but the Dark Dragon grew a deadly point on the index finger of her nightsilver arm and held it to Dax's throat.

The Dark Dragon had underestimated Dax and all that he had learned since she had last seen him. He twisted out of her grip and, with the power of his dragon leg he delivered a roundhouse kick, sending the Dark Dragon toppling towards Paisley, where she swiped her with the trident point of Næss. The Dark Dragon lifted her nightsilver arm, absorbing the blow with barely a scratch to the scales.

The Dark Dragon lowered her eyes and gave Paisley a deadly smile as the remaining mechanical dragons swooped behind her and focused on Dax.

Paisley gasped as she saw them heading towards Dax and she threw Næss towards them; the lance rotated like a blade as it grew shorter, and all along its shaft deadly points of nightsilver formed. Næss ripped through the remaining mechanical dragons, scattering their pieces as it flew out of the flame circle to rest point-down in the ground, a pole once more.

The Dark Dragon lashed out at Paisley; her sword now drawn. Paisley jumped back and reached for the sword on her back. As she drew it, she saw a movement above her. She expected it to be the rift, but she was surprised to see a flash of blue scales: Sterk-Natt swooped in and plucked Dax from the fray.

As she watched Dax ascend to safety, clutching Dóm in his arms, Paisley felt the Dark Dragon swipe her feet out from under her.

She hit the ground hard, her sword dropping as the air escaped from her lungs in a mighty rush. The Dark Dragon jumped on top of her, tightening the fingers of her nightsilver arm around Paisley's throat. Her small, delicate features shone in the most beautiful smile Paisley had ever seen as the ring of fire slowly died around them.

THIRTY-NINE

THE DOOMFIRE SECRET

Roach coughed as the smoke from the burning hall filled his lungs. He pushed with his arms up to all fours, debris from the roof spilling off him as he stood and coughed again, hitting the dust and muck from his coat. It was now looking as shabby as his old one.

As Roach staggered a little, his head swimming and the world coming back into focus, he watched Odelia grab hold of a beam and flap her wings, trying to lift it clear of Hal, who lay underneath. It moved only a little way as she yelled out with exertion.

As she mustered herself to try again, Roach came and stood next to her.

"Ready?" he said, bending his knees and rolling his sleeves over his hands before reaching under the smouldering beam.

She looked at him, her face full of ash and sweat, and Roach got the distinct impression that she would love nothing more than to headbutt him. But Odelia nodded. "On three," she said. "One, two, three."

Roach straightened his legs with a grunt of effort and Odelia did the same, flapping her wings, the two of them together lifting it high enough to be able to shove it away, exposing Hal.

Roach hooked his hands under Hal's arms and pulled him out, then Odelia grabbed his feet and the two of them manoeuvred him out of the hall. There was a group of Northmen fighting to stop the blaze from catching on the nearby houses, and some of them rushed to help Odelia and Roach as they coughed in fresh air and slumped to the ground with Hal.

As Odelia was fussing over the Krigare, Roach noticed the Heart Stone glimmering in Hal's pocket.

He hesitated for a second before he quickly swiped it and left as more help arrived, slipping around the corner of the hall, trying to figure out which direction Lorena had gone.

The smell of war was in the air. A few rows of houses stood between Roach and the Keep wall that encased the citadel. A loud *squawk* drew his attention, and he looked up to see a Krigare swoop down low, its dragon's mouth wide open, blasting the clear winter sky with fire. Roach sprinted across the frozen training grounds behind the castle, his breath coming in hot clouds of steam as he pushed through his pain and bruises.

He burst through a postern gate and out into the narrow streets. He saw the worried face of an old man, too frail to hold a sword, pushed up against a window. The sounds of fighting rang in Roach's ears, along with a rhythmic beating from the army beyond the wall, the army that he had aided the Dark Dragon in bringing here.

Roach turned away from the old man and continued down the narrow street along the wall towards the eastern gate. He paused for a moment. His quarry wasn't there, but still, he found his feet turn in that direction.

As he turned the corner of the street, he could see that the thick wooden gate was close to buckling. A few splintering rends had already appeared on the door, spitting wood into the ground like spiked fortifications.

A high-pitched scream came from above and Roach looked up to see Corbett hanging from the stone wall that surrounded the entrance. Roach could instantly see what he was trying to do – Corbett had climbed from the stairs that ran up the side of the wall and had shimmied out towards the chain that ran from the lever above. The lever should have dropped a metal portcullis into place, offering a new level of protection for the city, if the chain had not snagged and become tangled. Corbett was gripping on to the wall for dear life with one hand, the other tugging at the chain to try and free the tangle.

"Where's Paisley?" Roach shouted.

Corbett looked at him coldly. "What's it to you?"

"Do you want me to help you or not?"

"I don't know where she is – in the middle of all this paggering, no doubt. Lorena knocked me out and took Dax, so Paisley is no doubt hunting her down to save him. But if this gate is breached, then all the people in the keep will be in danger."

Roach sighed, shaking his head as he ran up the

stairs. When he reached Corbett, he saw where the problem was: the chain had twisted back on itself when it caught.

"I'm going to go and turn the lever the other way; that should give you some slack on the chain and you can untwist it," Roach shouted to Corbett before he continued up the stone steps that flanked the door. As he reached the lever, he looked over the top of the battlements: Corbett was still clinging to the wall.

"Now!" he bellowed at Corbett as he pulled the lever the other way and could hear the chain slipping.

"That's it, it's untangled!" Corbett yelled out. "Pull it again!" Roach flipped the lever and the chain pulled straight, snaking its way through the mechanism that would tip the counterweight and release the portcullis. As it began to gather speed, Corbett lost his footing.

Roach called out as Corbett screamed and fell to the ground, landing on his side. He rolled on to his back, winded.

Roach tried to pull the lever back, but now it had jammed in place; instead, the counterweight began to shift. He looked back down at Corbett, who was holding his side on the ground. As the counterweight reached tipping point, the sharp points of the portcullis were straight above him.

As they began their descent, Roach shouted, "Get out of the way!"

Corbett twisted to the side, rolling away as the points hit the ground, pinning his thick winter coat underneath.

Roach ran down the stairs. By the time he got to him, Corbett had slid his arms from his coat, leaving it pinned under the portcullis. He was sitting up with his back leaning against the latticed metalwork, taking short, shallow breaths and holding his side.

"Let me look!" Roach said as he kneeled next to Corbett.

Reluctantly, Corbett pulled his hand away. A large shard of wood from the door as thick as Roach's finger was sticking out from between two of Corbett's ribs. Roach pulled off his scarf and wrapped it around the wound. "Here, push down on this." He placed Corbett's hand back over the wound as a massive *crack* came from the door – the King's Men had been blocked for now, but they still continued their assault.

"You need a doctor," Roach said.

Corbett shook his head. "No, I need to get up there," he said, pointing to the battlements. Roach looked up, then back at the door as the assault continued.

"Fine. Come on, you can't stay here, and up there is probably as safe as anywhere right now." Roach put one arm under Corbett and helped him to stand, then led him towards the stairs.

"Do you think you can make it up?" he asked.

"I'll try," Corbett said.

Roach held tight to Corbett, half lifting, half dragging him up. Corbett gritted his teeth and groaned with each step. A soft sheen of sweat began to cover his forehead, and the higher they climbed, the paler Corbett became.

As they reached the top, a *crack* filled the air. Roach, holding Corbett up, craned his head to look over the wall. The door below had split open to reveal the portcullises.

"Will it hold?" Roach asked.

Corbett shrugged. "I hope so. But the King's Men might regret breaking through. The men of the North have enough booby traps to keep them at bay, now that the portcullis is down." He raised a shaking arm and pointed towards a Northmen behind the archers on the wall; he was busy with a large vat of boiling tar.

Corbett leaned against the back wall of the battlements, swaying gently as he clutched his side. "I never thought I'd see the day when I was fighting against my own people."

"They're not your people. They're hers!" Roach grimaced.

"She's out there, the Dark Dragon?" Corbett said, dropping his head to one side.

Roach nodded. "And I bet you that's where Paisley is, fighting the Dark Dragon."

"We should go and help her!" Corbett said, and he began to shuffle unsteadily along the battlements.

"We?!"

Corbett let out a large sigh as he stopped and gripped the top of the inside wall with his free hand. "Yes, we. It doesn't matter how much you try to deny it, Roach: your heart isn't in what the Dark Dragon is doing, and you know it." He shuffled slowly on, looking into the battle below.

Roach stayed still, his fists tight and his shoulders

up as he argued with the truth of what Corbett had just said. Then he stomped over to the edge of the battlements, looking out over the frozen mere in front of them, and the meadow that led down to it.

"I might not agree with all that she does," Roach said, "but that doesn't mean that I'm on your side. I'm not on hers, either. I'm on my side. I have my reasons for doing what I do."

Corbett looked over at Roach and gave a small shrug. "Whatever you need to tell yourself. Can you see them? Can you see Paisley?" He shook his head and rubbed his eyes.

Roach began scouring the fighting. Most of the King's Men had advanced close to the city, fighting on horseback and on foot as the Krigare circled above them on dragon back, and the army of the North met them in combat on the field.

"There!" Roach pointed over to the top of a small ridge rising in a ring of fire.

"Stay here," he told Corbett as he set off along the battlements, trying to get a better look at the figures within the circle of fire, avoiding archers and the young boys and girls who were stocking the arrows as fast as they were being shot.

As he ran, he saw a huge black rift deepen and grow above where Paisley and the Dark Dragon were fighting.

Roach paused at the top of the gatehouse, where he could see them clearly. The Dark Dragon, small and deadly, clutched Dax with her nightsilver arm, and all the time the rift in the Veil above her was growing.

"There they are!" He pointed, shouting back to Corbett, who had not stayed where he had told him but was struggling to join him, breathing heavily as he held his side and clung to the interior wall to hold himself up and guide himself along. Roach just had time to catch him as he pitched forward, his legs buckling under him. Roach guided him to the floor. His face was pale and his lips tinged blue as he tried to suck in short, sharp breaths. Roach placed his hand over Corbett's, pushing down on the wound to try and stem the blood flow, and Corbett let out a small yelp. The scarf was already full of blood that squelched up and ran through Roach's fingers.

"How do we get down? How do we get to Paisley?" Corbett asked,

"We don't," Roach said. "You're injured, you need

432

to stay here, and rest, and I need to go and get you a doctor."

"Maybe we could climb down the outside of the wall," Corbett said as he nodded towards the arrow slit in the wall. "Paisley needs us!"

Roach turned his head and looked through at a perfectly framed view of Paisley fighting the Dark Dragon on the top of the mound, surrounded by fire.

The Veil rift had doubled in size, reaching up high into the sky. Dax was in the air now, being carried by a beautiful deep-blue dragon.

"Paisley!" Corbett said as he tried to get up, and Roach pushed him down. He was too weak to try again, and his head rested back on the cold stone of the battlement.

Paisley was lying on the ground, the Dark Dragon sitting on her, pinning her down with her nightsilver hand clamped firmly around Paisley's throat. Paisley kicked her feet and hit out, but the Dark Dragon didn't move.

"I don't think she has enough stars for a third time around," Roach said his voice high as he felt a lump in his throat rise.

"Look!" Corbett lifted his free arm and pointed at

the Veil cloud. It was dissipating, breaking up around the edges, fading.

"Paisley!" Roach whispered as he realized that the Dark Dragon was going to kill her.

"This is all wrong!" Corbett whispered, his voice croaky and dry. "Paisley has the King Star, and only a George born of a dragon can kill Sabra, right?"

"Right?" Roach repeated, struggling to absorb this news.

"And Violetta was a Dragon Walker, or at least descended from the Soul Sisters. She had the piece of the Heart Stone, and Paisley, she's. . ."

"The only one who can end this, can end her!" Roach suddenly realized why the Dark Dragon was so focused on Paisley.

Corbett let out a low gasp. "Och, no! Of course!"

Roach turned to him, and his expression was one of revelation.

"Roach, do you know what my stars say?" Corbett asked as he extended his wrist from beneath his sleeve to show the gold splattering of stars.

Roach shook his head. "I haven't a clue."

Corbett smiled sadly. "They say that I will come to understand the secrets of the Celestial

Mechanism better than anyone, and you know what? I do." Corbett looked at Roach, his eyes full of tears.

Corbett set his jaw and pushed Roach away from him. "What are you doing?" Roach said as he placed his hands back on the wound that Corbett was no longer holding, the blood collecting in a small pool beside him.

Corbett's efforts had cost him, and he took a second to focus the little energy he had. "You don't understand. When I made the arm, the Dark Dragon's arm, I used her blood for the copperich so that she could control it. But I didn't use her blood for the nightsilver. In fact, it's still sitting in the pocket of my coat. Instead, I used my blood."

"And?" Roach asked in frustration, not comprehending where this was all leading.

"And when nightsilver is married to a host, bonded by their blood, it is intrinsically paired with the life of that host. If they are alive, then the nightsilver takes on some of their strength and characteristics. And when the host dies, the nightsilver dies too."

Roach's face fell as he realized what Corbett was saying. He remembered the cut he had seen on

Corbett's arm back in the forge and was angry at himself for missing the connection. The nightsilver in the arm was not bound to the Dark Dragon's life force, but to Corbett's.

"Why would you do that?" Roach wanted to shake Corbett for being so stupid.

"I thought my blood would make it weaker, make it useless to her, because I am not that brave or tough or strong, and I thought—"

Roach shook his head. "Corbett, you idiot! You are the bravest of all of us. Look at all that you have done, even though you've been scared the whole time. Do you know how much strength that takes, to face your fears and do what's right?"

"I hope so." Corbett was crying now. "We both know that my track is ending. There's no time to save me. But there's time for me to save my friend and she has a bigger destiny than mine. And my destiny, I can see it, you know, everything that's to happen, I was part of the Unknown Unfolding, and this, well, this way as my stars grow dark I know my track has counted for something, has made a difference."

Roach shook his head as Corbett placed his hands over Roach's.

"Tell her, won't you? Tell her about the Unfolding. . . tell her that I love her, and my mam and pa and brother too – let them know."

Roach nodded.

"And Odelia!" Corbett gave a small hysterical laugh through his tears. "She won't believe you, mind."

"Oh, she will," Roach said.

Corbett scrunched his eyes and let out a gasp.

Roach glanced over at the Veil rift; it was barely more than a whisper.

"I don't want to be alone. Will you stay with me?" Corbett asked, the tears flowing down his face now. "I'm scared."

Roach moved his hands away from Corbett's side and sat next to him. He gently placed an arm around Corbett and held him tight; they both kept their eyes on the wisp of Veil above Paisley. "I know you're scared. But you, Corbett Grubbins, truly are the bravest person I have ever known."

"Paisley," Corbett said in a small escape of breath. His lifeless body slumped in Roach's arms.

Then the black Veil cloud thrust back into being with a *boom* that rocked the fortifications of the keep and threw everyone to the floor. Roach twisted his body to protect Corbett; then, after a long moment, as the air cleared, he gently let go and stood to see Paisley lying in the centre of a radiating circle of fallen fighters.

FORTY

THE DARK DRAGON'S GIFT

Paisley stood alone on the top of the mound. In her hands she held the broken fragments of the Dark Dragon's arm. Paisley felt the electrica coursing through her. She looked up into the wintery sky, blue and clear and as still as the battlefield around her; the rift was gone. She dropped the pieces of the arm to the ground and crushed them under her foot, the brittle nightsilver crumbling to nothing. As she looked at the remains of the Dark Dragon's arm, she felt a weight fall off from her. It was over, the threat had passed, and Sabra was no more.

Her chest felt full and tight and as she breathed

out, she cried in relief. Paisley looked around; all she could see were the knights and Northmen who had moments before been fighting. They were now all lying on the floor, and her heart leaped into her throat: were they all dead too? Had she done this? Had their souls all entered the Veil?

Paisley closed her eyes and saw the Dark Dragon's face, she remembered how she had placed her nightsilver hand around Paisley's neck and squeezed so that she could not breathe. Paisley moved her hands to her throat and remembered the feeling of emptiness as the Dark Dragon choked the life out of her. She had seen stars and had thought, in that moment, that they were her first stars coming to claim her. Still the Dark Dragon squeezed till Paisley had felt a gentle tugging from deep within where the Veil resided in her, and she had willingly followed it.

Paisley opened her eyes to the light as she shook her head, not wanting to think about the darkness that she had felt herself travelling into – not the Veil, she realized, but the Veil rift that had floated above her. And then she remembered re-emerging from the Veil rift and rushing into her body as the Dark

Dragon's nightsilver arm broke, and the huge rift that had formed collapsed in on itself, sending out a mighty *boom* that blasted through the air and rung like the ripples on a pond.

Paisley spun in a slow circle, looking about at the battlefield around her. Then she saw with relief that the fallen warriors, both friend and foe, started to move and come back to their senses. She continued to search the ground for the Dark Dragon, but couldn't see her. How far had the blast thrown her? Had the Veil swallowed her, too?

As the knights and Northmen found their feet, a horn blasted from the trees that surrounded the keep and Paisley turned to watch the King's Men retreat towards the woods. Three small aerocopters landed in the field and began gathering the wounded.

Then, beyond the dip at the foot of the mound, moving in the direction of the aerocopters, Paisley saw the small figure of the Dark Dragon. She was being aided by Lorena and together they were running towards one the aerocopters. She could just make out Uncle Hector, his arms out, beckoning them towards him.

"No!" Paisley cried as she fell to her knees, the

lying nightsilver crunching as she crushed it. The idea of her fear and dread of the Dark Dragon still resting on Paisley's track felt too heavy to bear.

Paisley punched the ground, and as she did, she felt Corbett's nightsilver bangle shift over her stars. It was cold, and when Paisley looked at it, she saw that it had lost all of its lustre.

She clutched it with her other hand. "Corbett."

She turned, searching the battlefield. "Corbett!" she screamed, and suddenly she remembered him showing her the phials of blood back in the forge at Ord and the sheepish look he had on his face when he told her, *"I swapped it for someone else's when I made the nightsilver – I didn't think that making it from her blood was such a great idea."*

Paisley scooped up a handful of the nightsilver from the broken arm. At the time, she hadn't thought too much about what he had said; she had been focused on her lance and her stars. But now? Now it was everything. He had used his own blood to make the Dark Dragon's arm.

She was on her feet and running in the direction of the keep before the first of her fresh tears had fallen. She plucked Næss from the ground where it had landed, and as she ran, she screamed Corbett's name over and over again.

The knights that were fleeing in the opposite direction gave her a wide berth as she passed. Then Dax was suddenly above her on Sterk-Natt.

Paisley shouted up to him, "Find Corbett! Something terrible has happened to him!"

Dax flew off, and as he did Dóm-Fyr flew away from him and joined Paisley, flying alongside her as she carried on running, keeping one eye on Dax. His dragon had landed on the top of the citadel's walled defences and Paisley made for them.

Odelia and Hal were already there, crouched around Corbett.

Paisley dropped Næss to the ground as she walked over to her friend. "What have you done? What have you done?" She sobbed as she saw him slumped against the battlements, his glasses broken and lopsided, his hair dishevelled, blood blooming on his shirt from the large splinter of wood protruding from his chest. Paisley pulled it out, dropping it on to the blood-soaked scarf that sat on the stones of the battlement; she recognized it as the one Roach had been wearing at the Mechster in York, when he had taken her stars and had promised to keep Corbett safe.

Dóm landed on Corbett's chest. She looked up at him and nudged his jaw with the tip of her nose while Paisley crouched down next to Corbett and held him tight in her arms, sobbing. "This is not how your track was supposed to end," she told him as she straightened his glasses and smoothed his hair.

Odelia made to comfort Paisley, but Hal stopped her.

"I know what you did," Paisley said between sobs. "You told me back in your family's forge that when you made the Dark Dragon's arm, you didn't use her blood." She cupped Corbett's face in her hands. "You used your own. I think it's a cruel twist in the Chief Designer's plan that he would entwine our tracks so that when I was about to enter the Veil, you had to die to save me." Paisley's hands shook. "You shouldn't have needed to die, Corbett! Not for me. Never for me." And she hugged him to her and wailed in her grief in a way that she never had for her mother.

She felt as if her heart was breaking into pieces just like the parts of the Heart Stone, each fragment

444

powerful and full of a strong emotion that she would never be able to fully control.

It was Dax who finally moved her away from Corbett, his small hand gripping her shoulder. Paisley turned to him, her eyes puffy, her face pale. Dax had been crying, but she could tell that now he was being strong for her, and a little bit more of her heart broke.

She hugged Dax close, and he hugged her back before straightening up.

"Roach," Dax said, his voice hard and low.

Paisley turned to see Roach standing with his hands up.

"I was with him, Corbett, when he. . ."

Paisley flew at him, hitting Roach in the chest as he stood with his hands still up, and she sobbed and shouted: "You should have saved him! You promised me! You *promised* me!" And then she collapsed, sobbing, on to him, and he lowered his arms and held her as her whole track trembled.

"I know I promised you, and I'm sorry. He knew what he was doing. At the end, he knew his track was coming to a close, and he knew that by his stars going dark you had a chance."

Paisley pulled away from Roach, her eyes red, her tears still flowing. "You should have kept your promise," she spat.

Odelia was standing with her swords out, Hal next to her with his blade drawn, burning his gaze into Roach.

"I'm trying to keep my promise now," Roach said as he held out a small phial of blood.

Paisley's eyes widened when she saw it. "Is that *hers*?" she said in disgust, and made to knock it from his hand.

Roach moved fast, folding his fingers around it and pulling it away.

"I don't know if this will work," Roach said, "but once before, there was a woman. Her name was Jenika, and she worked for the Dark Dragon as I did— do, as I do. Everyone in the Dark Dragon's service is given the gift, and the gift is her blood. She makes us inject it." Roach gave a shudder as his lip curled in disgust. "It has certain properties, her blood: it restores youth and gives you extra energy for a time; it enhances you. Whatever you are good at, you get better."

"So, what, you're giving me this because you want me to drink it?"

"No, I'm giving you this because Jenika died, and then the Dark Dragon gave Jenika her blood and she came back. I'm giving you this because the Dark Dragon's blood can only bring someone back if they consume it close to their passing, and if they already have her blood in them. I'm giving you this because Corbett was in her service." Roach held out the phial again.

Paisley reached out a hand as she understood. "This will bring him back?"

Roach nodded. "Yes, but Jenika was not the same again; she wasn't wholly herself. She'd been altered."

Paisley unconsciously touched the place where the Dark Dragon had stabbed her, the place where she was not whole, the place the Veil now occupied, making her altered for ever.

She still held out her hand to Roach, and he placed the blood in her palm.

"If you are going to use it, you need to do it soon. If too much time has passed, it won't work. I've seen that too, with the Alchesmith Russell Hertzsprung."

"I want you to go now, Roach. I want you to leave, and I don't want you to come looking for me or to try and help me ever again. Do you understand?"

Roach put his hand in his pocket and looked as if he was going to say something to her, but instead he just turned around and walked away.

Paisley rushed to Corbett, crouching by him as she pulled the stopper from the phial. Dóm startled and flew from Corbett's chest, landing on Paisley's shoulder. The little dragon squawked at the glass phial.

"Shouldn't we think about this? He said that Corbett would be different," Odelia said.

Paisley shot Odelia a look. "I'm different, Odelia. But I'm here, and I'm travelling my track and finding a way."

"But you weren't brought back because of the Dark Dragon's blood," Odelia persisted.

"Time is running out. You heard what he said, and I'd rather have a Corbett that is alive than one that isn't."

Paisley poured the thick red blood into Corbett's mouth before anyone could stop her.

She sat there, holding her breath. Dóm climbed from her neck and curled herself in Paisley's lap.

They all watched, their cogs pausing as they waited. Paisley hoped that it wasn't too late, that the Dark Dragon could do this one piece of good for her. She picked up Corbett's hand and held it to her cheek.

Then Corbett opened his eyes and sat bolt upright, drawing in breath like a drowning man.

"Corbett!" Paisley ran her hand over his forehead and his chest, feeling his warmth, feeling his breath coming fast and his heart beating strong. Through the rip in his tunic Paisley could see that the skin was healed – no sign of a wound, and no black scar like on her own chest.

"Oh, Corbett." She threw her arms around him, and he winced. "Sorry, sorry," she said.

"You're all right!" he said, lifting a hand to Paisley's cheek.

She nodded. "So are you," she said through the tears. "We thought we'd lost you!"

He placed a hand over his heart. "I. . . I think you did for a moment there."

Odelia bent down and gently lifted Corbett in her arms. "Come, I'll take you to the infirmary," she told him, and extended her wings.

Paisley stood, holding Dóm-Fyr in her arms, and turned to look over the battlements. She searched the fleeing knights and quickly found Roach, his dark coat stretching out behind him as he headed for the aerocopters.

As if he sensed her looking, he stopped and turned and gazed back at Paisley.

Dóm let out a little jet of fire, then the little Dragon opened her jaws and let out a tiny roar – but deeper and more menacing than the *squarks* of before.

*

In the infirmary, Corbett woke from a dark slumber. It was early evening, and he had no idea how long he had slept for: hours, days, years? Part of him didn't care.

He closed his eyes against the soft lights in the room and tried to hold on to the dream he had been having. In his dream, the Dark Dragon had taken his hand and led him through the grove near his parents' forge where he had played as a child. She had sung to him, her voice so sweet and light and full of love for him.

He opened his eyes again and realized that he didn't need to close his eyes to see or feel or hear her. She was there with him and always would be, filling his veins, occupying a corner of his thoughts for ever.

"Bring me Paisley," she whispered melodiously.

AUTHOR NOTE

Dear Reader,

Each and every one of us has a sphere of power; that power comes directly for us, and it is up to us alone how we use it.

Sometimes we may feel that things outside of our spheres push down on us, dim our light, bend our tracks, or halt them entirely. These times are tough, but it is important that our lights never go out, that our small power is always there. We have the power of choices and can choose to nurture our light and find our own tracks.

Knowing that we are responsible for our power, our actions, our light, is a huge task and it can feel a little overwhelming. But it is also powerful and liberating, when we choose to take responsibility for our tracks and the light that we shine into the world. When we do that, then no Dark Dragons can ever stop us.

So, own your power, shine your light, claim your track and step forth knowing that though there may be dragons, you can choose to shine brightly and go boldly.

Ad astra,
Annaliese Avery

ACKNOWLEDGEMENTS

It has been almost a turning since *The Nightsilver Promise* spread its wings and made its way into the world, and what a fabulous time I have had on my track. Writing *The Doomfire Secret* has been a joy, full of surprises and unexpected turnings that I am so excited to share with readers, but as with all endeavours, I didn't get there on my own.

My amazing agent, Helen Boyle, has been the brightest and steadiest of stars; she has lit my track and guided me along the way. Every day I thank my stars for her and the courage, strength and friendship she gives me.

At the beginning of *The Doomfire Secret*, there was a twist in the track so fortuitous and unexpected that I am sure it is part of the Unknown Unfolding! Yasmin Morrissey, my magnificent editor, left me for a while to travel my tracks while she brought new light into the world. Congratulations Yasmin and Alan, I know that Isabella lights up your tracks with the power of a thousand king stars, and I am so happy for you both.

Much like the unseen tracks, Yasmin was still guiding me on, and she left me with two glorious editors to shine the way. Ruth Bennett, our time together was as fleeting as a falling star, but you burnt bright and true, and added so much glorious insight to Paisley's story, thank you. And Linas Alsenas, like a morning star you arrived to guide me through the final steps of the process. To you both I am so very grateful for taking me and Paisley under your wings.

Natalie Smillie has given as much intricate detail and beauty to the cover of *The Doomfire Secret* as the Chief Designer did to the looping tracks of the Mechanism; she is a marvel, assisted by designer Jamie Gregory, who by his title is already marked with creative genius! You are both magnificent and I thank you.

The whole team at Scholastic is as vast as the Mechanism itself. There are so many amazing people whose cogs affect the turning of my track, some that I have direct contact with and many that I don't; I am so grateful for all of the energy and excitement that they give. My particular thanks go to Hannah Love (and Fergus and Pekkala too!), Harriet Dunlea, Bec Gillies, Pete Matthews, Jessica White and Sarah Dutton, you are all quite extraordinary and have made my track an absolute joy.

To all of the booksellers, bloggers, reviewers, educators and librarians who have championed Paisley's story, I thank you to the ends of the universe. We have been through some rough tracks over the past few years and you have all made the journey smoother by sharing your love of stories with others.

To my fellow writers on Twitter and Instagram, in SCBWI, SOA, and especially those in Write MAGIC, thank you for all of your support and friendship. I am always in awe of the amazing community that we have. Never forget that you have the power to create worlds!

Two fabulous writers whose stories have not only brought me hours of reading pleasure, but their support has given me confidence and the impetus to be bold. Vanessa Harbour you are as handy to have around as a copperich lance! And Dominique Valente you are as inspirational as a Great Dragon!

Beta readers are an important part of writing; they help me to see when I have strayed from the track; my heartfelt thanks goes to Cathy Kelly, George Poles, Teara Newell, and Elizabeth Frattaroli, for all of your gentle nudges and for all of your excitement for this story too.

Nicki Marshall, (and Daisy too!) you have travelled far along this track with me and I am so blessed to have you, thank you for your friendship and guidance.

I am lucky to be part of a wonderful group of writers called The FBM's, each one of them has been such a comfort and strength to me over the last turning, they are as dear to me as Dragon Sisters!

To my fellow Undiscovered Voices 2020 finalists I give

my pen; you are all knights of the Order of Scribes and I am privileged to serve alongside each of you.

To my family, Jason, Liberty, Krystal and Oak, you are the light my track turns towards, and I am so proud of how brightly each of you shine. Thank you for keeping me in tea and food, for letting me talk at you about plot and characters, and for never giving up on me and this wonderful dream of writing.

And to you, glorious reader, thank you for visiting Albion again, for travelling with me to the Northern Realms, for finding new friends, facing old foes, and discovering dragons! I hope that your track is smooth and long, I am honoured that Paisley and her adventure has kept you company along the way.